CAUTION OR COURAGE?

Juniper's mind raced. Were they really going to traipse into a dark forest following these strangers—these horse-thieving ruffians—Anju or not? Yet what other choice did they have, if they wanted to get back their mounts? Juniper felt a sharp tug in her chest, a pulling match between risk and reason. What was the queenly thing to do in this case? What would Erick, her chief adviser, recommend—caution or courage?

Live bold! Risk big! screamed Juniper's heart. And: *They're your mother's people. Would they really do you harm?* And: *How can you pass up this opportunity to explore your heritage?*

It was true that she knew next to nothing about the Anju. They could be led right into a trap. They were unprotected settlers, and young ones at that—but by the goshawk, this lead was *all they had.* And they needed those horses. The longer Juniper thought, the more the feeling hardened inside her, the certainty that this was a trail leading her inexorably toward her destiny. She couldn't think of this as a risk she was taking, not really.

They'd keep going forward.

They would follow this breadcrumb path wherever it led.

OTHER BOOKS YOU MAY ENJOY

Princess Juniper

OF THE ANJU

Princess Juniper

OF THE ANJU

BOOK TWO

AMMI-JOAN PAQUETTE

PUFFIN BOOKS

PUFFIN BOOKS
An imprint of Penguin Random House LLC
375 Hudson Street
New York, New York 10014

First published in the United States of America by Philomel Books,
an imprint of Penguin Random House LLC, 2016
Published by Puffin Books, an imprint of Penguin Random House LLC, 2017

THE LIBRARY OF CONGRESS HAS CATALOGED THE PHILOMEL BOOKS EDITION AS FOLLOWS:
Names: Paquette, Ammi-Joan, author.
Title: Princess Juniper of the Anju / Ammi-Joan Paquette.
Description: New York, NY : Philomel Books, [2016] | Series: Princess Juniper
Summary: "Princess Juniper competes to win the leadership of the Anju tribe and
rescue her home of Torr from foreign invaders"—Provided by publisher.
Identifiers: LCCN 2015029571 | ISBN 9780399171529 (hardback)
Subjects: | CYAC: Princesses—Fiction. | Kings, queens, rulers, etc.—Fiction. |
Adventure and adventurers—Fiction. | BISAC: JUVENILE FICTION / Royalty. |
JUVENILE FICTION / Action & Adventure / General. |
JUVENILE FICTION / Social Issues / Friendship.
Classification: LCC PZ7.P2119 Po 2016 | DDC [Fic]—dc23
LC record available at http://lccn.loc.gov/2015029571

Puffin Books ISBN 9780147513786

Printed in the United States of America

1 3 5 7 9 10 8 6 4 2

For my dad:
too far away, but always near at heart

QUEEN's BASIN

Kitchen and
Dining Area

Great
Tree

Housing
Caves

Beauty
Hut

The Settlers of Queen's Basin:
Brief Character Sketches by Princess Juniper

Juniper Torrence—Queen: Three weeks ago, my father gifted me a little valley kingdom in the heart of the Hourglass Mountains, which I could rule myself for the entire summer. We have named our country Queen's Basin, and we run it entirely free of adults. Without a doubt, my best Nameday gift ever!

Erick Dufrayne—Chief Adviser: This bookish, brave boy-of-all-trades has become my best friend in the world. (Don't tell my Comportment Master, for he'd surely disapprove of me "consorting with commoners"!)

Alta Mavenham—Chief Guard: A baker's daughter who has achieved her lifelong dream of becoming a soldier . . . and she's one of the most skillful I've ever seen.

Tippy Larson—Personal Maid / Girl-About-the-Basin: Our youngest settler has become the indispensable sidekick (and sometime jester) we never knew we needed. I can't imagine the Basin without her!

Paul Perigor—Groundskeeper: Away from his father's strict soldierly eye, he has finally been able to indulge his love for all green and growing things, and a young crop of vegetables is currently being coaxed from the fertile soil of the North Bank.

Leena Ogilvy—Head Cook: This girl is a whiz with a cookpot—she and her helpers make sure we're all fed delicious meals every day. I don't know what we'd do without her.

Toby Dell—Animal Supervisor: A third-assistant groomsman back at the palace, here he has taken full charge of our chickens, goats, and horses (the ones not stolen), making sure their every need is tended to promptly and with tender care.

Roddy Rodin: His talent for craft and construction apparently has no limit. From bridge handrails to apartment doors to building an entire Beauty Chamber—this boy is the master architect of Queen's Basin, and that's a fact.

Sussi Dell: The youngest sister of Toby, she divides her time between helping Leena, Toby, and Paul. This shy, quiet girl has that lovely gift of seeing a need you didn't know you had and filling it a split second before you were going to ask.

Filbert Terrafirm: Our tallest, strongest member, this boy lends out the gift of his brute force wherever and whenever it's needed. You'd be surprised how often that is!

Jessamyn Ceward: Don't even get me started. If it's not about flowers, frills, and leisure reading of a summer afternoon, this noble-born girl has no time to partake. I'm still seeking a way to help make her a productive member of the settlement.

Cyril Lefarge: My snobbish bully of a cousin (also two years older than me, blast his wispy whiskers!) tried to steal the throne of Queen's Basin away from me. He nearly succeeded, too, imprisoning me along with Alta and Erick. But we outwitted him, and now he's the one locked up. Next task: figuring out what to do with him.

Root Bartley: Cyril's close friend and crony, and one-time henchman. But when it came to the showdown, Root chose Queen's Basin over his school ties, and helped us in Cyril's overthrow. Now that he's out from my cousin's shadow, I've been delighted to find what an interesting and clever person he is.

Oona Dell: Poor Oona. The middle Dell sibling's defining trait over the past weeks has been her all-consuming (and unre-turned) crush on Cyril, which led to her choosing his side in the final battle. Now they're locked up together, for all the good it may do her. (I have yet to see him speak a word to her directly, the poor dear.)

1

MY DARLING DAUGHTER:

As I write this, your party has just left the palace.

You know that our dealings with Monsia have been tenuous in recent decades, and reports of their activities have been increasingly difficult to obtain. Everything I have told you tonight is true: The raiding party at the gate is small, and I am confident we will repel them with ease.

And yet. Something in me is uneasy.

You will forgive me, I hope, for seizing this chance to swiftly send you and your subjects—this representation of the youth of Torr—as far from the fighting as possible. No other living person knows the location of the Basin. It appears on no maps. You will all be safe there for as long as is needed. I have taken the liberty of adding my own cart to yours, supplemented with further provisions, along with some items from the palace coffers and from our cultural stores which begged safekeeping.

I cannot say why I feel this need, and there is no particular event that demands this caution. You have often heard me say that as king I feel some connection with the land I rule, and if that is the case, then perhaps something in the wind or the sky or the call of the birds tells me that everything is not as it should be.

I am likely growing soft in my declining years. The moment I finish this letter, I will write another, dashing off the bright, happy notice that the invaders are put to rout and all is well. I will line both scrolls up on my desk. And I am certain that within a few hours I will return and toss this missive into the fire, while the good news flies to you on quickest of wings.

But for the moment, I will indulge my old man's worry and say: If you are reading *this* letter, time has passed and the worst has happened. I cannot think how, but the palace has been overrun. I implore you, do not do anything rash. Do not send a reply by return messenger, lest it be intercepted. Most importantly, stay where you are! I will find a way to come for you, but <u>by no means</u> must any of you leave the safety of the Basin until then.

Do I have your promise?

All my love,
Your father

Juniper finished reading the king's letter aloud and looked at the group gathered in front of her.

The morning sun was half risen over Queen's Basin, the little mountain kingdom they'd built with their own hands, bathing the surroundings in its comforting honey-sketch glow. The wooden posts of the dining area were twisted with bluevine and half-wilted wildflowers from last night's party, and more than one face still showed the pillow imprints of the night's sleep. But as Juniper's last words faded away, every eye was fixed on her, every face fully alert.

"So that's it," she said, trying to keep her voice from wobbling. However many times she'd read this letter, it still tore her up inside to think of her father penning those words while the Monsian army battered the outer gates of the castle. "Now you know everything I know. King Regis sent us this letter by messenger's flight two whole weeks ago. Every day since then, I've waited and scanned the skies for a wing from the palace—Erick and I both have—but there's been nothing."

There was an uncomfortable silence.

"Are we in danger, then?" Sussi asked at last, in a quavery voice.

"We're in absolutely no danger, hidden away here as we are," Juniper said firmly. "No one but my father knows this place even exists."

The group exhaled, which prompted Leena to pass around the pot of goat's-milk porridge for second helpings. As the slurping started back up, Roddy asked around a mouthful, "What're our options, then?"

"Yes," said Root. "What are we going to do next?"

It was a good question. For her part, Juniper felt torn. When she'd first received the letter, she'd been consumed with trying to figure out what they should do about it—or what they even *could* do. Her grief and fear for her father stormed in her chest like a living thing. The only way to keep from losing herself to worry was to force her mind away from things she could do nothing about, and to keep as busy as she could with what was close to hand. Then had come her bullying cousin Cyril's challenge to her rule, and after that she'd been so busy getting out of that jail cell and planning a devious party and reclaiming her throne that it had been a lot easier to lock her worries away into that safe space in her mind and not think about them at all. Now Queen's Basin was returned to her, and Cyril was soundly defeated.

Now the bigger problems were back.

Juniper looked around the circle. With Cyril—and Oona, the lone traitor who had stuck by him—off in a temporary holding cave, the group was smaller than ever. She had just eleven subjects here, none of them older than fifteen.

Every one of them was looking to her for direction.

That was the thing about being queen. You had to *know* things. Didn't you?

Juniper remembered something her father had said in one of his endless Political Discourse lectures, a trick he used when he was out of ideas but couldn't afford to show it. *People need strong direction from their ruler,* he'd said. *But the direction doesn't always have*

4

to come from you alone. A wise leader will use every tool available, brawn and brain alike.

"What are our options?" she repeated now, trying for a calm and collected tone. "That's a very good question. I'd like to turn this around for a minute. What *should* we do next? Does anybody have any thoughts? Ideas?"

Silence pooled out from her question, a silence broken only by the scraping of spoons on pewter dishes.

Juniper sighed. She looked over at Erick, who sat pondering a piece of parchment. He had the air of a dried corn kernel just about to pop. *Ah!* "Chief Adviser Erick Dufrayne?" she said encouragingly. Erick had gotten a lot bolder since arriving in Queen's Basin, but speaking up in a group might never be his top skill.

Sure enough, Erick's first look was one of undisguised panic. But then he blinked and refocused on the papers on his lap. He cleared his throat. "It isn't much. Only, I've isolated the main areas that need attention right now. To start us off, as it were."

"Perfect!" Juniper beamed. "Do tell."

"All right, then. So here they are. One: the messenger. Two: the invasion of Torr. Three: Cyril." Erick paused.

On the far edge of the group, Jessamyn shook herself out of a sitting sleep. "What about the stolen horses? Shouldn't they be on our list of concerns?" Her voice was as petulant as always, but an oddly sharp note in it snagged Juniper's attention.

"The horses, yes!" cried Tippy, quivering on the edge of her stone. "We *must* send out scouts to find our plundered beasts."

"Hmm, good," Erick agreed, scribbling on his list. "That is an important issue to deal with."

"Yet no one has given any concern for it up until now," Jessamyn countered. "Despite how much time has passed since the incident. I can't see why this has not been made a greater priority." A split second later, she shoved Root and shrieked, "Get your muddy boots away from my feet, you great oaf! These are my finest slippers—and freshly polished, too!"

Juniper blinked. For just a moment, Jessamyn's voice had sounded strangely . . . *earnest*. But there was no way; it had to be a trick of Juniper's sleepy mind. "Let's step back and look at the big picture," she said to the group. "What do we know for certain about all the events of the last few weeks?"

"Stealing our horses was the first attack on our camp," said Alta briskly. "And that's the one we know Cyril wasn't involved with. Everything that followed—the destruction of the dining area and kitchen, stealing the milk and eggs, and putting everything to waste—that was all led by him."

Red-faced, Root scuffed at the dirt with his boot, evidently wishing he could forget his role in the destructive pranks.

"The theft of the horses took place at the very start of our time in the Basin," Juniper mused. "So this enemy is aggressive, strikes fast and hard—"

"And is greedy!" snapped Leena. "Taking the very horses from a pack of settlers, and youngsters, no less? That's a low blow, I say."

"So why'd they stop, then?" asked Alta, opening and closing her sword hand in an apparently unconscious gesture. "Why take our horses and nothing else? They've never even come back, so far as we can tell."

"My question exactly," said Juniper. "Since then—there's been nothing. Not a mutter nor muster. So . . . could something have scared them off?"

"Our guard duty, maybe?" ventured Sussi.

After the attacks, they'd started up a strict guard rotation, headed by Alta, but Juniper wasn't so green as to think that alone could have warded off any intended attack. "I don't think so," she said, with an apologetic look at Alta. "But this is what we need to think through now. Are we still being threatened? Was it just a random attack, done in passing as the aggressors moved on elsewhere? Or is there some reason they have been lying low all this time? Could they be waiting on something before they return for more trouble?"

"Is the worst still to come, you mean," said Jessamyn dryly. She leaned back in her seat, fanning herself extravagantly with a lace-trimmed fan. But behind the bustle of finery, her gaze was steely and sharp-eyed, cut through with barely masked concern.

Juniper again noted this shift in character, but too much was going on for her to have any hope of interpreting it. In any case, Jessamyn's statement quenched the last spark from the morning meal. Erick shuffled his parchments and clasped his hands on top of the stack. Every eye was fixed on Juniper, every face filled with silent questions. The back of her neck felt hot as a griddle.

"So," Juniper stammered. "Er, those are the questions relating to our unknown attackers. But as Erick pointed out, that is just

7

one of the problems we face. The bigger mess—*by far*—is the situation back home. And figuring out what we should do to help our country."

"We've got to head back, do our part to liberate Torr. I think that's clear! Why wouldn't we?" Alta challenged.

"I can think of several reasons," said Paul reasonably. "Not least of which is that we know *nothing* about the situation at the castle. We'd be walking straight into the enemy's hands, and that's a fact. What good could come of that?"

"With so many of our horses taken," said Filbert, "do we even have enough left for us all to ride out?"

"Nine are gone. Five remain," said Alta. "Not everyone would be able to ride, but we can pack the rest into a wagon. We'll need it for food and supplies in any case."

"So you propose that we jig it back to Torr in a gift basket, the better to doff ourselves directly into the enemy's hands?" Jessamyn scoffed.

"Do you have a better idea?" Juniper asked, turning toward the other girl. It startled her to ask this question seriously, given all she'd seen of Jessamyn over the past weeks. But one thing Juniper had learned from her endless hours hearing petitions in the throne room back in Torr: Human nature could always surprise you. Just when you thought you knew a person inside out, she might go and unfold herself into someone completely new.

"What about sending a message back to the palace?" Jessamyn asked. She was filing her nails now with a small rounded stone, but her casual air looked just a little too studied. "That messenger of yours can make a return trip, I gather?"

"Send a message back? When the king expressly said not to?" Alta snapped. There was no love lost between those two, Juniper could see. "Why should we want to do that?"

"Well," Jessamyn said primly, "I'm sure I don't know. But we are discussing some form of action, or so it seems to me. A message is a far more prudent way to begin than launching our whole bodily selves out into the fray."

"We could write a letter in code!" Tippy chimed in, eyes sparkling. "Do it all sneaky-like." Sneaky was a state that Tippy knew extremely well.

But Juniper shook her head. "Who should we write to in this code? My father is held captive, and we must assume the main palace contingent is taken along with him."

"*Held captive*, you say?" Jessamyn cut in. "How much do you know of warfare, Princess Juniper?"

Juniper felt her blood turn to ice. "How much do *you* know of warfare, Jessamyn Ceward? My father is held captive because that is what happens to a king whose country is overthrown. The Monsians are cruel, despicable barbarians, it's true. But I can't believe they would commit outright and unprovoked regicide. They're bound to take the long view, and a king in captivity is worth far more than one who's been quickly disposed of." This was true, Juniper told herself. *It was true.* She would not—*could not*—bear even for a moment to consider the alternative.

Maybe Jessamyn saw some of this in Juniper's face, for she just muttered, "Still. Sending some form of message could be useful."

Juniper needed to bring the discussion back under control. "It's a good idea, but I can't see how that would work. The messenger's plainly no good without a recipient. We *have* got to find a way to help Torr. But if we exit the caves and set out toward home, we're risking any number of dangers. We've got to think this through before deciding—see if there is a way to gather more information before we head out."

"You should talk to Cyril," said Root. "I've been thinking a lot since everything went down with him. Looking back, I think he knows more than he let on, even to me."

"Yes," said Alta. "Cyril didn't just betray you, Juniper. He's a traitor to his own *country*! He's been working with the Monsians, helping them invade Torr—or his father has, which is one and the same."

Erick nodded. "Those papers we found in Cyril's camp showing the Monsian maps and their lists of troops and armaments? It's clear that he and his father knew the attack was to happen. I think Cyril must have more information about Monsia *and* their attack on the palace. Maybe there's something that could help us."

"Do you think we can get him to talk?" Juniper asked Root.

Root frowned. "It would be a matter of catching him from the right angle, I'd imagine. Finding a way where it benefits him. Cyril's slippery, to be sure, and he's smart as anything. But deep down, he's not a bad person."

Juniper bristled. Not a bad person? Based on the years of bullying and mean-spirited tricks she'd had from Cyril in years past—not to mention his forced takeover of Queen's Basin—she thought she might just disagree. Still. She'd beaten him once and she could do it again. Questioning that scalawag grew more appealing by the moment.

"Let's finish up our porridge and then hop to that straightaway. Root, will you come with me? And Alta, too?" Juniper looked down at the pale mass of congealed oats quivering on her plate. "On second thought, why don't we go now? I find I'm quite eager to drop in on our master usurper. Let's see what he has to say for himself."

2

FROM THE DINING AREA, IT WAS ONLY A SHORT
walk to the cliff base that led up to the apartment caves. Though
her mind was full of the coming confrontation with Cyril, Juniper
couldn't help admiring the smooth, stony path they'd recently laid
down. The ground here on the river's South Bank was cracked and
dusty, but walking on a proper road, even this skinny little one,
made her feel ever so settled. She herself had laid many of these
stones—and had the scuffed-up hands to show for it—but how
marvelously that backbreaking effort had paid off! *One rock at a time,*
she mused as she strode toward the cliff, with Root and Alta close
behind her. *It's the only way to get anywhere.*

That would be true of this confrontation with Cyril, too.

Up the bank they went, following the cliff-hugging trail. They
filed past the tiny cave-houses where the settlers lived, each one
bearing the unmistakable imprint of its owner: a cheerful mish-
mash of colored drapes and cloths and cushions in Sussi's; the scent
of dried orange peel and cloves wafting from Leena's; a clever

planter box hooked outside the window of Paul's, all abloom with geranium and marigold and moss rose. Finally they reached the end of the row: Cyril and Root's former cave.

At the woven-rush door, Juniper paused. It wasn't long at all since Cyril had locked her, Erick, and Alta inside this very space, and the memory still jarred her. No real harm had come to them, of course. But that moment when Cyril had shoved her inside the cave-turned-prison, when he had slammed the door shut, when he had twisted the lock and snapped it tight and laughed in her face as he flaunted his win, his power, his complete domination—

That moment, she would never forget.

It changes you, going through something like that.

Balling her hands into fists, Juniper unbarred the door and marched inside. Root followed just behind, with Alta taking up the rear. Alta had her sword belt on, which Juniper knew was just for show. But it made her feel better all the same.

The door shut behind them.

Juniper let out her breath. The inside of the cave was completely different from the bare, cold prison she'd been stuffed in days ago. As soon as she'd foiled Cyril's attempt to steal her throne, Juniper knew he would have to be contained, or he would just run off to join his father and the Monsian army. That was evidently why he'd come along on this trip to begin with—to try and gather information for the enemy. Still, Cyril *was* her cousin; Juniper had no wish to subject him (or his single devoted follower, Oona) to the rough treatment he'd given her. For all his treachery, she would not stoop to his low methods.

And so Roddy and Sussi had worked their magic on the two-room space, and what a job they'd done! The window bars were gone (it was too small and high to climb out of, and the bars did nothing but cast depressing shadows on the floor). They'd dragged in a pile of quilts and pillows, and installed a rustic table with two sitting stools in the front area. They'd brought in a game of jacks and piles of lacquered playing cards. Erick even contributed several of his well-loved volumes, one of which Oona was deeply engrossed in now.

As they entered, Oona set the book down and rose, smoothing her skirts and scanning their faces eagerly. "Is it mealtime?"

"Not yet," said Alta, walking through to the back room, where Cyril lounged on his pile of quilts. A pile considerably higher and fluffier, Juniper noticed, than the one in Oona's room.

"Well, well, well," Cyril drawled, tucking his arms behind his head with a lazy yawn.

"I see this cooling-off period hasn't sweetened your character any," Juniper remarked.

Cyril stuck out his bottom lip. This made him look less like an older rival who had made a play for her throne—and nearly won—and more like a sulky toddler. Juniper hid the urge to giggle.

"Cheer up," she said. "I'm here to talk business. You like business, don't you? I've got some things to discuss, and I thought we might go outside for it. Walk around a spell, let you stretch your legs. The air is powerful sweet this morning—some new fragrance on the wind that I haven't smelled before."

"Lunch, too?" Oona asked hopefully.

"Won't be long," Alta cut in. "But didn't you just have breakfast?"

Oona shrugged and scuffed the floor.

Root dug in his pockets. "I think—I might have some . . ." There was a rustling, then he yanked out a small woven sack. Except he must have tugged it wrong, because the bag exploded in a torrent of tiny round falling bits. In seconds the stuff was skipping and bouncing all across the room like a swarm of bees let out of their hive.

"Hazelnuts," said Root lamely. "Um."

"Oh, just the thing!" exclaimed Oona. "No, don't you worry," she said to Root, who'd crouched down to scrabble at his mess. "Just hand me over the bag, and I'll tend to it. It's like a new game of jacks, I reckon. That shall keep me busy the rest of the morning. Not much else to do in here, don't you know it."

Root smiled in response, but didn't stop picking up the nuts.

A few minutes later, Juniper and Cyril headed out, followed by Alta. Root stayed behind to see his cleanup job through. There weren't many places to take a walk in Queen's Basin. It was just a short climb down from the Cavern (as they'd named the enormous cave that connected the tunnel leading though the mountain to the Basin) to the animal pens, a near stroll from there to the dining area and kitchen, the same again to the Great Tree, and a little jaunt further to the Beauty Chamber and the bridge leading over to the North Bank. They hadn't put down walkways on the North Bank yet: The land was just as muddy and wild as when they'd first arrived (only now with a garden patch pushing out tiny vegetable shoots and an orchard picked clean of fruit). Juniper was wearing her brushed indigo slippers today, so instead of risking the mud across the bridge, she decided to take their walk up the slope to the high lookout point.

"We're headed where, exactly?" Cyril grumbled.

"Nowhere special; only there's a spot up here I like," said Juniper, "that is good for sitting and chatting. Plus, I figured you'd enjoy the exercise." She knew she could have questioned him just as easily inside his quarters. But truth be told, that dank cave was depressing. A brisk whiff of the fresh outdoors would not only be more pleasant for her, but would also remind Cyril what he was missing out on due to his poor life choices.

"Well, there's no point waiting for the sit-down," Cyril said. "Let us chat away. What's nipping at your ankles?"

Juniper would not let his pithy quips distract her. "Fine. Let's get right down to it: What I want is for you to tell me more about Monsia. Anything you know about their army, in particular. You had all those maps and troop statistics, and those shall be delivered to my father by and by—" She was satisfied to see Cyril wince at this. "But I'm looking for more up-to-date information. What's their overall plan in this attack on Torr? What do they really want and why? Most importantly, what can we do to stop them?"

At this, Cyril stopped and stared at her. "Seriously?" he said. "That's what you brought me all the way out here to ask? I could have answered that back in the cave. Or, more accurately, I could have *not* answered that back in the cave." He barked out a laugh.

"Whatever possessed you to think that I would give you any of those answers?" He cast a scornful look toward his cave, making it clear that he had a pretty good idea who had given her that idea. Turning his back, Cyril began climbing again.

"Wait," Juniper sputtered, scrambling to catch up. Alta was close on her heels. "I get it. Your father is working with the Monsians, and there's got to be something in it for him—something big. But what about you? What do you *truly* think of this invasion? I know we haven't always agreed on . . . well, on anything. But you can't truly believe that horrible country should overrun our own—can you? Torr is *your* home, too. Surely you wouldn't want to be part of a big bully picking apart something small and beautiful, maybe tearing it to pieces?"

Juniper was panting now, but they'd reached the crest of the hill. She stood next to Cyril, who gazed scornfully out over Queen's Basin, arms akimbo.

"Wouldn't I, though?" he drawled. But something in his tone belied the words ever so slightly.

"There's no denying you're made of faults, Cyril Lefarge," Juniper said. "But I've always known you for your fierce country pride. And there's also the matter of *right and wrong*. I really believe that deep inside you, there's someone who knows the difference, someone who can still make up his own mind. And that's why I think you're going to help me out."

A shadow crossed Cyril's face. But then he blinked and said, "I guess it's time you learned how wrong your thoughts can be." He set off up a near embankment.

17

Juniper exchanged a glance with Alta.

"That lout!" Alta muttered. "How do you put up with him? I would have socked him a good one by now."

"And then where would we be?" Juniper said. "Here's what I know about Cyril: More than anything, he hates losing. Right now he's been soundly beaten. He's my captive, and each time he sees me is a pinch to his middle. What I'm offering him is the chance to get back a bit of the upper hand, to let him feel in charge again for a moment or two, even just by giving his information. You'll see. He's wavering now, I can tell. We just need one more nudge to push him over. Maybe it's like Root said: We need to find a way that helping us benefits *him*. If we can make our needs line up with his wants, we'll be in business."

"No sweat, then," said Alta sourly. "With his wants being so noble and all."

Juniper perked up. "Nobles," she said, beaming. *When you hit a wall in the road,* her father always said, *find a way to meet it sideways.* A change of subject might be just the thing to muddle the tension a bit.

Clambering the rest of the way up the slope, she plopped down near Cyril, who was reclining on a grassy bank. "How well do you know Jessamyn?" she asked.

Cyril turned toward her, puzzled. "Jessamyn?"

Alta, hovering over them in a vaguely guardlike position, looked equally surprised. Juniper had no idea whether this line of thought would lead anywhere relevant. But Jessamyn's odd behavior that morning still nagged at her, and Cyril *was* awfully good at knowing things that others were hiding. So she just held his gaze with raised eyebrows, and waited.

"I don't know Jessamyn well at all. She's been at the Academy for a few years, but she's two grades below me. I scarcely see her."

"Go on," Juniper persisted. "Her father's some ambassador—that's all I really know of her, so you must have more on this than I do. What can you tell me?"

Cyril had burst out laughing. "*Ambassador*? Is that the word that's going around?"

"Well . . . yes. Isn't he?"

"Jessamyn's father is a *traveling merchant*." Cyril's voice dripped with scorn. "He's made himself a small fortune, apparently, if you can put that name to raw *coin*. The man invented some gadget that half the continent apparently can't do without." Cyril's eye-roll was practically audible. "Spends his days trekking from town to town, raking in the riches."

Juniper processed this. Had Jessamyn actually *said* that her father was an ambassador? Certainly she had never corrected that assumption. But why? Was it just general misinformation, a way to make herself look more important?

Or was something else afoot?

Juniper had no idea. But one thing at least had worked: The subject of Jessamyn had cleared the air and, even better, had gotten Cyril into an easy, talkative mood. *Meet it sideways,* she thought with satisfaction. But what next?

Then the answer came to her.

"Cyril," she said, leaning toward him, "I've been thinking." As long as she'd known him, there had been one constant in Cyril's life, one soft spot in his crusty shell: his vanity. Based on the admiring looks she'd seen him flinging at the looking glass outside the Beauty Chamber, that relationship was still going strong.

"Thinking, eh?" he scoffed. "Must be an odd sensation for you."

Juniper brushed this aside. "I've been thinking about your complexion."

Cyril's hands flew to his face. Juniper forced herself to keep a neutral expression.

"What about my complexion?" he said suspiciously.

"It's just," said Juniper, "that cave of yours. So dank and musty, isn't it? No proper sunlight or cleansing airflow. After my stay in there, I had to spend a great deal of time polishing my skin to get it back in shape, let me tell you." She squinted at Cyril's chin, then shook her head sorrowfully.

"What?" he yelped. "Do you see something? I thought I'd checked—"

"I'm sure it's nothing. Maybe just the smallest bit of . . . *you know*, on your . . ." She let her words trail off.

Cyril's fingers patted up and down his chin, trying to find the offending spot. Juniper saw Alta turn away, her shoulders moving silently up and down.

"Here's the thing," said Juniper, leaning in closer. "Sussi has come up with a marvelous facial cleanse mask using river clay. She *might* be persuaded to make a portion for your use. But if you stay locked in that fusty old cave for much longer, I don't know if there will be much more to be done for it. You see what I mean, don't you? So. I'm ready to make you an offer: We can move you back out into the air during the day, just as simply as you please. No more of that grim, clammy rock space."

Cyril frowned, still rubbing self-consciously at his chin. "You'd let me go free? In exchange for what?"

"Well, you couldn't be *free* exactly. You're still a traitor." She brushed away his derisive snort. "It's true, and you know it. Queen's Basin is rightfully mine to rule, and you came against that most treasonously. Took up weapons against us, even! And we can't forget about the Monsian angle. Still. Here's my plan—we'll need to put it to the group, of course, and make sure that all agree—but I propose this: You'd be free to roam the camp, with a guard. Alta will stay with you at all times, or one of the others . . ." She paused. "Maybe I could get a bell for your ankle? That would help—"

Cyril's back jerked straight. "I will *not* wear a bell!"

"Fine, no bell. But what do you say otherwise? All you need to do is provide us with the information you know to help us in our return to Torr. It's a very good offer! Your thirsty skin will thank you. *And*, though you'll say it doesn't matter one whit, you'll be doing good for your country besides."

Cyril let out a theatrical sigh, though his hand stayed guardedly on his chin. "Here's how it looks from my side. I will accept your offer of this so-called *freedom*, but here's what I can give you in return for it. *All* I can give you. I know nothing more about the dealings of Monsia with Torr, nor could you persuade me to share them if I did." He lifted a hand to quell Juniper's protest. "No. That's something I won't budge on. Say what you will about

21

my country pride—and I won't deny there's truth to that—still, you shan't get me to fink on my blood. Hear me out, though! I do have something important to share which I think you will find well worth my freedom."

Now that he had her attention, Cyril leaned back and preened a little. "Oh, yes." He lowered his voice ghoulishly. "And it's fairly juicy, to boot. Want to hear it?"

He paused again for effect, then raised his hands in a dramatic gesture. "I know who thieved your horses."

3

FOR A LONG MOMENT, JUNIPER WAS SPEECH-
less with shock. It was so exactly like Cyril to have known this
information from the start and said nothing until it could benefit
him! Then Alta dove for him with throttling hands outstretched,
and Juniper had to jump up and get very busy keeping her from
knocking Cyril's lights out—though it pained Juniper a bit to do
so, for never would a beating have been so well earned.

Still, this was sorely needed information.

And Cyril knew it.

The boy himself sat with arms crossed on his chest, watching
their tussle with smug confidence. At a suitable pause in the action, he said, "Bring me to your next gathering, and I shall share
my intelligence with the group. I guarantee they will be pleased
to hear me out."

Still in the act of blocking Alta, Juniper let go. Alta barreled
on through her own momentum and crashed into Cyril, who
toppled backward like a felled tree. Juniper ignored them. Her

focus sharpened to a fine point. *What* was she doing? If her father could have seen her now . . . Surely he'd raised her to be smarter than this! Why, she was acting no better than a thwarted schoolgirl in short skirts facing a threat to her sandbox.

Juniper drew herself up tall and steeled her gaze on Cyril. "Enough," she said. She did not raise her voice.

She did not have to. Alta fell away to the side. Cyril struggled to his feet, wagging his head in a last grasp at self-confidence. But his moment was gone. *He only has the power I allow him to take,* Juniper realized. Cyril had already been soundly beaten; it was time he learned his place.

"Let's get one thing very clear," she said, her words icy. "There is nothing that we *need* from you, Cyril Lefarge. You believe you have some information that would be of use to the group. You might, or you might not. That is for me to decide—*me* alone, as the ruler of Queen's Basin. The ruler both appointed *and* chosen by the people," she added, and saw him wince. She took a step forward, pressing her advantage.

"Now, I've made you an offer of guarded freedom around Queen's Basin, but that offer is quite conditional. I'm going to hear your bit of information, and I'm going to hear it *now*. And if I like it, if it proves useful, then we'll talk about what comes next. If not, you can stay in that cave till the snows come. And your pimply face with you."

Cyril swallowed. He glanced toward Alta.

"*Now*, Cyril," said Juniper. She stepped even closer, noticing Cyril's eyes widen and his head duck slightly on her approach. For once, she appreciated all those boring old Comportment classes. Acting like a pompous ruler could come in handy after all! She yawned theatrically. "Already I grow weary of waiting. Perhaps I should—"

"I can show you," Cyril said quickly. Stammered, really. Cyril! Stammering! Of all the little wonders. "Though, uh, it's possible I may not know *quite* so much as I implied just now."

Juniper huffed and started to turn away, but Cyril put a hand on her arm.

"Don't go—listen. I meant what I said; I do have information you will want to know. Hear me out."

"Go on, then."

Cyril swallowed. "All right. Root and I had gone back to my camp that night, and Root was already abed. But I was restless, and that infernal music from your party at the Great Tree didn't make sleeping any easier. So I set off to hike about the cliffs awhile." He looked at Juniper as though for approval, then lowered himself onto a nearby stone. Juniper stayed standing, hands on her hips.

"It was Jessamyn's shrieks that first caught my notice," Cyril went on. "I hurried over to the embankment, where I found I could see quite clearly down into the Basin. It was perilous dark out, but the stones carried enough light that I could see a cluster of man shapes gathered at the horses' pen."

"We know that already," Alta snapped. "That's the very story told by Jessamyn. What actual new information is it you've got, then?"

Cyril glowered at her. "As I said, I was not near enough to see any detail upon these thieves, but I did see them start to move very quickly away once Jessamyn began her ruckus. They were bathed in a certain orange glow that made it possible to track them in the dark."

Juniper nodded; Jessamyn had mentioned the orange lights, too. But Cyril had stopped talking.

"And?" Juniper said impatiently.

"And I followed them," said Cyril. "I cut across the pass above the waterfall quick as I could, and made to see where they might be headed. I will tell you straight out, I did not find much worth noting. But I did see their destination, such as it was." He paused. "And I can take you there."

After a quick stop to collect Erick, the group set off across the cliffside to investigate their new lead. Cyril navigated the rocky trails easily, scurrying up escarpments and across stony banks at an unwavering clip that Juniper found impressive. To Juniper, each mountain trail looked nearly identical. Cyril *had* probably spent more time clambering about up here than she had, given all the free time he'd had over the last weeks. Still, his sense of direction was unerring, and he kept up a stiff pace.

The path was upwind from the waterfall, which rattled and roared below them—it was, in fact, a fine vantage point for looking down upon the pool where the group had spent more than one relaxing day swimming and taking in the sunshine.

It did not escape possibility that Cyril might be taking them on a daisy-chase. But when he finally stopped by a shallow gap in the stone face halfway between the South and North Banks, Juniper saw, with quickening pulse, that the ground held the faint but unmistakable sign of hoofprints. And not only that . . .

"Look!" said Alta. "It's those mystery tracks—same as we saw around the horse pens that night, Erick, the ones you couldn't figure out."

Erick dropped to his knees and squinted at the hard-packed earth. "That's them, all right," he said grimly.

The tracks were vaguely foot-shaped, but unusually big and pocked through with sharp, clawlike ridges. Juniper shuddered, remembering how scared they'd been that night and how Jessamyn's screams had echoed all through the Basin.

And now they were going to follow these prints . . . where?

"There you have it," said Cyril. "As promised, so delivered."

"Where'd they go, then, your mystery bandits?" Alta said, obviously impressed by the prints but trying not to show it. "Tipped off into the falls, did they?"

Cyril cocked his chin toward the dip in the wall. His confidence was returning, but before he could say anything, Juniper pushed past him for a closer look. The spot where they stood looked like a simple rest area along this shingled trail that hugged the mountain face. But Juniper had not roamed the Hourglass Mountains these last weeks without learning a thing or two. The way the rock wall curved ever so slightly in, mirroring the pool beneath, suggested there was more to this spot than first met the eye. The heavy curtain of hanging bluevines looked familiar, too.

She'd walked through something very similar to reach that first cave that had led them, ultimately, to the Basin.

This was an opening in the mountain—a path. She knew it was.

Erick stood and caught Juniper's arm. "Are you sure about this?" he whispered. "These prints . . . We don't know anything about them. Or where they might lead."

Juniper pinched her lips shut. She *wasn't* sure, and that worried her as much as anything. "We're just investigating," she reassured him. "We're not going anywhere right now."

She looked at Alta, who nodded. Erick settled for a shrug. Cyril started drumming his index fingers on the stone in the vein of an announcer, until Alta elbowed him in the ribs and he broke off with a yelp.

Juniper plunged at the rock face.

As she'd suspected, the vine-draped wall was not a wall at all. Right in the center, where the faint prints disappeared on the stone track, the dense vines pulled aside to show the rock face narrowing to a V-shaped opening.

Juniper could see clear through the gaping mouth into the secret passage of a mountain tunnel.

After dropping Cyril back in his cave while they figured out next steps, Juniper and Erick and Alta gathered in the Great Tree to talk things over.

28

"What a marvel!" said Erick. His fingers were twitching in the way they did when he'd been away from his books for too long. "I've got six different things to research now, based on this new information. But another secret-passage cave? Astonishing!"

"I guess it makes sense," said Juniper. "The intruders vanished so quickly and quietly—and it explains how the tracks were just gone back when we were trying to follow them. Of course they would have a passage taking them out of the valley. The same way they came in, no doubt."

"So what's our next move, then?" Alta asked.

"We should take the final decision to the group," said Juniper, "but for my part, I want to follow these tracks and find out where they lead." She wasn't sure when she'd decided this, but suddenly, it was the truest thing she knew. Her heart thumped with excitement.

Alta nodded. "We need to, don't we? It's the best lead we've got."

"I'm not sure," said Erick. "We don't know anything about these people, and they're likely dangerous. I mean, they might not even *be* people; how can we know?"

"We've got to reclaim our horses," said Alta.

"The way I see it," said Juniper, "is that it's an exploratory mission. The cave's a tunnel, just like the one that led us here. So we'll send a group through. We'll move with care. And if anything looks risky, then we'll turn back. What do you say?"

It was clear Erick still didn't love the idea, but he gave a reluctant nod.

"All right then, we're agreed," said Juniper. "And we'll see what the rest say before we set any plans in motion. But first—just to change the subject a titch—there's one more thing I wanted to ask you both: Have you noticed anything different about Jessamyn these days?"

"Jessamyn?" said Erick. "I guess she just seems like . . . a regular *girl* to me. Ouch!" Alta's elbow cracked hard into the middle of his back.

"Oh, ex*cuse* me," said Alta sweetly. "Did that feel *girly* enough for you?"

"Come on, you two," said Juniper. "I just feel that something is off with Jessamyn recently. Since we left the palace, we've all gotten to know her, right?"

Alta snorted. "Such as is worth knowing."

"Exactly," Juniper said grudgingly. "I'm not one to badmouth others, but . . ."

"It's no secret that Jessamyn has been the perfect picture of a spoiled, indulgent little layabout," said Alta.

"Hmm," said Erick. "And now that I give it some thought . . . is that picture almost *too* perfect?"

"Yes," Juniper agreed. "That's just what I thought. Or . . . I guess I *didn't* think it, really, not until today. But you saw the way she was going on this morning."

Alta nodded, as though trying the impression on for size. "You're right. All those brash ideas and that talk of warfare and sending messages and so on. Very unlike her. Unlike the *normal* her, that is."

"Skipping back and forth, too, wasn't she?" said Erick. "Almost like another person was pushing out from time to time, only to be shoved back inside."

"Exactly," said Juniper. "And there's something more we just learned." She filled Erick in on the new information they'd gotten from Cyril about Jessamyn's father, even though it shed no real light on anything. "And that's all we know. What I can't figure is what we should do about it. If we even need to do anything. It all seems important, but . . . how?"

"We could have a look around her cave," suggested Erick. "See if there's anything in there that's out of the ordinary."

"It's right next to mine," Alta agreed. "And I happen to know that milady is off a-lolling by the far riverbank, slathered in some nourishing skin potion or other."

Juniper considered. "It doesn't seem right to go poking through someone else's belongings."

Erick cleared his throat. "I think that when something seems fishy in your kingdom, it's pretty much a law that you need to look into it. As your chief adviser, I recommend action in this case."

Overlook a wasp, and you will face the swarm, her father had once told her. With a war on and traitors recently uncovered, they couldn't be too careful. "All right," Juniper said. "Let's all go together, though. And no poking or prying. We'll be there strictly as investigators, not nosy parkers."

With that, she jumped up and followed Alta and Erick down the tree and along the path toward the apartment caves. When they reached Jessamyn's door, they found it shut but not locked. It swung smoothly on its hinges, and the three stepped inside.

Juniper took in the room at a glance: neatly made-up bed in the corner, several dresses and a rainbow-hued robe hanging from pegs on the wall, a small tabletop covered in a brilliantly white cloth and topped with a sturdy porcelain vase. Juniper had been in Jessamyn's apartment only once before, the night of the disastrous horse-thieving. But she'd been so distracted then, trying to calm the girl down and discover what was going on, that she hadn't paid any notice to her surroundings. Now, as she studied the space, she found herself surprised at how . . . *spare* it seemed. Where were all the frills? Where was the gaudy, garish décor, the visual froth to be expected from someone of her personality? Their everyday Jessamyn was a peacock on full display. Yet her dwelling was plain and functional, containing the basics and nothing more.

"Curious," murmured Juniper, running her hand along the bedspread.

"Look here," said Erick. He was standing by a shelf cut along the rock wall that held a row of books.

Of course he was.

Juniper moved closer. The full collection of *Flower Bard* epics took up pride of place, but Erick had reached a hand to feel behind them. From this rear spot he tugged several slim, cloth-bound volumes that were wedged behind the front display row. He held these books out to Juniper and she read their titles, eyebrows lifting higher and higher on her forehead: *Political Instability in Our Times*, read the first. And, *Bellamy Bellingham: On the Trail of the Lower Continent's Most Notorious Renegade*. And the last one was *The Face of Deception: How Your Body Betrays Your Innermost Thoughts*.

"A little light reading, with her peppermint bonbons?" said Alta doubtfully.

"Well, if this doesn't beat the cream to peaks," said Juniper. The more she learned about this girl, the more confused she became.

Who *was* Jessamyn Ceward?

And what was she *really* doing in Queen's Basin?

4

IN THE DINING AREA A FEW HOURS LATER, Juniper sat looking around the circle at her gathered subjects. "There you have it," she said. She'd given them the quick version of the morning's events, from the offer she'd made Cyril, to the information he'd shared, to the mysterious tunnel that seemed to open on the next step in their investigation. She hadn't mentioned their suspicions about Jessamyn, of course—what was there to say, after all? But Juniper kept a close watch on the girl in question, who lounged nonchalantly on the far side of the circle. "As for the new tunnel, we didn't venture past the opening, but the prints were plain to see. A whole group of horses went that way in recent weeks, and their kidnappers besides."

"You think Cyril is telling the truth, then?" said Leena skeptically. "He really did see all that hugger-muggery, just as he said?"

Juniper looked at Erick, who shrugged faintly. "Alta?" she said.

"He led us to the cave, didn't he?" said Alta. "And there were the prints. I mean, no offense to his pompous self, but I think making up a story that detailed on the turn of the moment would take a dab more creativity than he's got in him."

"I agree," said Erick. "More importantly, he wants to get out of that cave—and stay out—so he has nothing to gain by feeding us false information."

"So, assuming the lead is a good one," said Juniper, "we have two decisions to make. Do we all agree that Cyril can go about free, so long as he's got a guard with him to make sure he doesn't take off or start causing trouble?" She looked around the circle, where shrugs and head bobs showed general agreement. She nodded. "All right. And then, even more important—what should we do about the trail?"

This was met with silence.

Then Leena looked up, eyes sparking. "We need to follow it, don't we? There's a clue, you pick it up, you sniff it out, you dash after it, all madcap-like. Whatever else *would* we do?"

Juniper beamed. "I can't say I disagree. And that's pretty much what Erick and Alta and I were discussing this morning. But what about the rest of you? What do you think of the idea of setting out and doing some exploring?"

"I cry yes!" said Tippy, leaping to her feet. "Yes to the tunnel, yes to adventure!"

You could always count on Tippy for resounding enthusiasm, Juniper thought to herself. Between her and Leena, the spark of excitement quickly caught flame.

"Let's hear it for the caves!" said Paul. "For what is a seed without a harvest? We must follow this through."

Sussi clapped her hands. "We'll make a party of it—take a proper picnic basket and all."

"Those creature-thieves won't know what hit 'em!" called Roddy.

The circle dissolved into general giddiness and derring-do.

Finally, Juniper raised her hands. "I'm glad we're all agreed. There's just one thing . . ." She hesitated, hating to dampen the fervor of the moment. "You know, we can't *all* go on this scouting mission."

The group wilted visibly. Juniper rushed on, "Think it over—there's more than a dozen of us all together. How could we creep about anywhere in such a great pack? And what about the running of our own kingdom back here—the care of the animals, the gardens, the last of what needs doing to make Queen's Basin our very own perfect country?"

Leena looked up. "Is that still worth doing, then? With the invaders at the palace and all?"

"Just so," said Toby. "Our own families might be held captive or worse, and we're here spiffing up our summer place? Doing nothing to help? I don't like it."

"We could find a way to learn what's happening in Torr, as we talked about yesterday," said Jessamyn casually. It was the first she'd contributed to this discussion.

"Or we could make two groups," said Leena. "One to go after the horses and the other into Torr."

But Juniper shook her head. "You bring up a good and true

point. The last thing I want is to give everyone busywork. I already learned a thing or two about that." Her mouth twisted, remembering her recent lessons on the right and wrong way to be a queen. "We've got to find a way to help save Torr. But we can't just blaze out willy-nilly into the midst of a war without a proper plan or idea of what to expect. Our first step's got to be our bedrock, after all. If that's not solid, how can we hope to build it into a road that goes anywhere? We rate high on passion and fierce energy. But Monsia is a genuine army, a conquering kingdom. If we hope to make any difference at all in this fight, we'll need all the smarts and strategy we can get. And that will take time, thought, and going about things right. Erick, what do you say?"

Erick startled, then gave a firm nod. "So our first move is to send a team to follow these prints into the mountain."

"Precisely," said Juniper. "A small scouting team to gather information and see what there is to discover. I'm thinking Alta and myself, with Erick staying back to keep the home base running." She looked up to see what Erick thought of this. It didn't feel right to go without him, but she *really* needed to leave someone trustworthy in charge.

"That's cracking," he said. "I've been meaning to reread the *Ancient Legends* compendium, and now I shall have time for that . . . along with all the proper work, of course."

Juniper nodded, satisfied. "I think Cyril should come with us, too. For safekeeping." The slippery usurper would be a real nuisance to have along. But Erick would have enough to do running the camp without having to fend off Cyril's tricks, too. Plus, for all his orneriness, Cyril knew stuff. He wouldn't be nearly as handy to have around as Erick would have been, but hopefully in a pinch he would do.

"Oh, let me come also, let me!" pleaded Tippy. "For how shall you do without a maid, on such a wild and perilous journey?"

Juniper laughed. "This is barely a jaunt, Tippy. I don't expect we shall be gone even a full day. Certainly I won't need my hair and clothing tended to on the way. We'll be traveling rough, you goose! Anyway"—her voice softened—"you've got so many other fine and useful qualities to make you quite indispensable around here." She looked around the circle. Other faces were equally crestfallen at the lost adventure. Even Jessamyn looked oddly anxious. "Look, I know this seems like quite the glamorous expedition. But we're a team—remember? This early trek is just one part of it. We've got our proper venture back down to Torr soon to come, and that shall bring quite its own plenty of adventure and peril. But there's much to be done to get us ready to move out then. Not to mention fixing up the camp for our absence. Can I count on you all for that?"

The faces brightened; many actually seemed relieved. Maybe trekking the far mountains wasn't every kid's vision of an ideal day.

"What about Oona, then?" asked Alta. "I guess we won't leave her up in the cave once Cyril's been let out."

"Ah, Oona," said Toby. "My sister's always been one to follow her fool heart to all the wrong places. But in truth, she's mild as a mackerel. With Mister Fancy Pants out of the way, she'll give us no grief. I can vouch for her."

"I can handle the little rattlescap," Leena added. "She can work with me, and I'll keep an eye on her. But Toby's right—I can't see her causing any trouble."

"All right," said Juniper. "So Alta, Cyril, and I will set off at first light tomorrow, and I expect we'll be back before sundown." Then she paused. "But if we're not, everyone please carry on as normal. I intend to follow this trail wherever it leads. I *think* it shall be a quick and easy matter to get the information we need, which I'll then bring back to the group. But I don't want anyone mounting up a rescue if we come to some delay. Agreed?"

There were mutters of assent, and Juniper then gave everyone the rest of the day off to do as they pleased. With much enthusiasm, the group dissolved into twos and threes as all set about their preferred activities. Juniper stayed where she was, lost in thought. Suddenly, the prospect of following a set of unknown prints into the dark heart of the mountain, in hopes of tracking down a group of mysterious attackers, seemed vaguely overwhelming.

That wasn't a shiver coursing down her spine, she told herself. Simply a chill breeze gusting across the valley as the sun panned the arc of the overhead sky.

Tomorrow they would head out.

And find their answers, come what may.

Shaking off her apprehension, Juniper stood and looked out over the bustling bowl of Queen's Basin. A game of loggits was gearing up on the far field, with Paul ramming fat sticks in the ground at intervals and various others lining up with smaller sticks for throwing at the targets. On this side of the river, Sussi was drawing three big squares in the dirt for a barley-break game, with her fellow players pairing up and arguing over who would form the center group that had to catch those in the outer squares. Several other kids wandered alone or in pairs, reading or munching snacks or finding their own ways to relax on this sunny afternoon.

One figure in particular caught Juniper's eye: Jessamyn was walking along the river alone. Juniper smiled. The timing and opportunity could not have been better.

When Juniper reached the riverbank, Jessamyn had tucked her skirts up to her knees and was wading in the shallows with a series of little gasps and screamlets.

"Is it cold?" Juniper called out to her.

Something flashed across Jessamyn's face, but the next moment, she was her languid, carefree self. "Not a whit, wouldn't you know it? The rocks feel double pointy today, and they're doing a number on my feet. But the waves are splashy as bathwater! I have to hold myself back from toppling in headfirst."

"That's strange—I'm sure the whole stream was frigid when we first arrived."

Jessamyn shrugged and waded further out.

"Hold up a second," Juniper called. "I want to talk to you."

The other girl stopped, but didn't turn back to face her.

"Look, Jessamyn," said Juniper, "I'll get right down to it. I know you're hiding something from all of us. I don't know what or why—I haven't the faintest idea, to be honest. I don't *think* you're working with Cyril or the Monsians. But I do know there's some funny business going on, and I've got to know what it is."

"Oh, you!" said Jessamyn lightly, turning to splash an arc of water Juniper's way.

The wave washed across Juniper's face. It *was* unusually warm, she thought. But she didn't react, didn't shift her gaze from Jessamyn's, just went on. "I've talked with Cyril about your father. I know he's not an ambassador. Though why that should be a big secret—or if it even is, to be honest—I haven't the faintest idea."

Jessamyn tilted her chin, her face bright and glib, but Juniper held up a hand. "Wait," she said. "Let me tell you first what I think. I think you're a lot smarter than you look. I think you've got some information you could share with me—*if* you're willing—which could be a great help to us all."

"Why, Juniper, you simply—"

"Look around you for a moment," Juniper said desperately. "Won't you think about where we are, what's going on? We're on our own up here in Queen's Basin, with untold bedlam afoot back in Torr. All your talk of getting word back to the palace, and I *saw* that look when we talked about going for the horses."

Jessamyn scowled and skimmed her fingertips across the surface of the water.

"What is it, Jessamyn? What are you hiding? If you know something important, something that could be really useful to us right now—"

"I've nothing to say, and that's that," said Jessamyn stubbornly.

"Then you're going to have to tell me *why* you won't talk. Don't even think I'll believe that you truly have nothing to say, because I can see that *nothing* painted all across your face, bright as your precious rosebud lip salve." Jessamyn flushed. "I'm *not* going to take no for an answer, so you might as well 'fess up."

A moment passed. Then another.

Juniper held very still, not moving a muscle. She could be stubborn, too. She felt the water from Jessamyn's earlier splash pooling in the collar of her dress, seeping into the gathered lace, dripping down her bodice.

Finally, Jessamyn's shoulders drooped, her defiant stance crumpled. She sloshed over to the bank and sank down, not seeming to notice she'd sat right in a patch of gooey red mud. "Fine. What do you want to know?" The words were little more than an exhale, but her tone seemed different—deeper, as though a sharp mind had suddenly clicked into place behind this popinjay's body.

"The truth," said Juniper, plopping down next to her in the mud. "*All of it*. Who are you? What are you doing here? What on earth is going on?"

The story, when it finally came, was both simple and staggering. Jessamyn's father, Rogett Ceward, was indeed a traveling salesman. He'd invented a small multiuse item called a gnut— Jessamyn was vague about what it actually *did*, but apparently it was indispensable to nearly every facet of farm and village life. This fandangle had made the Cewards' fortune.

But that was not the deepest truth about who he was.

Rogett Ceward's visible profession was peddling gnuts. But his hidden trade—the one he did not reveal to anyone around him—was peddling information. He traveled the Lower Continent and beyond, accompanied by Jessamyn's older sister, Eglantine. Their mother hated travel, and ran a quilting shop near their home in central Torr.

But Rogett Ceward was a spy. A spy-for-hire, to be precise.

"Your father is a *spy*?" Juniper echoed. She'd expected something, but *this*? "Jessamyn, I can't even—"

Jessamyn raised a hand. "Please. Call me Jess."

"What?"

Jessamyn tucked her knees up to her chest. She squelched her bare toes into the mud, in such an un-Jessamyn-like manner that Juniper couldn't stop staring. "*That's* what I mean," the other girl said. "That look you just gave me. Who is *Jessamyn*? She's frills and swoons and lolling around morning till night. Jessamyn has never lifted a pinkie finger to help herself." She rolled her eyes. "Jessamyn is the coat I wear to keep out the prying eyes. *Jess* is who I really am. You've no idea how hard it's been to keep up that front—I nearly caved six times while you were cajoling me just now."

"I'd never have guessed," said Juniper dryly.

"Thank you, I try," Jessamyn returned. "I had actually decided it was time to come out with the whole story, given all that's going on back home. But when it came down to the moment, you looked so desperate and drippy. I couldn't resist making you wait for it a little longer."

Juniper knew this revelation should make her hopping mad. But all she could think about was how different this saucy, mischievous girl was from the flibbertigibbet she'd gotten to know over the last weeks. Then again, Juniper knew what it was like to feel your inner self being tugged in two separate directions. Somehow, she didn't think it was going to be hard to think of this girl as Jess. Not at all.

"All right," she said. "You got me good, I can't deny it. But let's go back to talking about your father: He doesn't . . . He's not working for Monsia, is he?"

"Fie, no!" Jess looked aghast. "My father has precious little loyalty, aside from his devotion to the Almighty Pocketbook. But there is one thing he will *never* stoop to, and that is dialogue with the Monsians." She frowned. "There is some history there, I believe, though he's not made me privy to it. I mean, who in the Lower Continent *doesn't* have a personal vendetta against the Monsians? In any case, that's what brought us to the palace—my father heard word of a looming incursion. He was planning to meet with the king and see if they might work out a deal."

"Get paid for delivering his information, you mean."

Jess nodded glumly. "As I said, my father's loyalty is to himself and his coffers first and above all. I don't doubt he knew a great deal about this attack well in advance of its happening. I only wish his timing had been better—or that he'd acted first and waited to secure his payment later."

This sent Juniper into a momentary tailspin. What if her father *had* been told of the coming attack? Might he have been able to guard against it, to nip the threat in the bud, to root out the traitors before they could make their way to the palace doors and let the enemy in? Such a small decision to bear upon such a vast end result!

Juniper shook those thoughts aside. What was done was done; they couldn't go back and change the past, not one bit of it. But the future, that was still within their power—if they acted smart. "So where is your father now? Do you have a way to contact him?"

"That's just it," Jess said. "My father was supposed to send me regular communications, but I've heard not a word. I always thought his greed would get the better of him one day. He's hopeless, you know! I can see how it must have gone: He waited too long to give King Regis the details and to pass on the full warning—maybe holding out for more coin—and then the Monsians moved quicker than he'd anticipated, so he himself got caught in the attack. I'm certain he's now imprisoned there himself, along with the king and all the others. I'm on my own."

Juniper frowned. "Why *did* your father send you along with our group?"

"That was my doing," said Jess. "My sister, Egg, is the smart one—indispensable to his work, she is. Father lets her join him on his journeys and help in all his escapades. Meanwhile, I've got to stay in school and learn to be a lady." She turned up her nose. "I'm out for the summer, and I got him to bring me along on his trip to the palace. He thought it would be good for me to be seen at court, but all the while, I was seeking my chance. If he could only see me in action . . . Well. Then I heard of your trip, and I told Father I should go along with you and . . ." She trailed off.

"You were spying on us!"

Unexpectedly, Jess grinned. "Yeah. That's why I had to act so persnickety—to throw you off the scent and all. How did I do?"

"You took me in for sure," said Juniper. "All of us, I think. But what information could you hope to gain from an all-kids settlement?"

"Why, anything. You're the crown princess of Torr, after all."

Juniper digested this. "So you were coming along to spy on us—on me—and . . . then what? How would you communicate any of your findings?"

Jess's eyes misted up suddenly. "That's the very worst of this whole thing. My own pet—he came with me on my horse. Why do you think I was so upset when they were all stolen? My own dearest Fleeter was in the saddlebag."

"Your *what*? You had a creature in your saddlebag?"

Jess nodded miserably. "Oh, Fleeter! I knew I should have brought him in with me that first night—but I was so worried someone would come to my cave and see him and there would be questions."

"*Fleeter* . . . is, um, a . . . ?"

"A cat. A very special cat, spy-trained and swift as anything. I planned to sneak down and remove him that first night, find him somewhere safe to sleep. That's why I went to the horses' enclosure to begin with. Instead I surprised those attackers but couldn't keep them from absconding with my darling." She dabbed at her eyes. "Now he's doubtless perished, my own love, *and* with him any hope of getting back in touch with Egg or my father."

"He was just . . . stuffed in the saddlebag?"

"Fie, no! The pouch was specially made, extra wide and

reinforced. We put a spiffy nest in there for him, with food and water aplenty. But it's days now they've been gone—even longer! Oh, Juniper, I've been positively frantic. Every moment you've seen me lounging around, I've actually been running over the whole knot in my mind, trying and trying to figure what to do. My father made me swear an oath never to reveal his trade. And how could I reveal myself without betraying him as well? I didn't know what to do."

"So when we spoke of tracking down the horses . . ."

Jess swallowed hard. "My Fleeter's gone, and my father's been taken—I know he must be captive, or he'd have found a way to contact me. I've got to find out if he's all right. I've got to do something. And—then there's my sister, Eglantine. Egg. She's there, too." Jess's head dropped to her chest, and her shoulders shook with silent sobs.

"All right, all right," said Juniper. "I'm glad you told me all this, Jess. There are times when an oath forsworn brings the truest honor of all. We'll figure this out—we *will*, all right?"

She leaned in and wrapped Jess in a tight hug, but all the while, her mind whirled with hopes and plans and possibilities. "Listen. You were asking about sending messages, before. I *could* get a messenger back to the palace, if there was cause to. Is there anything that—"

Jess's face lit up. "That's truly an option?"

"Why, yes—what you've heard me call the messenger is the most wily winged creature alive: a ghost bat, one of a small fleet that was trained up by my father's own hands. Our messenger can fly between two fixed spots, bearing its miniature message capsule, following a sound outside of our own hearing but loud and clear to those tiny bat ears. Our Beacon——that's what produces the sound—— has been set up here, and the other is back at the palace. But what good is a messenger with no one left free to receive its missive?"

"If your messenger can get to the palace, that may be the saving of us all. For Egg is there, and she will know what to do."

"Your sister? Why should she not be held captive along with your father?"

Jess waved that away. "Egg is a special bird, to be sure. She may be the smartest person alive today, never mind her age. For who would ever think to imprison a skinny runt of a girl, not yet fifteen years old *and* deaf as a doorknocker?"

"She can't hear?"

"Not a boom nor a whisper." All trace of tears was now gone from Jess's face. "It's one of Egg's greatest strengths. She has yet to meet a soul who suspects an inkling of her true worth. She'll be free and gadding about the castle, or I'm no Ceward. *And* by now she'll know every last cranny and hiding-hole better than the palace's own builders. If you've got a communication setup, I guarantee you she has discovered it. Only get me to your messenger, and I will get you a spyhole into the castle."

5

JUNIPER DID NOT NEED TO HEAR THIS TWICE;
she sprang into action lickety-split. In no time at all, Jess had
written up a note to Egg—one which would make their needs
plain, yet also not betray them should it fall into the wrong hands.

There was no guarantee, after all.

Jess and Juniper and Erick then gathered on the promontory to
see the ghost bat off, launching it on the wing just as the sun was
setting. Juniper had no idea how long it would take the creature
to fly to the palace, all those leagues away, but starting the journey under the cover of darkness seemed prudent. The creatures
were trained for stealth, so she could only hope it would stay safe
through the whole long journey.

"That's that," said Jess, once the pale dot faded into the horizon.
"And you are setting out tomorrow morning?"

Juniper nodded. "We'll find your cat—that'll be at the top of
our list, you have my word. Erick, you should keep a watch on the
skies while we're away. I can't imagine our messenger will make it

49

back before we return, but if some chance intervenes, you should be ready to gather in his reply."

Erick nodded and, their mission accomplished, the three clambered back down the cliff toward the sleeping caves. As Jess walked off to her apartment, Erick pulled Juniper aside and pressed a book into her hands. "Take this with you tomorrow," he said. "I was scanning my shelves earlier, because I knew I had something with good information about this area."

Juniper looked down at the volume. *Mountain Ranges of the Lower Continent.* What she thought was, *Oh, filch—more weight for my travel pack.* What she said was, "Many thanks, Erick. I warrant this may come in . . . useful."

"It should," he said seriously. "It's not terribly up-to-date—printed more than ten years ago—but how much will have changed out here in that time? The city maps and roadways are hopelessly behind, but I skimmed the Hourglass sections, and they look solid. At least you won't be traveling blind." He looked at the ground. "Oh—make sure to bring warm cloaks. It's a lot colder on that peak than this one."

"I do wish you were coming along," said Juniper. What was a queen to do without her chief adviser?

Erick shrugged. "Wishes are for fishes, as the saying goes. I'll keep Queen's Basin running at a tiptop clip, Juniper. You can count on me."

"I know I can," she said.

The Basin would be safe and well cared for until she could return for it. And she *would* be back within the day, just as planned.

So why was she so worried?

The next morning's sunrise found Juniper, Alta, and a yawning Cyril toting their day-sacks as they stood on the windy ridge, ready to venture into the dark unknown. On Erick's advice, they'd dressed for cold weather—impossible as it seemed in this sun-drenched summer valley. Juniper had on her forest-green gown of triple-spun sheep's wool, which had a pleasing pattern of hand-sewn peonies dotted down the bodice and splashed across the skirts. Best of all, the full skirt was split clear down the middle into a breezy set of pantaloons that were both stylish and practical. If they were to ride the reclaimed horses back—and Juniper resolved that they would—she intended to do so in maximum comfort. Currently her comfort level was hampered by several sets of underclothes *and* her thickest cloak. She felt rather like a stuffed and basted turkey dinner, truth be told. Alta, too, had paired her customary leather cap with a thick, mustard-yellow wool cloak. Even Cyril was puffy and rounded in a startlingly orange wool coat she'd never seen before. But if Erick was right—and when had he not been?—they would be glad of these extra layers before long.

Over the past few weeks, Juniper had seen more than her fair share of caves: passing through the twisty-windy rockway that had first led them up the Hourglass Mountains; going in and out of the huge Cavern, where they'd left their supplies and wagons before descending the cliff to the Basin; and, of course, there was her time in Cyril's prison cave with Alta and Erick. So it wasn't exactly a new experience, that held-breath moment of passing from light to dark, from summer-dawn warmth into the crisp, subterranean cool of the stones' embrace.

Not a new experience, but not one she could ever take for granted, either.

As Juniper parted the bluevine drapes obscuring the opening, she felt again that prickle down her back that she'd noticed the night before. This time, though, it felt curiously like excitement. Where would this pathway take them? What—or who—would they find? She knew she'd put her first skidding footstep on the path to a brand-new adventure.

She couldn't wait to discover where it would lead.

Where it led, at least at first, was *down*. Down and then up, to one side and then the other, as though the tunnel was a bucking horse trying to throw them off with its unexpected twists and turns. At least there were no splits in the way, so Juniper knew they hadn't lost the trail.

She walked in front, with Cyril behind her and Alta bringing up the rear. They each held a blazing torch high, but these were little more than puddles of light in the near-solid darkness. After some time, though, a flicker beyond their flames caught Juniper's eye.

It came from the wall beside her, and when she stopped and tilted her light a certain way, she saw it again. Something seemed to . . . glimmer.

"Hold on a moment," Juniper said. Putting a hand on the nearest wall to steady herself, she moved her torch up and down. Could it be?

She leaned a tentative finger to prod a strip of wall—yes, it was ever-so-slightly tacky. She brought her torch the rest of the way in, edged it right up to that dully glinting surface.

The wall caught fire. Or a strip of it did, anyway.

"Well, gobsmack me!" Alta yelped. "It's another flaming guidepost."

It was. Just like the one in the tunnel they'd followed to reach the Basin, this narrow patch of wall lit up and took off blazing. It was like a freshly wakened guide, rested after a long sleep and eager to be about his task of showing the way.

"Come on," said Juniper. She set off at a quick pace, the other two trucking right behind her.

They followed the flickering guidepost easily through the winding corridors. They'd found it just in time, too, for quickly they came to a fork, then another, then four more in short succession. Without this flare, they could have ended up anywhere at all—for the way was far too dark and rocky to see any horses' prints, even if they were there.

Then, quite suddenly and unceremoniously, the tunnel ended in a high-ceilinged cave. The lighted strip sputtered into its bowl-like ending point, sent up a hot bright blaze, then died out a few minutes later. In the waning pitchlight, a bluevine curtain was clearly visible along the far wall. Juniper pushed through it and out into eye-popping brightness.

The tunnel had led them straight through the mountain and out the other side.

In just this few hours' distance, the surrounding landscape had changed completely. They seemed to be a good deal higher up, and the air was sharper than they'd gotten used to in the Basin. Extinguishing her torch, Juniper pulled her cloak tighter around her neck (inwardly thanking Erick for his good advice) and climbed out onto the black stone cliffside. Here there was none of the Basin's silvery-gray rock that gave out so much light and heat. It was far from summer on *this* mountain. But that wasn't the main thing that caught the group's attention.

Barely fifty steps beyond them, a bridge yawned out into space.

Well, not *space*, exactly.

"Would you look at this?" Alta's voice was awed as the three moved closer to inspect the structure. The bridge was made of wide wooden planks and suspended by arm-thick ropes woven together in a complex pattern. The whole contraption looked solid enough, if it hadn't been slung precariously out over the gorge in a way clearly meant for human passage. As it was, it looked rather like a silk ribbon bridging two battlements.

"We're going to walk over on that, then?" Cyril said, clearly trying for bluster but achieving a sort of bleat.

Juniper didn't love the idea herself, but the bushy, overgrown mountain face made it clear that this was the only way to go. "We've come this far," she said, swallowing a lump in her throat.

She didn't move, though. Neither did the others.

Suddenly, from behind them came a scudder and squeal, then

a round, brownish ball of moving cloth came hurtling out of the cave's opening. It catapulted pell-mell down the rough trail and came to a quivering stop at Juniper's feet. The ball unrolled itself into . . .

"*Tippy?*" said Juniper, aghast.

The little girl sprang to her feet, seeming none the worse for her tumble down the bank. She dusted off her cloak, shook out her arms and legs, and flashed her hands in a pose. "Here I be! Didja miss me?"

"Why, you rugheaded bug!" Alta exclaimed. "What do you think you're doing here?"

Tippy looked from Alta to Juniper, then her cool, impish look melted into something softer and more pleading. "Your Merciful Royalty!" she cried, throwing herself down to clasp Juniper's ankles. "I couldn't be left behind, I simply *couldn't*! Not even the glorious prospect of another game of barley-break could tempt me, that's how devoted I am to you. Tear me limb from limb, Your Mountain Majesty, but never tear me from your side!"

There were actual tiny teardrops starting in the girl's eyes, so caught up was she in her own drama. Juniper groaned. "Oh, pish! Get to your feet, you sneaky weasel. What are we going to do with you now? That's what I want to know."

"Well, send her back home, obviously," said Cyril.

The look on Alta's face suggested she had been about to say something very similar, but at Cyril's suggestion she bristled. "And how's that going to work, do you think? Send this slip of a thing to trek back through hours of tunnels, all by her lonesome?"

"'Tis ever so dark in there . . ." Tippy quavered.

Cyril laughed. "You know, this whippet went to such trouble to soft-foot it behind us all this way—I'm not actually sure she *could* be persuaded to give up and head back."

Despite her misgivings, Juniper had to agree. "Very well. I suppose you're coming with us, then—oh, *no you don't!*" She grabbed wildly at the scruff of Tippy's cloak, for no sooner had the words left her mouth than Tippy was skittering off toward the rope bridge.

"But—but—'tis all ropy and dangly out there! So much of a party bridge! Now that I'm one of the scouting team—I am, amn't I?—I simply must go and give it a dance!"

It took all of Juniper's strength to hold the girl still. "You're not—going to—dance—on that *thing!*" she gasped.

Finally Tippy went limp. She tilted her head toward Juniper. "But we have to cross it, don't we? I can be your scout. Testing the way, as it were." She puffed out her little chest. "I'm ever so stealthy—remember?"

Laughing out loud, Alta moved past them both. "Haven't we all been shown up by this divvy, then? You can head out shortly, Mistress Tippy, only let us levelheaded types give it a gander first. We couldn't bear to end up with your toppling-over death on our hands if there's not the necessary support!"

For all her bold words, Alta's arms shook visibly as she set them on the rope rests. For the first time, Juniper took in just how high up they really were, how steep and deep the chasm's drop was between the two mountain peaks. From way down below, fog billowed up thick and frosty, cushioning the bridge and weaving under and around its every beam.

Juniper watched Alta's slow steps with a hitch in her chest, until the other girl turned and crooked an arm. "It's stiff as roads, Milady Juniper—not even a wobble." The bridge *did* wobble, then—groaned clear to one side and then the other. But even from where she stood, Juniper could see it was the whole structure shifting in the chilly cross-mountain winds. Through this, the boards stayed steady and the handrail taut. The overhead ropes barely moved at all.

The bridge was solid. It would hold them.

"Let's go on out, then," Juniper called, a thrill running through her. "We cross!"

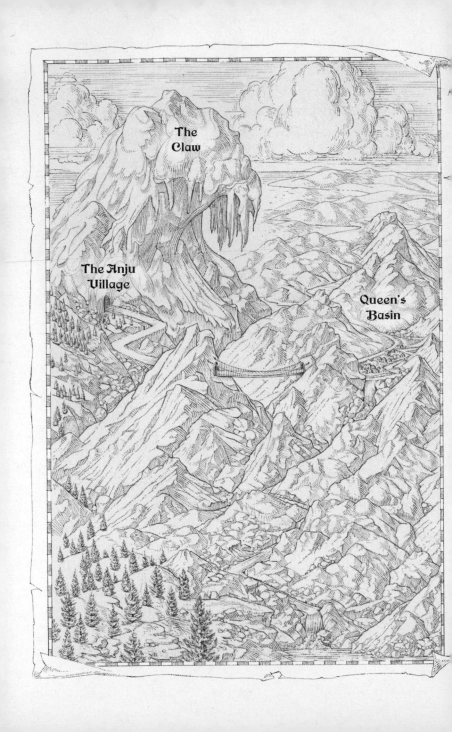

6

EVEN SEEING HOW SOLID IT LOOKED, EVEN
with Alta waving them to come, Juniper had to steel herself for
her first step onto the rope bridge. The fog didn't help, either: It
swirled in colder and thicker, shrouding them above and below so
they almost seemed to be stepping out onto the clouds. Still, there
was no way but forward, and Cyril and Tippy were right behind
her. So Juniper rolled her shoulders, set her hands firmly on the
rope guards . . .

And strode into the void.

The first step was awful: like putting her feet on a mass of
quivering jelly. Maybe you couldn't see much swaying, but, boy,
could you feel it! Could the thieves *really* have persuaded the horses
to cross this way? It seemed hard to imagine. Yet where else could
they have gone? There was no sign of any outlying trails. So Juniper
kept placing one foot after the next after the next, until before
she knew it, she found herself in the very middle of the sky. Alta

had nearly reached the far peak by now, and Juniper could feel the others' cautious steps behind her. But for this magic moment, she felt entirely alone, just a girl in the fog in a slow, chilly dance: finger by foot by step by stride, as she moved toward that gradually nearing peak.

Then a gust of wind blew past.

Juniper's hands tightened on the handrest as the bridge shivered from side to side. In the next step, the puffy surrounding clouds gusted away completely. A glance behind showed the mountain they'd left, still shrouded in mist—with a determined Tippy inching out of it—but the up-ahead was clear and sharp as a mountain stream. And down below them . . .

Juniper allowed herself one quick look. That was enough.

Far beneath her swinging feet, the mountain face dropped off altogether, cascading down a hundred-hundred leagues to fade into a filmy blur. Something soft nudged her arm, and Juniper turned to find Tippy slithering up next to her. The little girl slung her arms around Juniper's waist and held on tight.

Juniper slid her hands along the guardrail and kept walking. "See how near we are," she said brightly. "Not two dozen more steps, I'd say. Wouldn't you think so, too?"

Tippy didn't reply, but her grip on Juniper's waist tightened.

"Tosh, you goose," Juniper teased. "Only see how safe we are on this finely crafted structure! We shall be to that peak in no time. And what would your big sister say to see you here, venturing out all the brave explorer?"

Tippy's chin went up at this. "Elly would be as proud as a pea-hen, she would!"

"That's a certain fact. What stories we shall have to tell her when we get back to the palace!"

And so, backset by this busy patter, the last few steps fell away, until abruptly the bridge was behind them and Juniper was stamping her boots on solid stone again. Tippy launched off the last few steps and flung herself at the ground. Seizing a nearby tree stump, she wrapped her skinny arms as far around as they would go and clung on for dear life.

"Oh, sweet stony earth!" she murmured. "Never again shall I complain of you! Sweetest land of my heart . . ."

Alta shook her head. "For the dough's sake, Tippy!"

Juniper hid a grin and studied their surroundings. They were in a wide clearing that seemed at least partially manmade, to judge by the many tree stumps scattered across the wide-open space (including the one from which Tippy was now rising). The ground bore a thin quilting of snow, and the peak that crested high overhead was scratched out of the same stark black stone as on the other side of the bridge. Tippy blew out, and her breath swirled around her head in a chilly white cloud, making her clap in delight.

If it was this cold in summer, what must the place be like in winter?

Juniper reached into her carry-bag and pulled out the volume Erick had given her. *"Mountain Ranges of the Lower Continent,"* she mused, turning from page to page and trying to connect the carefully mapped-out zones with the land around them. After a moment, Cyril snatched the book from her hand and flipped the pages expertly.

"There we are," he said, tapping one with a manicured finger (though when he'd managed to groom his nails on this expedition was beyond her). "Midrange. Those three mountains clustered so tight like that? Mount Ichor, Mount Perichor, and Mount Lung. Your Basin is cupped right in their apex, the spot where the three come together. We scaled Ichor, tunneled clear on through it following that cave, and came out the other side. So here we have Topmost Bridge, linking us to Mount Rahze. And that peak aloft there can only be the Claw." Cyril sniffed. "A pretentious name if ever I heard one."

"You *would* know," quipped Alta.

"The Claw!" Tippy swung around to face the peak in question, gasping out another puff into the frosty air. "Only look at that shape—do you not see such a very claw-shaped Claw? For I can spot it, plain as day, casting its long and sinister shadow over us all."

The rest of the mountain visible from where they stood was steep and lumpy, with bands of snow-dusted forest striped across its stone face. But this all came to a sharp peak much higher than the other mountaintops in the near distance. The peak rose, then crested over like the top of a foaming wave, like a menacing down-turned scowl.

Like a claw.

There was no denying it was aptly named.

"Well, ain't that the bright and shining welcome," said Alta into the silence.

As Juniper gazed at the Claw, she could have sworn she saw a wisp of dark smoke curling out of the opening and drifting into the hazy blue sky. She shuddered. "I think we'd best be—" she began, then cut off abruptly.

As she refocused on the clearing around her, she noticed three things in quick succession: First, Alta had gone very still, eyes wide. Only her hand settled down to rest on her sword's scabbard. Second, the bushes around them began to rustle— almost as though there was something within them, something on the way out. Last of all came a loud voice, booming from the trees and echoing across the clearing: "Halt, intruders! Lift your hands high above your heads and do not move another muscle."

Juniper did not need to be told twice. She raised her hands slowly in the air, but her mind took quick stock of her surroundings. Tippy still sat on her stump, her jaw dropped open and her eyes wide with fright. Cyril had been in the act of sitting down himself, and the command froze him in an awkward half crouch, which would have made Juniper laugh at any other time. Alta seemed to be wrestling with her better sense; her hand hovered above her sword belt, then her shoulders slumped and she raised her hands as well, for which Juniper gave silent thanks.

Confident that no one was about to do anything rash, Juniper narrowed her eyes and addressed the rustling foliage. She kept her hands high and steady, but made her voice as sharp as bone. "We are *no* intruders! We are citizens of Torr passing time in these mountains by the command of King Regis, my father. We have broken no laws and done no harm. Now *I* demand that you show yourselves so that we might know with whom we speak."

She caught Alta's gaze, and knew they were both thinking of the intruders Cyril and Jessamyn had glimpsed on that dark, fateful night—the ones who had brazenly stolen their horses and had made the tracks that led to this very spot. Had the horse thieves been found at last? And, if so . . . *then what?* Juniper wished she had thought a little more about exactly who or what she was expecting to meet, if their journey was successful. And what she planned to do next.

Still, this was the Lower Continent. Folks were civilized around here. She hoped.

The rustling increased, seeming to come from everywhere at once.

Juniper's gaze was drawn to a point directly opposite her.

The snow-capped branches parted, and a figure stepped out.

Juniper blinked. It was a young man—impossibly tall and slim with long pale hair, wrapped in furs that engulfed his entire body, nearly obscuring even his face. The furs were the same scattered white-on-black pattern as the snow in the trees, so that he—and his companions, for Juniper quickly realized there were at least three of them—blended nearly unnoticed into their surroundings.

"Children of Torr," the stranger boomed. His voice was rough and gravelly, with none of the lilting accent of the Gaulians, nor the harsh staccato tones of Monsia. "What brings you so far from your home? This is no place for unwashed youth to play!"

Juniper's hands dropped to her hips in a rush of queenly indignation, but Tippy got the first words out: "Unwashed?" She shook a churlish fist. "Why, this very yestermorning I went a-dipping in our own stream, good and warm it was, too. If I were any more *washed*, I shouldn't know myself in the darkness."

"Hush, pet," said Alta in an undertone, inching over to swallow Tippy's further comments in the crook of her arm.

Juniper narrowed her gaze on the newcomers. "We are *not* children!" she snapped. "We are delegates of Torr, but we are also citizens of Queen's Basin, of which land I am the queen."

"Queen's Basin?" the stranger snorted. "I know of no such place." He exchanged glances with his nearest companion. They rode no animals, and Juniper couldn't see any visible weapons, but their air carried menace enough.

They did not comment on Juniper's lowered arms, however, which she took as a positive sign.

Composing herself, she stepped forward. "We are a new country, that's true. A dependency of Torr, if you will. My father, King Regis, endowed the land to me and my citizens, and we have established it this very summer. Today we venture out from our appointed land in search of certain aggressors who have done harm to our settlement." She met the stranger's gaze head-on. "Not two weeks past, our valley was invaded and our mounts taken by force. Do you know anything about the theft of nine fine riding horses?"

There was a beat of silence. Juniper noticed the tall youth again exchange glances with one of the others.

As they shifted in place, Juniper's gaze was drawn toward the ground. Their feet! Even from this distance, she could tell that the tall one had extremely large feet—they all did, come to that—and wore an odd sort of shoe she couldn't quite make out. What she *could* just make out was the prints left by those shoes, very familiar prints: the same ones she'd seen around the horse enclosure back in the Basin.

Juniper clenched her fists. "I can see that you know what I am referring to. We have introduced ourselves to you, yet I have heard no such return from your side. Who are you, that we may know our aggressors?"

The tall stranger gave her a superior smile. "Who are we? Why, we are the Anju."

Juniper felt her entire world tilt, then flip over in a full somersault. *The Anju?* Her mother's people, the ones of whom Juniper had heard tantalizing stories in her youth but nothing further since her mother's death so many years ago?

Juniper's breath fluttered shallow in her chest.

The tall Anju was watching her with concern, clearly wondering at the emotional tug-of-war that played across her face. After all these years, all her wanting and wondering, all the questions and the doubts and uncertainty . . . after all this, to be so casually faced with her mother's living heritage, *her own* heritage.

It was quite a lot to take in.

But Juniper was born a princess and crowned a queen. She would not let herself be so easily ruffled. Quashing down her emotions, she kept her voice as even as she could. "You have committed an offense against our settlement," she said. "I demand that you take us to your ruler. We must have our mounts returned to us or due recompense made."

There was a shifting behind Juniper as the other kids lowered their hands to match hers. Juniper glanced over in time to see a flash of admiration on Cyril's face. Before she could properly enjoy this rare treat, however, the tall Anju spoke again.

"We cannot confirm this offense of which you speak. You come to us saying—"

"No!" Juniper cut him cleanly off. "We will not be trifled with like this. Take us to your ruler immediately, or suffer the consequences." She swallowed. *Consequences?* Hopefully they wouldn't test her on this.

But the stranger dipped his head a fraction, then nodded at the others. "Very well," he said to her. "Follow where I lead. *If* you're able to keep up."

With that, he turned on his heel and seemed to quite literally vanish into the woods. Before Juniper could blink, his companions were gone as well.

The four adventurers stood alone at the mountain's edge.

"That went well," said Cyril. "Exceptionally lovable, that group."

"The *Anju?*" Alta whispered. "Juniper, are you all right?"

Juniper's mind raced. Were they really going to traipse into a dark forest following these strangers—these horse-thieving ruffians—Anju or not? Yet what other choice did they have, if they wanted to get back their mounts? Juniper felt a sharp tug in her chest, a pulling match between risk and reason. What was the queenly thing to do in this case? What would Erick, her chief adviser, recommend—caution or courage?

"I'm fine," she said to Alta, fighting down the pressure to move, move, *move*, knowing that every moment was taking the Anju farther from them. "But what do you all think of their 'invitation'?"

"You know me, Juniper," Alta said slowly. "I'm not one to shy from adventure. Trek me through the hills, put a sword in my hand, and I'm happy as a bun in an oven. But those fellows looked right fierce, and no mistake. Your mother's people or not, we've no idea where they're leading us! And if they *did* take our horses . . ."

Live bold! Risk big! screamed Juniper's heart. And: *They're your mother's people. Would they really do you harm?* And: *How can you pass up this opportunity to explore your heritage?*

She looked at Cyril, who snorted. "Far be it from me to agree with the baker's wench, but I have no interest in the Anju, nor do I trust them any farther than I could throw them." This seemed to distract him, and he started flexing his biceps like he was trying to calculate his throwing distance.

It was true that she knew next to nothing about the Anju.

They could be led right into a trap. They were unprotected settlers, and young ones at that—but by the goshawk, this lead was
all they had. And they needed those horses. The longer Juniper
thought, the more the feeling hardened inside her, the certainty
that this was a trail leading her inexorably toward her destiny.
She couldn't think of this as a risk she was taking, not really.

They'd keep going forward.

They would follow this breadcrumb path wherever it led.

7

ONLY MOMENTS LATER, THOUGH, IT SEEMED like their trek might be over before it had properly begun.

"We'll never be able to keep up with them!" said Alta.

"Keep up with them?" Cyril grumbled. "We'll have to find them first."

"We know where to start, at least," said Juniper, darting over to inspect the tracks the Anju had left in the light snow on the edges of the clearing. Large, oddly shaped prints they were, lumpen and tipped with strange sharp points.

"It's like they've got claws all over their feet," said Tippy with a shudder. "That can't be normal."

"All over their *shoes*, Tippy," said Alta. "They're people just like us." She didn't stop frowning at the prints, though.

"Take your eyeful here," said Cyril. "For that's all the prints to be found about these parts. I cannot see another anywhere."

"That's impossible," said Alta. "How could they leave no tracks at all?"

"There's no snow under the tree cover," remarked Cyril. "They kept to the dry patches. Obviously they didn't want us to follow, whatever they said." His voice indicated this was perfectly all right with him.

Juniper wasn't so sure. "I agree they don't really want us to follow. But what they said . . . it sounded almost like a challenge. Like they didn't think we *could*, but that we might just prove them wrong—if we're able."

"Hiyo! Lookie down here," said Tippy suddenly. She'd squatted by a bush, and was now gleefully doing the chicken-walk around it.

"What is it?" said Juniper, leaning down to look.

"They *are* leaving us tracks," said Tippy. "Can you see them?"

Alta squinted. "That bent-off twig?"

"It's not bent—it's *snapped*. And all twisty-turny, so it's pointing ahead. Do you see?"

"What a little dreamer," griped Cyril. But his jibe lacked its usual punch.

"Here's another," Juniper called. "I do believe you're right, Tipster! How do you notice so much?"

"I'm closer to the ground, maybe?" she said mischievously. Never had Juniper been happier about the little girl's freakish attention to detail.

The trail—if it even was that; it was hard to tell for sure—did seem to point a way through the stark, frosty greenery. As Cyril had noted, there was little to no snow on the ground here, but the green that was there stood out all the more clearly in the sparse landscape. Still, it took all of them working together to keep track of the faint guideposts, which often seemed like little more than the markings of forest creatures. Eventually, though, one or the other of them would notice an outlying branch set like a pointing finger. Stripped for visibility, the mere tip broken off, the whole thing bent to show direction.

Subtle, but effective.

So they continued along their way. And when they finally crested a rise and heard the high, warning crack of a whistle coming from the trees, Juniper knew they had arrived.

"Stop!" she called to the others. "I think we've reached our greeting party."

She strode to the front, with Alta and Cyril just behind her and Tippy weaving around them like a wobbly gourd doll. The forest they'd been crossing had looked much the same for their entire trek, but the copse they entered now felt different: The trees were fatter, the foliage thicker overhead, the air noticeably warmer, as though better protected from the elements. And . . .

"Is that roasting meat I smell?" Tippy whispered, lower lip visibly quivering. The smell *was* there—faint and far-off, but unmistakable to their growling bellies.

"Shhh," said Juniper.

The whistle came again. The far branches parted. In moments the adventurers were faced with a long row of strangers— a full dozen of them, men and women alike. Each was beanpole-tall, clad in heavy, pale furs, with a chiseled face and eyes as silvery-hard as stone. The row flexed and parted, and a figure stepped to the front: a wizened old woman whose long fur cap and robe swept out to both sides, revealing a pair of snug leather trousers.

Her voice, when it came, was sharp as flint. "Name yourselves, intruders."

Juniper stepped forward, casting her legs wide in as firm a stance as she could manage on the uneven ground. "We are no intruders. We are citizens of Queen's Basin, a dependency of the land of Torr. We are here upon the invitation of your scouts"—she indicated the tall youth skulking (the coward!) on the far edge of the row—"who have led us to this spot by their identifying markers."

"What is this you say?" the old woman demanded. "Kohr?"

The Anju in question shuffled forward, head down. "We encountered the strangers at the bridge. They demanded a meeting. We imagined they would become lost among the trees."

"You challenged us to follow and left a clear path that we might do so," Juniper retorted. "Thus, we are here at your invitation. I should have thought you would also communicate this to your superiors, but no matter. Let's get down to business. Why are we here? To reclaim what is rightfully ours. I believe your people know something of the nine horses that were stolen from our settlement these weeks past? We require the return of these animals immediately."

The old woman narrowed her eyes. "Your settlement? And who are you, then?"

Juniper straightened further, lifting her head high. "I am Juniper Torrence, only daughter of King Regis of Torr, appointed ruler of Queen's Basin of the Hourglass Mountains. And who are *you*?"

A murmur ran down the row, and Juniper shifted uncomfortably. What was going on?

"Juniper . . . Torrence," the old voice creaked, then the woman barked out a laugh. "Well, the way turns as the road leads. I should not have thought it, but . . ." Before Juniper could react, the woman strode with surprising speed across the open space toward her. She stretched out both arms. "You are welcome in our settlement, Juniper Torrence. My name is Odessa, daughter of Amadia—Mother Odessa, they call me. Well met."

The moment felt slightly off, but Juniper couldn't place why. The old woman seemed almost to be waiting for something. Juniper mentally scanned her Political Discourse lectures—was there some sign-and-call response particular to these mountains? Her father had never lectured on the Anju people or customs in particular, only on their place in the general history of the region. Juniper felt woefully out of touch.

Finally, she settled for inclining her head and reaching out to grasp Odessa's outstretched forearms. What else could she do? "And to you, Mother Odessa."

They embraced, then each stepped back several paces. Juniper thought the woman looked disappointed, but she seemed to quickly steel herself. "I speak for my people," she said. "At least, at this time I do. We are a peaceful tribe, as you will find for yourself. We mean no harm to you or yours, this I swear."

Juniper nodded. "I think we shall have a great deal to discuss, you and I. But first, we must know what it is we are faced with. You appear to recognize my name, so you must know that my mother was one of your own. You have just guaranteed our safety and spoken of your tribe's peaceful nature. Yet how is it that your people have brought this attack against our camp?"

"As you say, there is much to discuss. For your first concern: We do have your mounts, and they shall be returned to you. They were taken . . . in error." Odessa paused and studied Juniper, as though sizing her up. "Times and seasons, my dear, times and seasons! So much can turn upon the span of a moment. You have come to us at a most auspicious time, and that cannot be disregarded." She stood taller, suddenly looking less like a bent old crone and more like the fierce leader of a mountain tribe. "Will you return with us to our settlement?"

Juniper hesitated. "Go back just a moment. Our horses were taken . . . *in error*, you say? How is it possible to converge upon someone's camp and steal their animals *accidentally*? You're either a peaceful people or a warlike one—there's no middle ground."

In answer, Odessa flung her arms wide. "Look around you, girl! You see where you are? The Hourglass Mountains! This is *our* land and has been so for generations. We are peaceful, that is a truth. Did you see any weapons upon those guards you encountered? Do you see any around you now?" It was true. Juniper didn't. "We do not instigate; we do not launch petty skirmishes; we do not venture where we do not belong. We keep to ourselves, and thus we live in peace. Yet we also do not take kindly to encroachments upon our spaces. That valley you chose for your settlement is itself an old Anju camp, albeit long deserted. Can you blame us for keeping an eye out for trespassers on our territory—and for retaliating against those who occupy it without right? We will not mount an unprovoked attack, that's a fact. But we will defend our own to the death."

Juniper felt quite lost for words.

"You see how much can change depending upon the angle of view? Your settlement was spotted by our scouts, who saw it as the trespass it was. Only after the horses were taken did further observation lead us to realize your . . . particulars."

"Particulars?"

Odessa lifted an eyebrow. "Why, your youth, of course. You're all children over there!"

Juniper bristled, but Odessa ran quickly on.

"This put the whole situation in a different light. Still, we decided to keep the beasts, hoping their loss might encourage you to go on your way sooner, to return home without further delay. And now . . . well, now we have still more information, and the image has shifted again." Odessa heaved a weary sigh. "Ah, your mother! Mountain blood runs through your veins, girl. It turns out you've as much right to the territory as any of us. Now—will you come and learn more about this blood tie? Will you come and see your mother's people for yourself?"

Would she? Juniper had taken three quick steps before Odessa had finished her last sentence. Turning back to the others was almost an afterthought, and seeing the hesitation in Alta's and Cyril's faces did nothing to quell her enthusiasm.

She was queen, by the goshawk! This was *her* call to make.

"Come on," she said. "Let's go meet the rest of the Anju."

Avoiding their eyes, she turned to follow Mother Odessa into the trees.

8

"WHAT *CAN* YOU BE THINKING?" CYRIL HISSED in Juniper's ear as the fur-clad Anju melted ahead of them into the dense forest canopy.

"I'm doing what I must," Juniper retorted. The idea of unsettling her brash, boisterous cousin just made her decision a happier one. Anything Cyril disliked couldn't be that bad.

Cyril's mouth twisted. "I see," he said with distaste. "Leaping at the chance to return to your savage roots. If you knew the things I do about these *people*! You've no idea what you're getting into."

"Don't I? How about you tell me, then, if you know so much."

Cyril shifted uncomfortably. Underneath that pompous arrogance, Juniper caught a flash of something else.

"Wait," she said. "You're not *afraid* of the Anju, are you?"

"They're wild!" Cyril said hotly. "They're unprincipled—they live in the *forest*! We might expect anything at all from them. How can you venture off into the boondocks like this, with absolutely no sense of where we might end up?"

Alta looked anxiously between the two of them, as if hesitant to commit to one side over the other. Tippy just seemed to be enjoying the show.

"Cyril," Juniper said patiently, "*we ourselves* live in the wilds, just at this moment. These are my mother's people. Surely many of them knew her, even! It's not twenty years since she went away. If they meant us harm—and why would they, after all?—but if they did, then surely they would have shown so by this time. Why should they lie about their peaceful natures, when they have it well within their numbers to overwhelm us anytime they choose? Look around you. They're nowhere to be seen at all. We are following *them*."

"More fools us," Cyril muttered.

"I didn't see any sign of weapons," said Alta, but she sounded like she was trying to talk herself into agreement.

Cyril persisted. "I know all about the Anju. They've got a whole network of clans like this scattered through the Hourglass range. One tribe? *Pssht.* That would be no concern. But they're all *connected.* Maybe they don't go around mounting attacks, like that old woman said. But when they need to defend themselves, they are fearsome to behold! And who can say what they might consider a threat?"

"What are you saying, Cyril?" Juniper said, but she was only half listening. Her focus had snagged on his first statement. A network of clans, which might be called together at a moment's notice?

"I'm saying you can't just go skipping into their den like an ignorant schoolgirl. You'll be eaten alive."

Ordinarily, Juniper would have caught that barb and batted it right back into Cyril's face. Instead, she couldn't hold back a smile. Far from talking her out of meeting the Anju, Cyril had just added a great and shining new reason to do so.

Could there be an answer here to their Monsian problems as well?

"How is it that you know so much of the Anju," she said finally, "since you evidently have never met one in person? Aside from my mother, of course."

"Why, don't you recall where I've been the last five years? I took Cultural Perspectives twice weekly at the Academy all last quarter."

Juniper considered him. "Learned a lot about them, did you?"

"All there is to know. I was top of my class, obviously. Anything you like—history, topography, cultural customs, relationships." He tapped the side of his head. "It's a treasure trove in there, I'm not too proud to say."

Juniper rolled her eyes. "You've got pride enough to spare, I'm sure. Still," she said cheerfully, "there's one great thing about you, Cyril: The more trouble you try to cause, the better things usually end up for the rest of us. We may find a use for you yet, pompous noggin and all. Now, our guides are getting away. Try and keep up, will you?"

In the end, they didn't have far to go. Dense as the copse of trees had been where they first stopped, the Anju's trail led them even deeper: into the darkest patch of forest Juniper had seen yet. Moss crawling along the ground was so dark as to be nearly black, and the hanging vines gave off a lightly perfumed scent. While the air still held a little bite, it was far warmer than when they'd first crossed over to this mountain. Though not nearly so warm as the Basin. Unlike the secretive scouts, Odessa didn't let herself get too far ahead, but waited for Juniper and the others to reach the group before pushing on further.

Finally, Odessa came to a stop. "We have arrived," she said.

"Here?" said Alta doubtfully. "Where are we, then?"

Tippy bounced on her toes, then let out a sudden gasp, her eyes wide and round. "Only look up, everybody! Oh, the wonders!"

Tilting her head back and scanning the treetops, which glowed gently with pops of glimmering light, Juniper saw flashes of walls and roofs and frosted wooden structures peeking out of the dark green bristles.

The Anju village was everywhere above them. It was *in* the trees.

While Odessa stood and waited, smiling at their gapes of wonder, the rest of the tribespeople kept moving. Some slipped behind and into the verdant bushes. Some grasped hold of ropes or low-hanging branches and pulled themselves up various nearby structures. Every one of them seemed perfectly at home in this rustic outdoor paradise.

"Too much," moaned Tippy. "Too very much happy for one expedition!" Her hands opened and closed like she couldn't wait to start climbing. She did wait, though, turning to Juniper to see what came next.

Odessa faced Juniper as well. "Juniper, daughter of Alaina, will you and your companions come up and tour our village?"

Juniper felt excitement ripple through her. So this was her mother's village—where young Alaina was born and lived her whole early life! Juniper had always loved climbing, had always felt freer looking down on the world from a height. Was this something she'd inherited from her mother, too? She looked at Alta.

Alta met her eye. "If I may speak for us, Juniper?" Juniper nodded, and Alta said to Odessa, "We are greatly pleased by your welcome, as our queen has stated. However, as her chief guard"—Alta had to notice the tiny smile that quirked the old woman's lips, but she barreled on—"I find myself wishing for a little more information. I can see that we have arrived at your settlement, and a fine settlement it does appear. But before we ascend, I'd like to know a little more about what we should expect. Where are you taking us exactly, and to what purpose?"

"Another thing," Cyril cut in. "Back upon our first meeting, you said you spoke for your group, but just 'at this time.' What the deuce did you mean by that?"

"You've posed two very good questions—and very big ones, besides," Odessa said, acknowledging the others but still facing Juniper. "I'd hoped to get a little more comfortable before delving into historical matters. But if these answers will ease the transition, I am happy to oblige. To address your last question first: We, as a tribe, are in a state of mourning. Our beloved chieftain has died, only seven days past." She lowered her head slightly. "Our rulerships are set in place for three decades, but Chief Darla wore the leather band for a mere seventeen years. This has been our week of remembering, our week of preparation before the new ruler takes control of the tribe. Until that ruler is chosen, as a former chieftain myself, I am the one to fill the gap, along with the other members of our Council of Elders."

"You have my sincere regrets on the loss of your chieftain," Juniper said quietly. "It seems like a poor time for your tribe to be entertaining visitors."

"Not at all," said Odessa. "The only thing better than a life well lived is a death well met. Chief Darla left us too soon, but her passing was not unexpected. It was some months ago now that she contracted the yellow flux, which left her in a delicate and declining state of health. But she had lived a full life, and we are not ones to lose time weeping. This week is her tribute: a time of remembrance and honor and commemoration. We are celebrating her life, as she wished for us to do and as is our custom. As I have said, your horses are safe and being kept in a secure location. We shall take you to inspect and retrieve them by and by. But first I would like to offer you a tour of our settlement. And I invite you to join us at our feast this eventide. For the company and to share the experience, but also because we have quite a delectable spread lined up, and you have the look of those who could use a hearty filling-up."

Juniper opened her mouth. Then she paused. She knew their first priority was to get to the horses, to check on Jessamyn's spy cat and see if, against all hope, it was still alive to be rescued. Yet the thought of gathering their mounts and leaving the Anju behind, so soon after she'd come, was like a punch to the gut. She turned toward Alta. "What say you, my chief guard?"

"For my part, I should like to see the horses first thing. But . . . I can see the value in touring the settlement as well."

Juniper brightened. Of course—retrieving the spy cat and the horses was no longer the only possible value to be gained from meeting with the Anju. What if there *was* a way to enlist the tribe's help in the fight against Monsia? Returning to Torr with the backing of a larger group could make all the difference. More to the point, Alta had to know how badly Juniper wanted this connection personally, and she loved her friend for justifying it for her aloud.

Suddenly, she had a way to make both operations possible.

"Mother Odessa," said Juniper, "I should be glad to accept your offer of a guided tour of your settlement. I shall bring young Tippy along with me. At the same time, might Alta be conveyed to retrieve the horses?" She paused. What about Cyril? Alta nodded and patted her scabbard reassuringly. Juniper grinned. Cyril had shrunk visibly since entering the Anju's settlement. Whatever information he'd learned about them at the Academy, it seemed fairly clear he wouldn't step out of line while they were here. "Take him along with you," she mouthed, and Alta nodded. Cyril folded his lips at being so unceremoniously parceled off, but he said nothing.

"And the evening meal?" asked Odessa. "You will stay long enough, I hope, to join us in this time of celebration? It seems to me there is no better way to know a people than to share their table. And this will be a feast like few others."

"Oh, let us stay," cried Tippy, "for that roasting meat has been piping its sweet smell at me and fairly begging me to answer!"

"Evening meal means evening dark," Alta cautioned.

"Then we shall put you up for the night, and you may head out tomorrow at first light," said Odessa. "Even if you left now, you should not reach the bridge before nightfall, which would leave you to camp out in the open. Enjoy our hospitality, humble as it is, and you will set out refreshed on the morrow."

"Very well," said Juniper. The idea of a longer stay with her mother's people was very pleasing. And when that came complete with a delicious meal? Well.

It was no decision at all.

They decided that Odessa would take Alta and Cyril to fetch the horses, which were penned up on the far side of the village. The Anju had little use for livestock, Cyril informed Juniper before they went their separate ways. They prided themselves on their foot power, and it was said they could outrun a carriage at full tilt. Juniper thought that was something she would quite like to see.

Juniper and Tippy were introduced to a newcomer, a girl of about Juniper's age who was to be their guide. She'd materialized from behind the tree's trunk as though she had been lurking there all along, just awaiting introduction.

"I am Zetta," the new girl said. "With your permission, Mother Odessa, I should be happy to provide escort from here." She inclined her head to the older woman, then looked challengingly at Juniper. "Shall we climb?"

While Odessa led the others away into the tree cover, Zetta motioned toward the nearest trunk. Juniper saw a low branch jutting out near her at about waist height. It was smooth and worn and sturdy as a well-built bench. It beckoned. She looked up beyond it and saw that the first branch led to a second, which led to a third, and on up this fat friendly tree in a winding sort of stair. The stair led to a landing and, just visible through the leaf-heavy branches, a polished walkway that was very like the wooden rope bridge they had crossed not an hour before.

She thought of their own Great Tree, back in the Basin, and how the branches led up like stairs to the big tree-house platform. These steps showed a similar kind of shaping—though how someone could make branches grow one way or another, Juniper had no idea.

Tippy bounced on her toes, but Zetta waved a hand for Juniper to head up first.

So. This was it, then.

She started to climb.

9

DURING HER AWKWARD ASCENT, JUNIPER HAD to stop more than once to steady herself against the rough bark. There were no handrails, and the step ledges grew increasingly narrow, but it was clear from Zetta's steady pace that *she* found this as easy as treading a garden path. Juniper loved climbing as much as the next girl—and more than many, in fact; it was one of her favorite ways to clear her mind and anchor her thoughts—but this was less of a climb and more of a vertical tightrope. Not to mention the way the wind tugged at her billowy split skirts and her thick cool-weather cloak. Juniper ground her teeth, gripped the trunk for support as best she could, and clambered on.

When they reached the top, Juniper was panting and off balance. She needed to figure out how best to get around in this treetop kingdom. Frowning at Zetta's feet, she saw the girl was wearing the same type of footwear as the scouts had back in the clearing. Zetta caught her look and lifted a foot for Juniper's inspection.

"Thrice-toughened rawhide," she said. "Strong but flexible."

"And these?" Juniper touched a finger to the stiff prongs that extended all along the bottom of the shoes, and out from the front tip as well.

"For traction," she said. "We're a climbing people, if you haven't noticed. It works fine for walking tough terrain, but it's magic on bark." She smirked.

Juniper looked down at her hobnailed boots, with their hard, unbending soles. She considered taking them off, but it was a bit too cold for that. Well, there was nothing she could do for her feet. Her gown, on the other hand . . .

"Do you have a knife, by any chance?"

Zetta looked startled, but shook her head. "Not on me," she said. "We don't hold much with weapons here, as you will no doubt discover."

"I'm not looking for a weapon, only a way to make my climbing efforts tolerable. Just a minute." Tugging the wide sash off from around her waist, Juniper held it up by its end and considered the neat stitching. With a pang of regret, she chose a spot at the narrow end and began to work at it with her teeth. It took a couple of minutes, with Tippy and Zetta staring on in confusion, before the delicate fabric frayed and a small tear appeared. Juniper grasped one side in each hand and yanked them smartly apart. The sash gave a satisfying rip straight down the middle. Juniper pulled the tear through to the end of the long band of cloth. Then she took one of the two newly narrow ribbons and laced it around her right calf in a crisscross pattern, fixing the billowy material snug to her legs. She did the same with the left side, then gave a proud twirl.

"That shall do well enough," she proclaimed.

"Oh, Mistress Juniper, you do look a picture!" said Tippy. She had hiked her own skirts up around her knees and tied them into a serviceable knot. Her knobby knee bones peeked through her undergarments, but Tippy was young enough that no one could possibly take offense.

"Well. If we're done with this precious grooming moment," said Zetta dryly, rubbing a hand along her sleek pantsuit, "perhaps we can resume the tour?"

"Indeed we can," said Juniper, "and I thank you for your patience."

Zetta shrugged, but with another look at Juniper's freshly created trousers, she added a tiny smile of approval.

Now that Juniper was comfortable, she took in her surroundings. They had come up through a hole in a plank floor onto a wooden balcony edged in a smart carved handrail. Again she was reminded of their own dear Great Tree, back in Queen's Basin. But while their tree house's floor was made of hewn wood and nailed-down planks, the construction around them seemed to have been coaxed out of the living tree: a bright, rounded structure that was solid and gleaming and daringly wide open. It was a lot like the tiny rooms in the Great Tree's trunk, actually—the way they seemed to have been hollowed out with no sign of human intervention, almost as though the tree itself had grown up that way. The result was breathtaking, and made Juniper feel quite at home.

Their height was astonishing, too, for now they were right in the ice-crusted shoulders of the sturdy tree. Above them, the leaves spread wide and fat, so that a mere dusting of snow showed on the roofs of the nearby dwellings. The floorboards and stairs had been brushed clean, with no slick surfaces at all. Far below, the ground looked leagues away.

"It's a wonderland!" Tippy squealed, and shot off down the nearest walkway.

Juniper soon saw that the Anju village was constructed entirely of wood. It was strung across the interconnected treetops like a woodland fairy paradise: webbed bridges and delicate banisters; gleaming halls with polished turrets and stepped bark roofs; walls and columns and apple-round windows to let in the sun. There were people, too, scattered here and there, busy villagers going about their work and play with little concern for the visitors in their midst. Small cabins and huts were built around the tree trunks, linked to the main settlement by a network of narrow airways. Or sometimes—

"Look! A swing!" Tippy leaped onto the miniature platform and swung herself breezily from one landing to the next with the ease of a native.

From within each home, faces appeared at windows, bodies filled doorways and then moved away: lean, slender, strong-shouldered men and women, boys and girls. Their eyes were frank and curious, but where Juniper would have liked to linger, introduce herself, hear a little about them, Zetta moved briskly on by. She passed each one with a smile and a nod, but led the way steadily forward.

As they progressed through the settlement, Juniper silently took in the information shared by Zetta: here lived this family and there that one; here the Littles took their morning lessons; over yonder was the Memory Wall, a giant historical record on the trunk of one great tree; there was the Climbing Tree.

"Climbing Tree?" Juniper interrupted, for she couldn't help herself. Tippy, a dozen steps in front, cocked her head and turned back.

A smile creased Zetta's sharp face. "Do you wish to try? If there's a better way to pass an hour or two of leisure, I don't know it."

Juniper tilted her head back, taking in the trunk in question. Unlike the other picturesque, well-crafted Anju structures, this tree was a welter of slapdash construction: there were bars and handles and knotted ropes and swings of all shapes and sizes. Brightly colored dye had been rubbed into the pale bark in various looped, overlapping patterns.

"Never should I snub the chance of new adventure!" Tippy trilled. "But how do you tangle out all this zig-a-zag color stuff?"

"Here is the starting platform," Zetta explained. "You simply pick one color and follow it through to the end. Start with the green track—that's the simplest. Then you move up to red, violet, and then black: the most daring of all. Will you attempt it?"

There was a challenge in Zetta's eye that settled *that* question for Juniper right quick. Glad for her newly appropriate climbing outfit, she gripped the first rope and began to climb with fervor. She fell behind Zetta almost immediately, of course, but that hardly mattered.

The moment her hands closed around the pull ropes, she was hooked.

Her Anju roots might have been left deep in her past, little more than the stuff of her mother's tales and legends. But right now, in this moment, she climbed like she was born to it.

In the end, Juniper completed the green and red tracks, and half the violet, before she set her boot down wrong and skidded sideways. She plummeted off the ramp, toppling head over legs to flop down on the thick rope net that was strung up around the course.

"My Lady Juniper!" Tippy screeched from above. The little girl scurried down the Climbing Tree after her, but Juniper just flapped a hand to show she was fine.

Juniper found that she enjoyed the floaty sensation of resting on the knotted ropes nearly as much as she had the climb. She bobbed gently, arms wide, taking in the leafy roof above with its peekaboo stretches of blue sky edging through, and wondering if she'd ever felt this light, this carefree. There was something about the Anju that went right to the core of her, like a half-remembered dream coming unexpectedly to life in the waking world.

A few moments later, Tippy flopped next to her, and Zetta joined them last of all, first looking down with disapproval, then finally picking her way over to sit primly alongside them. It was, Juniper thought with a giggle, quite nearly as though Zetta had been the one raised in the Royal Palace, and Juniper herself out in the wilds.

What on earth had become of that overscheduled, super-organized princess of Torr who had not a moment for leisure nor ever edged one foot off its prescribed path?

Juniper had no idea. But she felt no hurry to reclaim that version of herself.

Eventually Zetta said, "You see how our whole life is in these treetops? I told you that we climb for fun, and that is true. But more than that, we climb out of necessity. I made my start up the Climbing Tree before my third summer. You didn't do poorly for a first climb. Both of you," she added. "And with your barbarian footwear, no less." She wiggled her own flexible, sharp-edged monstrosities—which Juniper thought had never looked more practical or appealing.

Still, shoes notwithstanding: "I enjoyed it ever so much," Juniper said, still feeling the strain in her arms and legs. She couldn't help thinking how different her life and upbringing would have been had her mother made different choices, all those years ago. Of course, then her mother wouldn't have met her father, so there was no sense going down that path.

Zetta cleared her throat. Offhandedly, she said, "Chief Darla was my mother."

This woke Juniper clean up. Darla, the newly deceased chieftain? "Oh, that's awful," Juniper said. "Zetta—I'm so sorry. You must be . . . I mean, are you all right?"

Zetta shrugged, though some play of emotions struggled across her face. "We were not close," she said simply. "I entered the Littles cabin before my fourth summer. Earlier than some, but a chief's life is not as others'. My mother was a busy woman."

She went silent then. Zetta's revelation loosened something inside Juniper's own chest, so that she wasn't even sure what she was going to say before the words were spilling out.

"I lost my mother when I was seven. But before that . . . we were inseparable. She was the queen, of course, but I was with her nine hours of every ten. She didn't even let me have a maid—imagine? She took all of my care upon herself, sat me right next to her during any royal function she was required to attend. Except for the long boring ones, of course, or those that went until the early hours."

Zetta was looking at her curiously. "Your mother was Alaina."

"Yes," Juniper said. "I know she was a chief's daughter. I don't know much more about her than that. My mother told me stories, of course, but I was so young. It was all trees and rivers and loving life in the wild. It was places, not people. I suppose that's what I wanted to hear, at the time. I wanted adventure and action and silly tales. By the time I figured out what kinds of things I most needed to know, it was too late."

"She was to have been the next chieftain, you know."

Juniper propped herself on an elbow. "What?"

Zetta nodded. "Our chiefs rule for a period of thirty years, as Mother Odessa said. During the last half of the period, understudies are appointed—three or four, usually, young girls of the Bloodline who have the qualities for leadership."

"Wait—girls only?"

Zetta smirked. "Of course. What do you think, a man would be our chief?"

"Well . . . I suppose I never thought of it. You only have women rulers, then?"

Now it was Zetta's turn to frown. "It's different in your country?"

"In Torr my father is king. My mother was the queen, of course, but he was the direct heir to the kingdom. He carried the load of rulership."

Zetta shook her head, as though such an alien custom was beyond her understanding. "In any case, Alaina was one of those appointed. The main one, I heard. Your mother was Firstblood, and my mother only Secondblood. They trained together, but Alaina was far superior. Or so I've been told."

"Firstblood and Secondblood? What's that, then?" Tippy cut in, startling Juniper. She'd almost forgotten the little girl was there.

"It's the oldest way of measuring bloodline," Zetta said. "Legend says the first Anju sprang from the earth and rock of the Hourglass Mountains, and every one of us who came after is one of their descendants. Much has changed among us since those days; people come and go, and that earth connection does not extend the same across each one of us. Those who are chosen to lead our tribe must first show that their link to this land is rock-solid. Blood-solid. We are not just born to these mountains; they're a part of our very selves." Her eyes narrowed. "As you would know for yourself if you'd ever bothered to come here before now."

Juniper shook her head. She wouldn't rise to this bait. "Go on with your story," she said. "My mother was Firstblood, you were saying."

"All right. Well, Alaina was so much the frontrunner—by blood but also by skill, you know, she was that gifted—that the others were barely more than afterthoughts. That's why she was chosen to accompany the group going to launch a dialogue with the lowlanders."

Juniper digested this for a moment. "So then when she decided to stay in Torr . . ." She could imagine how that must have gone over.

"Yes," said Zetta. "Our whole tribe was thrown into disarray. The other candidates weren't nearly ready; my mother admitted that herself. She was so angry with Alaina; everyone was, for a terribly long time. Thoroughly irresponsible, she was—everyone still thinks so. Who would ever choose to put her *own* wants before those of her people?"

Juniper tried to imagine her mother, not even ten years older than she herself was now, being so swept away by the romance of this dashing man and his kingdom (lands, but it squicked her stomach to think of her father that way!) that she unexpectedly, impulsively decided to leave behind everything she'd ever known and start a brand-new life with him. Not only leaving behind her people and their leadership, but also knowing she would likely never see her home again. What must have gone through her mind? Juniper swallowed. "And what do *you* think of her?"

"Truthfully? It sounds like the bravest thing I can imagine.

Callous and irresponsible, to be sure, but awfully brave. To follow your heart like that, with no regard for where it might lead? She must have been iron-hard, your mother." Zetta sighed. "I don't deny I hated her a bit. Every time the other mothers gathered for Evening Hours and mine was off occupied with tribe business, I blamed her. Darla shouldn't have been the one wearing the leather band; Alaina should have. But eventually . . . I guess I got used to it." She smiled wanly. "And now Darla's gone, and Alaina as well, and here we are, both of their daughters together again. Who could have predicted it?"

"Who indeed?" said Juniper, pushing gently at the rope net on which they rested. Then a small, Tippy-shaped ball landed squarely in the middle of her stomach and knocked the wind clear out of her.

"Augh!" cried Tippy, unfolding herself. "I am bright pink with apology, Your Shamefully Bruised Royalty! I went back up to try to finish the violet track, but that last twist is powerful tricky. I can't believe I landed right on you . . ."

"It's quite . . . all right," Juniper said, pulling herself off the nets and easing back up onto the course. All this talk of the past was messing with her head, so the rude dash back to the present was actually a welcome relief. "I suppose it's time we got moving anyway. Is there more of the village for us to see?"

Zetta had already hopped onto the platform, and extended a hand to hoist Juniper up after her. Tippy monkeyed right alongside, crushing a heel into Juniper's ear but managing to avoid further damages after that.

So they continued on through the rest of the tour. But much as she enjoyed the sights and oohed and aahed when appropriate, a certain part of Juniper stood several steps back from the action, observing with an odd, detached wonder the small kingdom for which, had her life's course run just a little differently, she might have been in line to rule.

10

JUNIPER MET UP WITH ALTA AND CYRIL JUST
as the sky was beginning to pink and the sun was dipping toward
the far cliffside. With so much of the village under the cover of
trees, the sunsets weren't so clearly visible here as in the Basin.
The Anju did have one concession to ground-based living, however: a raised, rounded hillock where the entire tribe appeared
to gather for meals and occasions. This was where they were all
coming together now. It was colder here, out from under the
shelter of the trees and undergrowth. When two runty youngsters bustled up to the Queen's Basin group bearing heavy fur
wraps, the adventurers accepted them gratefully.

Once she'd wrapped the silky furs over her cloak, Juniper
leaned in close to Alta. "How went your time?" Juniper asked.
"Did you find—"

"Yes," Alta said, face aglow. "We found the horses. They're
all safe and well cared for. They shall be ready to head out at

morning's first light. The Anju have been as good as their word, and I foresee no troubles at all."

"What about the"— Juniper lowered her voice—"you know, the *cat*? Was it . . ."

"See for yourself." Alta tilted her head toward where Tippy sat, muddy skirts blooming out in a poof along the ground around her. In the hollow of her lap sat a dollop of gray fuzz.

Juniper sank down beside Tippy, after pausing first to unlace the ribbon from her calves. The self-styled pantaloons had been indispensable during her climb, but now they were making her feel clumsy and off balance (plus, she couldn't help thinking the puffball look didn't quite flatter her figure). This task completed, she reached out to prod the wobbly creature that sat licking Tippy's hand.

"If that's not the ugliest mongrel alive, then I'm no true Lefarge," said Cyril with distaste, from Tippy's other side.

The cat was skin and bones, but its distressing looks actually went a good deal deeper. It had blotchy gray fur that was worn away in large patches, a crooked tail, and ears like wilted sunflower petals. It also had what could only be described as a snout, which it now bared, showing pointy yellow teeth. Juniper leaned back involuntarily.

"Such a little love," gushed Tippy. She draped the unfortunate creature across her forearm and lifted it up to nuzzle her cheek.

Cyril shuddered.

Juniper, swallowing, ran a finger across the cat's back. "It looks surprisingly . . . healthy," she managed. "Where did you find it?"

"Still in the saddlepouch, for the wonder!" said Alta. "Say what you like of Lady Jessamyn, but she looked out for her beast. 'Tis a roomy little nest she made, and the way the bag hung down between the horse's legs, the Anju must not have even known it was there."

"Poor baby," Tippy crooned. "Were you *quite* forgotten?"

"It would have been disastrous if left much longer—the creature was clearly half mad with thirst, but unable to escape the latched bag. Still, there was a clever water pouch with a suckling tube that must have been quite full on the outset. The cat seems to have rationed itself so that the last bit only ran out quite recently." Alta tilted her head. "Else it wouldn't be alive now, would it?"

Juniper looked at the cat with new respect. "A survivor," she said. "Good. That's my favorite type of creature. So, tomorrow then, we set out bright and early."

There wasn't time to say anything further, as Zetta arrived and settled herself on Juniper's right side. Also, it was clear that mealtime was approaching, and Juniper was too hungry to give attention to anything else. Two large flanks of meat—wild boar, Zetta whispered sidelong—had been spitted on long green branches and slowly roasted all day over a bed of flaming coals.

Several men now began digging at rounded tufts of earth scattered at the hillside's base. The one nearest to Juniper was pocked all over in little steam holes, from which mouthwatering tendrils of scent wafted out in their direction.

"They have cooked food growing under the ground?" Tippy asked doubtfully.

"Watch and see," said Zetta.

A bony man wearing thick leather gloves tackled the near mound, clearing off the earth and then lifting out heavy, steaming rocks. From within came bursting clouds of fragrance that made Juniper go weak in the knees.

"Only I shall die of the goodness, never even having eaten it," Tippy moaned.

"How does it work?" Juniper asked, speaking a little louder to drown out the noisy growling of her stomach. The smell really was *too* good.

"It is one of our specialties," said Zetta, looking pleased as pudding. "The pits are dug well in advance, and first thing this morning, they were filled with coals fresh from the fire. Meat and roots and whatever else we had ready for cooking were all set above the heated foundation in layers. The whole thing then was covered up and left to steam-cook all day. You've smelled the tantalizing result, and only wait until you taste it. I myself cannot wait!"

"Ugh," said Cyril in an undertone. "Surely there is as much dirt as food in that pit. I shan't come anywhere near it."

"Cyril!" Juniper hissed at him. "We're guests here—you can't go saying stuff like that. Or didn't they teach manners at your precious Academy?"

Zetta laughed, while Juniper died a little inside to think she'd overheard the exchange. But all Zetta said was "All the more for those who do."

The food that was pulled out of the pits, however, showed no signs of its time underground. "The stones are scrubbed first," Zetta explained, "and all the food is layered all around in wide papua leaves before being covered over with earth. This serves to keep in the moisture *and* keep out everything else." She turned her nose up a little in Cyril's direction, but he only huffed.

The leaves were now being peeled away, strip by strip, and if the smell that had drifted out till this point was good, what came next was staggering. When the final steaming layers were pulled off and the full aroma burst out, Juniper forgot the roasting boars altogether and fell into the throng pushing toward the table. They all did—except Cyril, but Juniper decided to ignore him; he could fend for himself. The table was really a raised woven mat covered in a fresh layer of the same wide papua leaves. Upon this the food was scattered as it emerged, piping hot, from the pits, and those nearest to hand began heaping it onto thin bark plates. Soon the boars were ready, too. These were carved up and layered onto the table in crispy, sizzling strips, ready to be snatched up and eaten with scalded-hot fingers.

"It is a rare thing for us to eat meat," said Odessa, who had moved beside Juniper as they awaited their turn for food. "Our diet consists chiefly of roots, vegetables, and legumes. Meats are reserved for our feast days. This may explain the rather . . . *extreme* enthusiasm you see among our people."

Juniper grinned. *Enthusiasm* was a mild description for the joyful brouhaha going on all around them. In the hubbub, Juniper lost sight of Tippy and Alta as they angled nearer to the well-filled table. Even Cyril seemed to be overcoming his reluctance and stood with well-filled plate in hand, poking at his meat with cautious interest.

"One at a time—there's plenty for all!" came a deep voice. Several wizened men and women were directing the crowd, keeping things smooth and orderly.

"Those are the other Council members," said Odessa.

"They are the ones in charge now, right? Along with you?" Juniper asked. She wasn't sure this was the right time to broach the subject that had been lurking at the edges of her mind—now, with the smell of roasting meat wafting around them like life's biggest temptation. But she didn't know when she'd get a better chance. "I don't know if you've heard about this yet, but I thought you should know. Not a month ago, the Monsian army invaded Torr." Juniper swallowed, all her fear and uncertainty rising in her throat like a giant choking lump. "My father—the king—is in gravest danger, and our whole kingdom near to being overthrown."

Odessa turned away from the food, giving Juniper her full attention. She didn't look surprised, so at least some of this was not new information.

"I know this isn't the time for too much detail—only, before we leave tomorrow, I wonder if I might speak to the Council, to you and them, to see if . . . well. Our country needs help, and that's the truth. We're just a small group, those of us at Queen's Basin. I guess you know that. And we who have turned thirteen are adults by the laws of Torr, but in reality we are all very young.

What can we hope to do against an entire invading kingdom?" To her dismay, Juniper could feel tears starting in her eyes. "We need help. *Fighting* help. We need an army. And . . . you're my mother's people. We don't have anyone else to ask," she ended miserably.

For a moment, Juniper thought she saw a look of pain cross the old woman's face. Almost in the same moment, though, Odessa shook her head. "I realize that you know little of our ways, child," she said gently. "But this thing you are asking is impossible. I meant what I said when we first met. We are not a people to launch an attack, not for any reason. You don't know our history, but the Anju have seen war and bloodshed enough for a hundred-hundred generations. Many years ago now, our people took a solemn oath that never again would we raise arms outside of our own defense."

"But if—" Juniper began.

Odessa cut her right off. "War and violence stalks aplenty, child, without us raising ourselves to go seek it out. There is no need for you to talk to the Council, for they will never agree to this request. No Anju will ever take up arms willingly in such a cause. I'm sorry."

"Last call for the roasted boar," came a loud bark.

"Now, come along," said Odessa, grabbing Juniper's arm, "for I don't mean to miss this opportunity to feast, and you should not, either. The world turns as it will, and we can but follow its broken path. Let us eat while we may." With this said, she elbowed her way to the front of the table, dragging Juniper along with her toward a choice cut of well-seared flank.

When at last the food had all been eaten and every belly bulged round and full, Juniper followed the others in letting the weight drag her down to a reclining position. She was still raw with disappointment at Odessa's rejection, but giving up was the last thing on her mind. She needed a fighting force, and here was a fighting force—solemn oath or no. *Won't* fight is very different from *can't* fight, after all. She knew there was a way around this problem; she just had to find it. Meanwhile, she shook the despair from her mind and let herself think of nothing but enjoying the feast.

After the food, a bowl of coriander seeds was passed around ("For sweetening the breath," Odessa whispered. "Try some!"), and everyone settled back on moss-covered wicker seats and soft grass pillows. It reminded Juniper of the slumber parties she'd had with her mother on special occasions. Now she knew where that idea had come from! The meat-roasting racks and sticks had been cleared away and the coals built up into a roaring fire, around which the whole group gathered, warming their hands against the extra chill that came with the setting of the sun.

Next came the music, and Juniper's pulse quickened in anticipation. She had known many different kinds of music in her life: The court musicians and their polished stringed and woodwind instruments whose notes dipped and swanned in perfect harmony.

Her own harpsichord lessons, with which she had something of a love-hate relationship. The Musicker, that new-fangled portable music device that had been her mother's wedding present, and had brought so many hours of dance-party joy in Queen's Basin.

The music of the Anju was different from all of these; the instruments, rustic in a way that should have sounded paltry and thin. But oh, it was far from that! One man played what looked like an upside-down saw, running a hardwood stick along the teeth to produce a zesty, vibrant sound. A woman blew into an actual hollowed-out root vegetable, coaxing from it a rich cushion of velvety notes that rivaled any palace chorus. And there were xylophones and tambourines and triangles of varying sizes. The melodies, too, were altogether new—the notes were haunting, raw, and peeled open in a way that Juniper had never before experienced. It made her heart ache and her head buzz. It made her heels twitch and her toes tap, too. But dancing didn't seem to be part of Anju celebrations in the way singing was. So Juniper kept her knees folded and her hands clasped tight, basking in silent enjoyment. Beside her, Tippy bounced in time to the melodies; Alta kept solidly to her role as guard—she didn't even seem to hear the music, instead scanning the audience from one edge to other, then back again; Cyril just looked bored.

Juniper smiled. All was as it should be in her tiny transplanted bit of Queen's Basin.

Though in this quiet moment, she did feel the lack of Erick— not for his chief adviser's role, but for his solid friendship. He would, she knew, have had the same response to the Anju that she did: an eyes-open appreciation for each difference and a warm welcome for each familiar echo, each thing that brought them all together as one great people.

After the music came the stories: exploits, tall tales, boisterous adventures shared loudly and with gusto. Many of these were told in praise of their late chief Darla, who by all accounts had been strong as an ibex, fierce as a wolf, and stealthy as a forest cat. As the hours passed, Juniper kept sneaking glances at Zetta. How could she be so calm and unruffled, with her mother just days gone? But then would come a moment when Zetta turned her eyes to the trees, blinking rapidly and fighting visibly for that composure. And then Juniper knew that just because someone's face shaped a smile, it did not mean there were no tears hiding somewhere deep inside.

The revelry ran on, as the moon inched across the bright sky overhead. At last, when all the songs had been sung and all the stories told, when voices began to crack and increased pauses started to replace the laughter, Odessa stood up and moved onto the raised hillock. Her movements were slow and majestic, pulling in every onlooker's attention without her needing to say a word. This was evidently the moment toward which the entire night had been building.

Juniper sat a little straighter and saw the other Queen's Basin members beside her do the same. Even Cyril unslitted his eyes and raised a curious eyebrow—a height of emotion, for him.

"My people," Odessa began, "this night of remembrance nears its end. Our chieftain Darla has been a mighty force in each of our lives across these years of her rule. The greatest among us show their worth in a hundred small ways for every one large. And this was never truer than with her. Chief Darla ruled with unparalleled strength and wisdom, and wrought more within our tribe than our halting words could ever express. For this reason we have kept watch across this night, *her* night; for this reason we have held vigil in her honor through this last moon's waning, until it is gone forever and we see it no more. Now the moon has crested and nears its bed. The light of a new day trembles on the far horizon. And so we join our voices to bid farewell to the old and to greet the new with wide-open arms."

A chorus of shouts followed Odessa's words: a rough, hoarse call that lingered and rang as, before Juniper's eyes, the moon sank below the edge of the far mountain. Under the blackened sky, the cries quieted at last. In her mind, Juniper was tiny again, tucked into her mother's lap as they sat on a blanket under the star-studded sky. She'd always known that her mother loved the night; now, for the first time, she understood why.

The group sat in darkness for long minutes as the shadows pulsed around them. Night birds called to each other from the trees. An owl hooted in the distance. The wind lifted Juniper's hair and tickled her eyelashes. She felt Tippy shifting beside her and reached out to squeeze the little girl's hand.

Around the hushed night noises, the Anju's silence stretched, as thin and brittle as a twig in frost.

Finally, when the moment seemed it might snap under the sustained pressure, a ray of light pierced the sky: a single beam from the eastern peak that bathed Odessa's upturned face in its russet glow. She spoke then, in a rough whisper: "Yesterday's moon is gone; the sun of today arises. It is the start of a brand-new day. With sorrow, with reverence, now with dawning joy, we turn our backs on the old and make way for that which is to come." She sighed, a sound that seemed to come from deep in her bones. Bathed in the warmth of the rising sun, Odessa seemed to relax.

"As you have all heard and seen, we have welcomed visitors to our camp today. These visitors have come to share in our vigil, and now they will be witness to our momentous next step. The first act of this new day shall be to launch the Trials."

"The Trials!" the group shouted. Juniper could almost feel their collective heartbeat quickening as one. Across the dying fire, Zetta's eyes were flame-bright.

"For the sake of our visitors, I shall spare a few moments for explanation," Odessa continued, sitting down with a muffled groan and stretching her legs stiffly out in front of her. "Since time began, we the Anju have been led by those of the Blood. Heritage is our first true calling. But the Blood is not the only factor in determining our ruler: Our leader must be sharp, and strong, and true. Our head, but also our heart. Our master, but also our minister. If I may say, she must be the best of us all." She smiled across the circle at Juniper.

"And so we come to the Trials."

"The Trials!" came the reply. Juniper noticed to her

amusement that Tippy joined in this time. The cat was a sleeping weight in the little girl's lap and her eyes were latched on Odessa's, mouth half open as though awaiting the next call.

"Tradition beckons, my people! And we arise to meet it. Let us now move to the meat of this day's gathering. Three Trials shall prove our new leader," Odessa went on, shifting back to a more formal tone. "The Trial of Might. The Trial of Mind. The Trial of Mettle. Each of these tests shall last for a day and a night, preceded by the preparatory period and launching in earnest on sunrise three days from this one. Let she who is the greatest rise in triumph above the rest! Let this be the forge that proves her worth. The victor shall earn the right to be our ruler."

Odessa swept her gaze around the circle, and Juniper thought she paused an extra moment when their eyes met, before moving on. "Our candidates are unusually young this cycle. Chief Darla was taken from us only two years into their training period. They should have had a decade more in which to hone their leadership skills. The Council shall have an active role in guiding our new chief through her early years of rule, of course. But in the meantime—for these Trials, and for taking the step to assume rightful leadership of our people—for today, I believe our candidates are ready. *Must be* ready. So let us hesitate no further. Let our candidates rise."

Zetta stood first, sharp and quick as a drawn blade. "Zetta, daughter of Darla," she said. "I accept the Trial. May the best prevail."

No sooner had she finished than a stocky, curly-haired girl arose. "Libba, daughter of Xia," she said. "I accept the Trial. May the best prevail."

"Tania, daughter of Oula." The third girl was already standing, and her words nearly overlapped with the last. "I accept the Trial. May the best prevail."

This was followed by silence. The three girls—the candidates to be ruler of the Anju, apparently—stood with chins raised and backs straight and proud. Juniper thought of what Zetta had said of her mother's time as ruler. Did Zetta look upon this forthcoming challenge with anticipation, or with regret?

Odessa resumed speaking. "Zetta, daughter of Darla. Libba, daughter of Xia. Tania, daughter of Oula. You are accepted into the Trials." She paused then. Was it Juniper's imagination, or did Odessa's gaze keep swinging back *her* way? It was almost as though a challenge lurked in the old woman's eyes. Odessa went on. "Three things each of you bring to these tests today, three qualifications which every candidate must have: the heritage of bloodline, the fire to lead, the will to prevail. For whoever emerges from these Trials shall hold within her hands the power to command the Anju, to make of our people whatsoever she wishes."

Now Juniper knew she wasn't imagining it. Odessa punched her words across the circle, directly at Juniper.

"And not our tribe only, but all the greater Anju who are blood-bound to come to our assistance at any call of need. This all and more lies within the grasp of the victor of these Trials.

For an attack upon one of our members is considered an offense upon us all."

The three candidates shifted in place. There was a faint murmur around the circle. Apparently Juniper wasn't the only one confused by the direction of Odessa's speech.

Odessa paused. Then she said, with a carefully casual air, "Are there any further candidates who wish to join the Trials?"

Like a landing thunderclap, Juniper understood. What had Zetta said about Juniper's mother? Alaina had been Firstblood. Juniper had no idea about the two other girls, but Zetta's mother had been only Secondblood. This measuring of bloodline was their primary recommendation. And what of the rest—the fire to lead, the will to prevail? Juniper had been raised to rule her whole life. She was already queen of her own tiny kingdom. And what was more, she *needed* the Anju. Even now her father was being held captive—or *worse*, but no, she couldn't allow herself to think that, not for a second—her palace and home were overrun, and who knew what havoc the Monsian army was wreaking upon Torr?

Odessa had told her the Council could never be persuaded to join an attack upon Monsia, for the Anju would take up arms only in self-defense. But what if Juniper was their ruler? The attack on Torr, then, *would* be seen as an attack upon one of the Anju—upon her, their leader. So how could they then disagree with sending an army in response? It wouldn't be an offensive attack at all, but a defensive one. The greater army would be hers to command.

Juniper needed to rule the Anju.

To be their ruler, she needed to win the Trials.

Heart pounding wildly, Juniper leaped to her feet. In a loud, clear voice, she proclaimed, "Juniper, daughter of Alaina. I accept the Trial. May the best prevail."

11

AS THE WORDS LEFT JUNIPER'S LIPS, THE crowd erupted as half the gathered Anju leaped to their feet in outrage and dismay. The Queen's Basin group was stunned to silence; even Cyril sat slack-jawed with shock. Odessa stood a little to the side, a satisfied smile on her lips as she waited for the gathering to settle. Juniper's attention, however, was fixed on Zetta. At Juniper's words, Zetta had reeled back like she'd been slapped. She gaped in shocked betrayal; an instant later, her eyes narrowed and her open face slammed shut.

The answer to Juniper's earlier question was plainly visible. Zetta wanted this rulership *badly*. And now Juniper was pushing in to fight her for it. One thing was abundantly clear: The sliver of friendship that had started growing between the two girls was over and done.

Now they were rivals—nothing more, nothing less.

Swallowing a pang of regret, Juniper straightened her shoulders and met Zetta's gaze head-on. She wished her decision hadn't come with such a knife's-edge cost, wished she could have continued getting to know this girl who, in different circumstances, might quickly have become a friend.

But when it came down to it, Juniper had a father to save and a country to rescue and a war to win. Nothing could get in the way of that.

Nothing at all.

"Bring out the stone!" came a call from within the crowd. "The impostor will not pass the Blood test!"

"Quiet, all," said Odessa at last, waving her arms. "I recognize Juniper, daughter of Alaina. Her heritage and bloodline are well known to us all."

"*She's* not one of us!" said a lanky, bearded man whose face was marked by a puckered scar.

"Who is she? Where did she come from?"

"We can't let an outsider push into our tribe and demand to be our ruler, no matter what her blood. It's not right!"

If she was perfectly honest, Juniper didn't feel it was entirely right, either.

This didn't deter her in the slightest. She was her father's daughter; she would do what needed doing. She *needed* this rulership. And what was more, she thought, they needed her, too. Already ideas were crowding her mind of ways she could help improve their everyday lives.

"People of the Anju," she called out, never more aware of her rounded southern accent, so much in contrast with the Anju's sharp-angled tones. She made her voice as neutral as she could, drawing upon her memory reserves from her mother's story-telling times. "I recognize that my challenge here today is unconventional, may perhaps even be seen as irreverent. But it is with utmost respect that I offer myself as a candidate. I have no wish to change your ways or to make you into something you're not. I only know that you are in need of leadership, and this is something I can provide." Juniper carefully avoided Zetta's gaze. And that of Alta, Tippy, and Cyril. It was true—there was no end to the good she could do for this people and their tribe. Both of their groups would be infinitely better off in the end!

But first, she had to *win*.

"Right now you don't know me, or anything about me. But if I win these Trials, I guarantee that I will work long and tirelessly on your behalf. I may look different from you, I may sound different, but I *am* one of you in the truest way—by the Blood."

"The stone shall tell," muttered the scarred man darkly.

Juniper didn't have a spare moment to wonder about this, for just then a scuffle sounded behind her. Two strong men—one of whom was Kohr, the guard who had first come upon them by the bridge—lugged a rounded, flat-topped stone between them. This they deposited in front of Odessa, who held up a wicked curved knife.

"Candidates, approach!" called Odessa.

Libba was the first to hold her hand over the stone. Odessa's knife made a quick, clean stripe across the meat of her palm. A bright crimson drop fell upon the stone's outer edge. Before Juniper's fascinated gaze, the red spot trembled and then quivered upward, pushing through what she now saw were concentric circles of rock. One, two, three lines and more it passed, finally settling four bars from the heart of the stone.

"Fourthblood, confirmed," said Odessa. Libba withdrew, her chin raised proudly.

Zetta was next, and Juniper watched as the blood traveled to the second concentric circle. "Secondblood," intoned Odessa.

Juniper made to move up next, but a hand grabbed her arm.

"What's happening here?" Alta's voice was sharp. "I thought we were leaving at first light! What about Queen's Basin, the horses, the cat—Juniper, what are you *doing*?"

"Don't worry," Juniper said, ducking to the side with Alta as Tania took her turn at the stone. "I need to do this. *We* need this."

"Why? What are you talking about?"

She lowered her voice for Alta alone. "How did you think we were going to attack Monsia? Saunter down across the plains with our motley crew of kids, yelling them a command to lay down their arms and surrender? For days we've been trying to come up with a good plan, and you know what? I didn't have one. Not a real, true option that had a chance of working. Did you?" She looked at Alta, who shook her head. "And now this. Don't you see? The combined Anju are a force to be reckoned with. You and the others can still head back to Queen's Basin as we planned, and I'll join you as soon as I can. But first I've got to see this through."

"So you're going to use the Anju long enough to get what you need from them, and then cast them aside."

"Of course not," Juniper said. "Only think of all the useful progress I could bring to this tribe as their leader! Torr is light-leagues ahead in so many ways—timepieces and fountains and even schedules, in moderation—to name just a few things of countless many. All I need to do is win this tournament, get their help in defeating Monsia, and then . . . well, then we'll figure out what happens next."

"I don't know, Juniper. Your logic makes sense, but something about it just doesn't feel right to me."

Juniper drew herself up. "I'm sorry you see it that way. But you know what? I'll be more sorry if I don't end up winning this contest. Because if I lose, we all lose. And the whole of Torr with us. It's that simple."

The cut hurt less than she'd expected. Odessa's blade was whisper-sharp, and the slice was straight and sure. Juniper watched, fascinated, as a drop of blood bubbled up from the edge of the wound, trembled a moment on her palm, then dropped down to soak into the far outer edge of the stone.

It began moving almost immediately, pushing through the concentric rings without an instant's pause, before Juniper had time to properly worry, to wonder—her mother had married her father, after all; would this dilute her blood, possibly disqualify her? She had no idea how the blood markers worked, after all. There were maybe a dozen stone rings in all and the blood stripe bypassed each in turn—the eighth ring, the sixth, the fourth . . . finally it passed the second ring from the center, where Zetta's blood shone out dark.

Juniper's blood embedded itself in the heart of the stone.

Firstblood, she thought with a thrill. Her mother had been.

And she was, too.

Her father hadn't been Anju—how was that even possible? Juniper had no idea; nor did she really care. She qualified, and right now that was all that mattered. She couldn't deny her thrill at seeing that truth spelled out in blood and graphite.

"The Bloodstone has made its pronouncement," said Odessa formally.

"So recognized," replied the Elders, who had gathered in a semicircle facing the four candidates.

The rest of the crowd, though, was not nearly so placid. Several of those nearest to the action leaped to their feet; more than one face held looks of shock and dismay.

"What is this treachery?" called the scarred man who had complained earlier.

"Is this not the child of the deserter?" said another. "Is not her blood tainted by default?"

Odessa waved all of this away with a curt chop of her hands. "You have seen the results with your own eyes," she said. "The matter is closed. The Trial begins upon the third day's sunrise. Candidates, you will be shown to your quarters momentarily. You may then use the between-time in whatever way you see fit. You have each chosen a second?"

Juniper looked at the others. Each girl nodded in turn, and Juniper now saw that another person stood near each of them—a rounded woman with Tania, tall male figures near both Zetta and Libba. Juniper opened her mouth.

"Your second must be a blood relation," said Zetta frostily. "If none are available, the role is forfeit. And no one may be chosen who has previously held the role of chieftain."

Juniper's mind raced.

"Your second is to go with you on the Trials," Odessa said, her composure ruffled for the first time. "Providing counsel and guidance and strength when needed. No chief will need to rule alone, and so the sharing of the burden is integral to the testing."

Juniper reached for Alta, who stood just to her rear. "Alta Mavenham shall be my . . ."

Odessa shook her head. "Is she a blood relation? Else it cannot be so."

Juniper blanched. Would she really have to go up against Anju competitors not only knowing nothing about their culture, but now also having to face three teams of two competitors all on her own?

This may not have been such a great idea after all.

Then she noticed a shifting of bodies behind her. Several people moved aside. Into the gap stepped Cyril, a toothy smile on his face. "Of your blood? Why, I believe I qualify for that role, do I not, little cousin? I shall be glad to be your second."

12

THROUGHOUT JUNIPER'S LIFE—FIRST AT THE
palace in Torr, and more recently during her rulership of Queen's
Basin—there had been many times when she'd had to bite down
some particularly edgy retort that she knew wasn't right for the
moment.

Never had that act been quite so difficult as it was now.

Cyril Lefarge, her *second*? For long moments, Juniper pondered
whether she really would be better off alone than saddled with her
double-crossing lug of a cousin.

And yet . . . Cyril *did* know a lot about the Anju. He'd studied
at the Academy. Who knew what sorts of things he'd been taught
that might come in handy out in the wild woods? For certainly she
had no idea what kinds of challenges would be thrown at her. The
more tools in her arsenal, the better.

The truth? His help was an offer she couldn't refuse.

As to his loyalty and how to keep the self-professed traitor in
line, she had a few ideas about that, too.

123

So she swallowed her distaste and gave a graceful nod. "Cyril Lefarge is my cousin by blood. He will be a suitable second."

The Elders frowned, then clustered together in a knot to discuss this. They called Cyril over and bombarded him with questions; much of his time seemed to be spent reciting long strings of information—names and genealogies, Juniper had no doubt. Cheered by the thought of his discomfort, Juniper moved off to the side to await the next step in the proceedings.

Instead, she came face-to-face with Zetta. The shock and hurt Juniper had glimpsed earlier was nowhere in sight. The girl's face was as expressionless as tree bark. Clearly she had plenty of experience tamping down her emotions and keeping them well below the surface. And if her posture was a little more forced, if her eyes sparkled a little too brightly, it could easily have been blamed on the light.

"Juniper, daughter of Alaina," Zetta said formally. "It is my honor to compete against you in the Trials." To her credit, she only choked slightly on the word *honor*. She nearly spat the next words, though: "May the best prevail."

"Zetta—" Juniper began. But what could she say? She hadn't set out to fight for the other girl's throne. Having just been through a challenge to her own rule of Queen's Basin, Juniper hated to think of putting that pain on someone else. But too much was at stake. Every day that passed might spell disaster for her father, destruction for her kingdom. *Live boldly,* her father had always told her. *Move decisively. Act and then push forward, without hindsight or regret.*

Today, she had no other way to live.

Zetta leaned in. "I was born to this rule. It's my birthright, and I won't see it stolen away by some outsider. You may think you're special now, having Mother Odessa on your side. But *everyone* knows what you two are up to."

Juniper frowned, glancing over at where the older woman stood, eyeing them askance. "What are you talking about?"

"Oh, yes," said Zetta. "I am onto your little game. The way you arrived here, so conveniently, just at this very time. *Her* daughter should have been chieftain, in the last cycle. It's a matter of pride, surely you see that? But she lost the chance; she lost face. Firstblood or not. And now she thinks she can get all of that back by conniving the crown for her *granddaughter*."

Zetta's words dripped with scorn, but inside Juniper's mind, everything flashed white.

Granddaughter?

Odessa was Alaina's mother. Juniper's grandmother.

Was this really true? Her father's parents had died long before Juniper was born; the idea of grandparents had never really occurred to her before. To discover one now, so unexpectedly, was almost beyond imagination.

"It won't work. Do you know what Odessa's rule was like? Her tribesname was Odessa the *Merciful*." Zetta spat the word out like venom. "She had grand plans of treaties and joining forces with the lowlanders. And you see where that got her? Defection by her own daughter." Zetta drew herself up and looked Juniper over from hair to hemline. "You come from weak stock, Juniper, daughter of Alaina, daughter of Odessa. You may have the Blood, but you do not have the *spine*. I will take you down."

Before Juniper could reply, Zetta was gone, her tall bodyguard a shadow on her heels.

"I hope you know what you're doing," Alta said in her ear.

Juniper let herself wilt inside, ever so slightly. "I hope so, too," she whispered.

But really, just then the only thought going through her mind was: *My grandmother?!*

The first thing they learned was that the next three days, until the start of the Trials, were to be spent cloistered away in seclusion. Quarters had been prepared for all the candidates, and a Council member informed them that they should proceed there without delay. When Juniper looked across the crowd, however, she saw Odessa moving in her direction. Thanking the elder and assuring him she would follow momentarily, Juniper turned toward Odessa. She took in every aspect of the old woman's appearance—her long slender fingers, her quicksilver eyes, the graceful lope in her stride.

How had she not noticed these traits, not recognized them for what they were? It was nothing like seeing her mother again— what specifics she could even remember, from her long-ago child's-eye view. This was entirely different: not a call but an echo, not a vision but its shade, brief disconnected bars of a melody long forgotten that now swelled a chorus inside her very soul.

The old woman met her gaze head-on, face unreadable. Juniper's mouth was dry. How was she supposed to start this conversation? But she hadn't come so far to lose words now. *You are a princess and a queen and a challenger to the throne of the Anju,* she told herself sternly. *Now grow up and act like it!*

"Zetta told me something just now," she said carefully. Odessa's expression suggested she ought to tread lightly. "Something about your—*our*—shared past."

Odessa expelled a long breath. "So. You've heard."

"It is true, isn't it? You—my mother—we—" Words were such slippery things, Juniper realized. How had she never understood this before?

While she grappled, Odessa put a hand on her arm. "Child," she said, low and gentle, "it is true. And there is much we need to talk of, you and I. Much and more." For a moment her eyes seemed almost to brim, then she brought her features under control. "But now is not that time. Currently I am in my role as Council member. And you are in yours as candidate for chieftain. You understand why we must not be seen spending time together in conversation?"

Juniper did see, though she felt her heart plummet down to her rib cage. "When, then?" she croaked.

"Go through the Trials. Prevail. Let them see what you are made of, my blood."

Juniper's head swam. A cluster-welter of words scrabbled inside her, all wanting out at once, leaving her tongue-tied and awkward. "Is there . . . anyone else? Of my family, here in the village?"

Odessa's eyebrows knit in confusion.

"You know—aunts, uncles, cousins . . ."

"Ah. No, I'm afraid not. Your mother was an only child, and her father passed on many years ago, may the wind take his ashes. You are . . . I suppose you are the last of our proud line." Her breath came out in a rush. "Which is why I mustn't, I *can't*, lose you now. Girl, you were *meant* to come here, to be here at this time. It was clear to me from the moment I saw you back in that clearing and realized who you were."

Juniper had no reply to this.

"Afterward," Odessa said, "when all of this is over, we shall have a long talk. Many of them. For of a certainty we have much time to make up. But for now—you must go with the other candidates. No more delays."

"All right." What more could she say? Time, she hoped, would help her process this bright new world and the freshly discovered grandmother it now contained.

Odessa's grasp tightened on her arm, a squeeze that was warm and sure. Then she gave a brisk nod and started to turn away, and Juniper dropped back into the present: the Anju, the Trials, Alta and the others. "One more thing," she said quickly. "Can I have a moment with my group before going to our quarters? This all came about most unexpectedly, after all . . . We just need to sort out a few things."

Odessa looked sympathetic, as though she felt responsible

for getting Juniper into this. Which she partly was, in point of fact. "You may speak with your friends, but do so in haste," she said gently, then lowered her voice. "Once again, we cannot afford any room for misinterpretation. Your challenge already lies rather delicately upon the group."

Juniper nodded and rushed over to where the others had been standing off to the side, watching her exchange but apparently not wanting to intrude.

"Oh, Mistress Juniper!" Tippy gasped. "The pride of you, bursting into that fiery circle all aglow! I nearly fainted dead away, just to behold . . ." She, at least, seemed to have no complaints about Juniper's rash change of plans.

Alta sideswiped Tippy on the shoulder, and the little girl swallowed her final words. Juniper could spare only a quick smile; then she was all business.

"I know this is unexpected," she said, "and I am aware that you might consider this my worst decision to date."

"Which is saying something," said Cyril dryly.

Juniper ignored him. "Yet I'm sure you can also see all the reasons why I *had* to do it."

"We support you, Miss Juniper," said Alta wearily, in a tone that didn't quite match her words. "Only, what will those back in the Basin think? We were to be gone mere hours, and now 'tis a day and a night gone by. And you're staying away even longer to boot. Cyril, too," she said, as an afterthought.

"You've got to return to the Basin, Alta, just as we planned," said Juniper. "You and Tippy both. Tell Erick and the others what's going on and have the group start getting ready for our trip to Torr upon my return. Bring the horses with you and deliver the spy cat to Jess. Help her out in any way she needs with her messages to the palace. You heard the time frame here? Three days of preparation, then three days for the Trials. It shall be over in no time at all. If all goes well, we shall be ready to move out within a week's time, and with a full tribe of warriors at our back."

Alta frowned. "How can you be so sure it *will* go as you hope?"

"I am sure of nothing," said Juniper. "But it's my job as ruler to prepare for success, and then to handle what does come to the best of my ability. That is what I will do." She softened her tone. "The fact is, we *must* return to Torr, and the sooner the better. Don't you see? The fate of the whole kingdom rests in our hands alone. If it must be that fourteen youths form the whole of that resisting force, then we shall seek out a plan to make the most of that narrow advantage. But if I have my way, we shall meet that venture with the strength of a half-dozen tribes or more. And then we shall show Monsia that we are a force to be reckoned with."

Alta nodded, while Cyril preened nearby. That was as much agreement as she would get from him, Juniper knew. Tippy shadowboxed across the grass, evidently rehearsing for her imagined role in the battle to come.

"We'll keep in touch somehow," Alta said, and Juniper relaxed to hear the resentment ease out of her tone. "We must! Maybe Erick could find a way for your father's messenger to deliver you messages from us at the Basin? After it's back from the palace, that is."

"Perhaps," said Juniper. She wasn't sure if that could actually work, but they *did* need to find a way to communicate. The more important thing right now was that Alta was fully in agreement with her at last. "Your support means everything to me, truly it does! With luck and guts on our side, the outcome will not take long."

"And will go in your favor," Cyril observed. They turned to look at him, and his mouth puckered. "What? What did I say?"

Alta looked at Juniper, then said bluntly, "Is it quite safe leaving you alone with him, Juniper? Not many days ago, he was locking you in a moldy prison cell."

Juniper met her cousin's gaze squarely. "I fancy that Cyril thinks he has the upper hand now . . . maybe even thinks he can pull some kind of a fast getaway if the moment is right. But he's not as smart as he thinks he is."

Cyril frowned.

"I noticed that discomfort—dare I say, *fear*—that you showed upon our first meeting with the Anju. And I thought to myself, What could give a big, strapping boy like Cyril the shivers when it comes to this reclusive mountain tribe? I may not be Academy-tutored, but lucky for us all, I pay attention in my lessons. And Political Discourse is one class my father never let me skip. You know where I'm headed, don't you, Cyril?"

Cyril's cheeks had paled by several shades, and he swallowed audibly. He didn't reply, though.

Juniper went on. "Here's what I remember from my historical studies: The Anju didn't always live scattered throughout the Hourglass Mountains. Long ago, they traveled up and down the Lower Continent's western coast. The Horn of An, does that sound familiar? It's what the Anju claim as their point of origin. Of course, once Monsia took over, there was no question of sharing the territory or coexisting. This was all centuries and centuries ago, but it's my understanding that among the Anju, the hatred for Monsia runs *extremely* deep. Wasn't that the main purpose of my mother's group venturing down from the mountains to parley with the King of Torr, trying to negotiate a partnership? Joining forces to present a unified face to the Monsians." Juniper nodded, though the others already had her full attention.

"I know the Anju are peaceful and shy away from confrontation; that's the whole reason I even need to go about gaining control to enlist their help. But they also don't seem the type of people to pass up the opportunity for revenge, should it land in their laps. Perhaps in the form of a dyed-in-the-wool Monsian spy?"

Tippy clapped her hands in dawning realization. "You mean to expose Cyril and hand him over to the Anju if he steps out of line!"

"I certainly do," Juniper replied. "I wonder how they might respond to that . . . a curious conundrum, wouldn't you say? What *do* you say, Cyril?"

Cyril made one last attempt at bluster. "I was the one who offered to be your second, don't forget. You need me more than——"

Juniper raised a finger. "You shall certainly be of help. But don't for one instant forget who is in charge. And if you even think about running off on me, trying to escape to the lowlands with further betrayal in mind, remember that the Anju know these mountains like the back side of a branch. You wouldn't get sixteen paces before being hunted down and dragged right back."

And how would my grandmother react to hearing how you tried to take over my throne and locked me up in a prison-cave? she thought, with a silent smile. It was quite a pleasing thing, the idea of having blood relatives at your back.

"So maybe I *was* thinking some of those thoughts when I signed on as your second," Cyril snapped. "What of it? I'd expect no less from you if our positions were reversed."

"They're not, though, are they? I think you and I can get along famously, Cyril, as long as you can respect these boundaries and banish from your mind any thoughts of a double-cross. Now, what do you say?"

Cyril slumped, then gave a shrug. "It's not in my interest for you to win their challenge, though, is it? If your goal is to get their help in fighting Monsia, why should I be any part of that?"

"You should be—you *will* be part of that because, deep down, your first interest is your own health and self-preservation. If I lose the challenge because of your efforts, what do you suppose is the first thing I'll do?"

Cyril's mouth twisted in acknowledgment. "I still don't see any real benefit in helping you win."

"You make a valid point," Juniper said. She pondered a moment.

"Very well, then. Help me win this challenge—throw your lot fully on my side in every way. And if I win, I give my word that I will set you free to leave our company and go as you please."

Alta's eyebrows shot up to her hairline, and Tippy let out a gasp of horror. But Juniper kept her focus on Cyril. Surely gaining the rule of the Anju people was more than worth the loss of one traitorous noble. "What do you say, cousin?"

Cyril held out his hand. "You've got yourself a deal. Let's take these Anju down a peg or six."

13

EACH CANDIDATE WAS PROVIDED WITH A pouch of food, two horns of water, a pair of flint stones for starting a fire, two wool blankets, and an expandable oilskin frame that could be erected into a makeshift shelter. They could bring whatever other objects of their own that they deemed needful, but only what they could carry on their person. Juniper had her journal and charcoal stylus, her trusty bone-handled comb tucked up the hidden pocket in her sleeve, as well as the valuable tome, *Mountain Ranges of the Lower Continent* (which she had been studying with a fierceness that would have made Erick proud). Beyond this, Juniper and Cyril had little of use in their carry-bags; she could only hope what they had would be enough.

The quarters set up for the four candidates and their seconds were a series of small rooms clustered around a high-ceilinged common area inside a giant fallen dropsy tree. The heart of the tree had been hollowed in a silky, natural-looking finish reminiscent of Juniper's cozy bedroom back in the heart of the Great

Tree—only on a much bigger scale. With a pang, she realized how she'd come to think of Queen's Basin as home, and how much she missed it.

Juniper and Cyril spent the next three days resting, exercising, and preparing as best they could for the Trials to come. From time to time, Juniper glimpsed Odessa across the clearing or on a nearby tree-porch, and the pull was so strong, she had to wrap her arms tightly around her middle to keep from chasing her grandmother down on the spot. To be so close, and yet so far removed . . . it was the purest form of torture.

Once the Trials are over, she told herself over and over, *there will be time then. Time aplenty.*

It wasn't nearly enough, but for now, it had to do.

For the most part, they avoided the other competitors across the narrow passageways of their shelter. Juniper peppered Cyril with endless questions and found him to be a fount of knowledge about Anju history and culture, which she soaked up like a thirsty plant under a new watering pot. Unfortunately, Cyril knew nothing about the Trials themselves. Grudgingly, Zetta admitted during one of their more cordial exchanges over an evening meal that the other candidates were not much the wiser.

"Nor would we speak of it if we knew," she said. "It's a sacred tradition, and the details of the quest are bestowed in confidence at the start of each cycle, from chief to candidates. Because Chief Darla is not here to share the terms with us, as would ordinarily happen, we will hear them from Mother Odessa instead. But to talk of it among others, to scavenge and scrounge for information is simply not done!" She glowered, but Juniper met her gaze levelly.

"I understand, and I will respect your traditions fully. They're my traditions now, as well." She paused. "Look, I'm not here to be your enemy, Zetta. I just—why shouldn't we all be as one? Why do there have to be so many dividing lines: people and tribes and borders?"

Zetta looked at her stonily. "I don't know why there *have* to be. But the fact is, there are. And you trying to take over as ruler of *my* people will not change that in the least."

"They're my people as well as yours, you know," Juniper snapped. Then she felt a touch on her arm—Cyril, of all people, checking her temper. The world was tipped completely on its head!

"All I know is this," said Zetta. "It must be very easy to sit on your side of the line, looking longingly at my tribe and wanting them as part of one big happy group—*your* group. I wonder if you would think the same if such an invitation came your way from a different direction—oh, from Monsia, say?"

To this, Juniper had no reply.

Despite such minor upsets, the three days passed quickly enough. On the last night before the Trials, Juniper tossed sleepless on her pallet bed, wondering if she was prepared enough. So much rested upon this contest—perhaps even the fate of all Torr! Once again she saw her father's face as she'd seen him for the last time: his hug, his grave look as he wished her safety and godspeed, the shine in his eyes like his very heart was tearing loose from his body. Had he really looked like that? Or was she just projecting her own terrible longing upon that memory?

Oh, Papa! she thought. *I will see you again, and soon.*

She had to win the chieftaincy of the Anju. She just *had* to.

To clear her head, she walked out into the dark, cool night. She meant to take several turns around their dwelling, to stretch out her legs, which were cramped from the day's bout of calisthenics. Instead, she'd barely cleared the doorway when a nearby bush began to judder violently, then expelled a roly-poly girl with ragamuffin hair.

"Oh, Your Perfectly Timed Majesty!" Tippy exclaimed, catapulting across the open space and into Juniper's arms. "Hours and hours I've been haunting this spot, only hoping your royal self should venture out one last time before the big day!"

Juniper's heart warmed at the words; she hadn't realized how much she'd missed Tippy's madcap exuberance. Being cooped up with only Cyril and six Anju rivals for company had sorely chapped her soul. Hugging the little girl tight, Juniper said, "What brings you back here so soon? And where is Alta?"

"Why, she's back home, with the rest!" said Tippy, puffing up like a proud bullfrog. "I knew I could make the trip and I did—bridge-crossing and all. Here I am, ain't I? Alive and in one piece."

"They let you make that whole trip alone?" said Juniper, aghast.

Tippy cut her eyes to the side. "Not *let* me, exactly. They *might* not have noticed when I crept off all sneaky-like. They

138

were plotting a proper long expedition, only they weren't sure how it should best work, and so I . . . you know. But never mind that. I left them a letter, so they shouldn't worry. And here I am now, but I mustn't talk long. The Elders said I could await you, but only through nightfall. For then your focus must be all upon the Trials, and I should be a distraction. So they said, anyway."

Juniper nodded; she'd heard from Zetta that mingling with non-contestants during the Trials was frowned upon, if not actually forbidden.

Tippy brightened. "That's why it's peachy you come out now, see? For I can jabber my mouth on all I like, just so as I'm off before sunrise."

Juniper squinted at the muddy skyline, but Tippy was fumbling in her bag. "Only it may be I haven't many words for you after all. *Here's* what I've truly come to deliver. A letter from Erick!" Triumphantly, she thrust a rolled parchment into Juniper's hand. "Those back home are well, awaiting with eagerness word of your victory to come." Tippy looked from side to side, as though the victory might be hiding in the bushes.

"Hush, you goose! Who knows how the Trials shall go? But thank you for this. I shall take it inside and read where there's some light to see by. Can you wait while I do so and then while I write a quick reply to take back?"

In reply Tippy lifted her skirts, and Juniper saw a gray, furry lump twining around her ankles. "Jess's cat!" she whispered.

"Fleeter," Tippy agreed. "He's gotten even prettier these last few days, imagine that."

Juniper couldn't imagine it, in point of fact. "What's he doing here?"

Tippy puffed out her chest. "I'm trying out a 'speriment. Jess says he's trained to carry messages just as quick as a flick. He's fleet of foot, get it? *Fleeter*? Only he needs to travel the path first, so he knows where to go. Then he can be let loose and is just as speedy and trusty as can be. So I've brought the handsome and clever Fleeter here along with my message, and if all goes well, he shall be the one to deliver our responses up ahead. So we can write each other freely back and forth while you're about the Trials, see?"

To Juniper, this idea seemed optimistic at best, but she didn't bother arguing. "Will you come in, then, while I pen a return message?"

Tippy shook her head. "You go on. I'll just dally out here in the fresh air."

Juniper nodded, her mind already in Queen's Basin, and ducked back inside. With eager fingers, she cracked the pitchstones together and lit the fat beeswax candle that sat on the common room table. By the winking light, she read:

Dear Juniper,

Alta and Tippy made it safely back to us in Queen's Basin, though I hope you won't think me a mooncalf when I say that without its queen, this place is a Basin and little else. (Apologies: I have been reading too much poetry of late.)

On to practical matters: The last of the roadways are finished and all repairs done to the roof of the Beauty Chamber. We've done some strengthening on the handrail for the bridge so it no longer wobbles. Next, we turn our attention to moving foodstuffs and other travel necessaries up to the Cavern, and preparing to pack for our trip back. The reclaimed horses are all in good health, and saddlebag-stuffing duty begins tomorrow. Incidentally, I have discovered a fine chapter in one of my miscellanea tomes on "The Art of Saddlebag Stuffing." Did you know it was considered a bona fide art? There is apparently a method to being able to fit a large number of items tidily in——

Ouch. Tippy has run into me from behind, jarring my thoughts. I had better stick to the point, for I am also near out of parchment.

Jessamyn and I continue to watch the skies, but there has been no sign of the returning messenger, upon which we hope so highly for word from her sister, Eglantine, and the palace. Time only knows what shall come of that venture. Meantime we work and pack and await with anxious minds the word of your portending contest.

Do keep us abreast of events as they unfold.

Unflaggingly yours,
Erick Dufrayne

By the time Juniper finished reading, her face hurt from smiling. How she missed her jovial, bookish friend—and the rest of the rowdy group, for that matter! She herself didn't have much news to share, but she pried a sheet from the back of her journal and scratched a few words with her stylus. She explained what she had learned about the Trials (too little), her conversations with Zetta (unpleasant), and how things fared with Cyril (slightly more tolerable than usual). She told him about the Anju footwear and filled in the mystery of the tracks left around the horse enclosure. She drew a quick sketch of the shoes for his further edification. She thought about mentioning her connection with Odessa, but in the end decided to wait; it was simply too precious a fact to entrust to this bald parchment sheet. She assured him that she would be in touch and that she knew the camp would hold up splendidly in her absence.

She hoped that would be the case.

Then again, keeping her settlement's key rabble-rouser with her was surely a productive step in that direction.

When Juniper came back outside, Tippy was where she'd left her, only curled up in a ball and snoring lightly. Juniper felt bad disturbing such peaceful sleep, but above the treetops the sky was blushing toward lavender. She didn't have much time.

Barely prodded, Tippy leaped straight up into the air, landing in a crouch with balled fists up. "Oh, Your Reassuring Royalty!" she said, sagging in relief. "'Tis only you. I seem to have snoozed off. But I'm all a-joy of your timely return. Have you done with your lettering?"

"I have," said Juniper, putting the rolled sheet in Tippy's

hands. "And here it is. Now, tell me about this Fleeter creature. You say he might have some way of carrying messages for our future exchange?"

"Of the very yes," Tippy gushed. The cat in question was draped over her shoulders like a warm, purring shawl. "Just wait until you see this beauty in action!"

Juniper lifted an eyebrow. If ever a creature seemed less reliable for a delivery service, she couldn't picture it. But Tippy pulled a burlap sack from her belt, opened it wide, and made a clicking sound. Fleeter blinked stonily at her. Then, with something like a shrug, he extended his paws and oozed into the bag.

Juniper absorbed this in silence.

"That were Jess's instructions," said Tippy proudly. "He travels by scent, Fleeter does. So you don't want to confuse him with too much trekking and trucking about. What you'll need is a proper settling point. You get him to that spot and start things off from there, as it were." She looked up expectantly.

Juniper thought for a moment. "I know just the place. Do you remember that clearing we first reached, after crossing over the bridge—where we ran into those Anju scouts? There was a whole scattering of cut-down tree stumps there, all overgrown and weedy."

Tippy bobbed her head eagerly. "Oh, how I do! In fact, I like to stop in a bit each time I pass there, to practice my toe-pointy dance as I leap from one to the next, you see?"

"Right you are. I think that would make a fine settling point, don't you? I'm sure to find a cranny in one of those stumps that's big enough to stow Fleeter and his message besides. But . . . you think he will be able to journey out from there? How does he, er, work? Did Jess explain?"

"It could not be easier. Only take him to that hidey-spot and tuck this food morsel inside. He will recognize that as his homing place." Tippy pressed a moist wad of dough into Juniper's hand. Recoiling slightly, Juniper stuffed it into her waist pouch. Tippy went on, "When you have your message ready to send back, simply attach it to him and let him go upon his way. He traveled with me from the Basin, so he shall return thence to QB and his message along with. And bearing our reply, he shall return to his hidey in the clearing."

Juniper shook her head. The whole idea seemed to be stitched in wishes and hopes and very little else. "You really think this little spy cat can manage that?"

"I am sure of it," said Tippy heartily. "Jess has described the process in much detail—none of which, mournfully, do I actually recall. Nevertheless, Fleeter shall not fail in this task, of that I'm certain. I will take this letter you've written now, and if you'd like to put kitty to the test, send him our way at your next chance. Jess and I shall be waiting to greet him at home base. With goodsy treats aplenty for my little pet," she crooned, with one last reach into the bag to ruffle the unfortunate animal's patchy fur.

"Very well, then," said Juniper, stifling a laugh. "But you should probably get going now—I need to head back inside, for the sun is not three blinks from rising."

"Wait!" cried Tippy. Leaping up, she shot her arms around

Juniper's shoulders and squeezed tight. "Be well, my own queen. Come on back to us safe and soon, and wearing that Anju crown."

Back inside the common area, Juniper nudged open the mouth of the sack and peered at the mangy cat inside. The bagged beast felt warm and mushy in her arms. From within the small dark cave, its red eyes blinked owlishly.

Juniper heard footsteps behind her and looked up to see Cyril approaching, tousle-haired and bleary with sleep. Outside, a piercing horn's call broke the silence, sending a flock of birds lifting into the air with a flurry of beating wings that echoed the roiling in Juniper's stomach.

Juniper pulled the drawstrings shut and hooked the bag over her shoulder.

It was time for the Trials to begin.

14

"WE ARE GATHERED ON THIS MIDSEASON morning to bear witness to the history of our people, as it is forged before our very eyes," intoned Odessa, looking exceptionally majestic as she addressed the gathered group. Juniper pictured her mother as she used to sit next to her father in the great throne room in the palace, and couldn't hold back her smile. They were two of a piece for sure!

The four candidates were lined up with their backs to the crowd, facing Odessa with arms stiff at their sides, legs straight, heads high. The three Anju girls had adopted this pose immediately, and Juniper, alert to all she didn't know about the nuance of Anju culture, had moved quickly to copy them. The ramrod posture soon took its toll, though. Her muscles felt stiff and pinched, her shoulders heavy with the weight of Fleeter's bag and her own carry-sack, and her head aching from the sleepless night. Her mind might be well prepared, but her body had seen better days. Odessa's speech began to seem less majestic and more plain *long*.

Still: The Trials were about to begin!

"There will be three tests," Odessa went on. "Each must be accomplished within the span of time from sunrise to sunrise. The first shall be a Test of Might—judging your physical strength and fortitude, which is imperative in governing a body such as ours. The second shall be a Test of Mind—measuring your sharpness, quickness, and stores of intelligent memory. And the third shall be a Test of Mettle—determining what you are made of, what lies at the core of you, testing who you are as a leader and what you would bring to the position."

The gathered group was so quiet, Juniper could hear the wind ruffling the leaves. She swallowed around a lump in her throat.

"Any candidate who fails to be present here, at sunrise on the day following the appointed test, with the task completed as designed, will forfeit her place as candidate. Of course, to return early is perfectly acceptable, allowing you a time of rest before the next day's task.

"During these three days, you may use only the items you can carry on your person, with the exception of any tasks which require external elements, and also the gathering of such additional food and drink as might be desired or necessary for survival. You may not receive assistance from anyone outside of the Trials. You may not venture outside of the boundaries appointed—that is to say, this mountain. Know that you shall be under observation at all times, for we shall have silent watchers assigned to you, to ensure that all the rules are kept and the bylaws followed." Odessa shifted, scouring the candidates with her eyes.

"Upon the sound of the horn, you shall venture out from this point. You shall travel each in your assigned direction: to the north and the south and the east and the west." Odessa pointed to each candidate in turn, and Juniper saw that her direction was north. She grimaced; the exact opposite of the clearing where she needed to deposit Fleeter. Oh, well.

"Above all things, an Anju chieftain must comport herself with dignity and integrity, acting always in support of her people, down to the smallest member. Honor first; honor above all else. This is the primary rule, and the one that shall be paramount to all others. And now the Trials begin. May the best prevail!"

"May the best prevail!" roared the gathered onlookers.

Juniper couldn't manage more than a feeble squeak.

The Chieftain Trials: Test of Might

Candidates shall journey in their appointed directions for no less than a league.

From there, they shall locate an active sweet crystal mine.

Using only such tools as they may hold on their person or gather in their immediate surroundings, they shall extract from the mine enough sweetcrystal to provide the tribe with a year's supply.

They shall return bearing this material in full before the morrow's sunrise.

May the best prevail!

Juniper looked down at the parchment sheet, now sweaty and crumpled from her tight grip, and frowned. She and Cyril had quickly covered the required league's distance from the camp, then had turned to head for the clearing, the meeting spot she'd agreed upon with Tippy.

Which meant pretty much going back the way they'd come.

Cyril voiced loud complaints, but Juniper was adamant. "We have a full day and night to complete this task. And over three days have now passed since we launched that messenger back to Torr. We need to establish contact with Queen's Basin as quickly as possible. What if word has already returned from the palace?"

"But to go so far out of our way," Cyril grumbled.

"It must be done," she said. "Gladly, there is nothing on this parchment to say we must select a sweetcrystal mine in the direction we are first sent. I have read my infernal mountain volume from cover to cover in the past few days, and thus I can tell you there is a mine quite near to where we shall dispose of Fleeter. Two birds with the same berry, don't you see? Anyway, what's an extra league," she taunted, "for a big strong roustabout like you?"

Cyril growled and stomped on ahead of her. It *was* galling to retread the very ground they'd walked that morning: hours of rough trekking in vain as they passed the same landmarks on their way back. If there had been any other option—if the need to be in touch with Queen's Basin had been any less pressing—Juniper might have abandoned this plan altogether. But there was nothing for it. She just hoped that once the cat was settled, it would perform as Tippy and Jess had predicted. How could you beat such a quick and reliable means of information exchange?

If it worked.

As they walked, Juniper leafed through Erick's *Mountain Ranges of the Lower Continent*, trying to take in more of the massive amount of information: diagrams of edible plants; lists of wildlife and their habitats; detailed maps and etchings of each mountain in the Hourglass range, including Mount Rahze, across which they now wearily trudged. Then she turned to see Cyril looking at her disapprovingly, and burst out laughing.

"Lands," she said. "I've become Erick Dufrayne, haven't I? Bookwalker extraordinaire."

But she didn't stop her reading.

When the sun was high overhead, they reached the clearing at last. In the frosty morning glare, it looked less inviting than ever. Still, Juniper scanned all the stumps until she found one with a hollowed-out crater at its base. Into this she poured the little spy cat, which turned twice in place and started licking its haunches. On Fleeter's neck hung a small pouch. Juniper pulled out her stylus and scratched a few words of greeting, keeping it short and sweet until she could be sure this method would function as promised. Next she reached into her waist pouch and extracted the moist treat Tippy had given her. She placed it gingerly in next to the cat, who sniffed archly, licked his chops, then swallowed it in one bite.

Juniper waited expectantly, but Fleeter seemed to have no other immediate plans.

After a moment, Cyril said, "Isn't the beast supposed to *go* somewhere? Back toward the Basin, ideally?"

"That's the way I understood it," Juniper said wanly.

Cyril nudged the toe of his boot into the hollow, prodding the little cat. Fleeter yawned, turned his back rudely, and appeared to fall sound asleep.

"Maybe we should pry it back out?" Juniper asked.

"I've never trusted cats," said Cyril. "All those quivery whiskers . . ." He shuddered. "This mongrel has caused us hours of extra travel, and now it looks to be good for nothing more than a leisurely nap."

"It will work, it will," Juniper muttered. But her reassurances rang hollow in her ears. What if it *didn't* work? What then? Anything might happen at Queen's Basin, and she would be none the wiser.

"We can't wait here any longer, Juniper," Cyril said. "If this beast is broken, then so be it. We've got to get moving. Once we finish this test, we can come back for another check, and decide then what to do."

Juniper glared at the cat for a few more minutes, seeing no difference except louder and louder snoring. Finally she turned away. "All right," she said. "Let's have a quick bite to eat and head for the mine."

Thankfully, the mine Juniper remembered was nearby, and they got within sight of it by the time the sun had just crested its midday peak. By now, Juniper ached from head to toe. Her gown was crusted with dried mud, and her underdress felt damp and sticky on her back. Thankfully, Cyril looked even worse than she felt—scarlet-cheeked, panting, with a dark stripe running down his once-fine orange coat—which brightened Juniper up a great deal.

"There we are," she said, pointing to the mine's shadowy opening up ahead. Less than a hundred paces on, the cliffside fell away in a sharp drop. Far to their left, they could just make out the rope bridge over which they'd crossed into this particular adventure, and which Juniper now regarded with a nostalgic sort of fondness.

Next to her, Cyril collapsed onto a boulder. "High time for a break, wouldn't you say?"

He sounded like such a pitiful, wrung-out version of himself that Juniper was unnerved. She had to get things back on track. Yawning extravagantly, she fanned herself with her book. "I didn't take you for a sluggard, Cyril Lefarge. I myself find that this casual stroll has quite restored my equilibrium!"

She tottered past his rock, though it was all she could do to lift her legs from one step to the next. But her ruse worked. There was a loud snort from behind her, then Cyril barreled past her like a boar after berries. "Is that your mineshaft up there, then, Missy Moribund? I'll reach it before you do, I wager."

Juniper let him have at it. Truth be told, at that moment she couldn't have blocked a croquet ball from a wicket. She could barely keep herself upright. Reaching the mine's entrance, too, meant that their actual task would have only just begun. Cyril's idea of stopping to rest seemed, in hindsight, a beautifully wise one.

But she couldn't admit that aloud *now*, could she?

They trudged the last distance in silence. When they reached the little dell overlooking the entry, they both plopped down to catch their breath.

"We should plan," said Juniper.

"Yes," agreed Cyril. "Figure out exactly what we're doing before venturing in."

Juniper's legs felt taken over by a swarm of tingling bees. "Five minutes," she gasped. She leaned back and closed her eyes.

Juniper awoke with a start. From the sun's position, she thought an hour might have passed. "Cyril!" she yelped, and he shot upright.

"Bother," he said, then yawned. "I guess we needed that rest."

Juniper jumped up, instantly wide awake. She collected her things and began to move. "No, no, no! Come on—we've no idea how long it will take us to find and collect the sweetcrystal."

"Look, we can't do our best if we're falling-over asleep. I'm not the one who chose to stay awake and gad about last night, after all."

"Never mind that," said Juniper. They reached the cave's entryway, and Juniper studied it carefully. The space was wide and well-traveled, the ground tracked with the pale greenish-white of trampled sweetcrystal powder. The very air gave off a rich, sweet scent, as if begging to be harvested and shaped into a confection.

Then Juniper cocked her head. "Do you hear something?"

"Footsteps," Cyril said. "Coming from . . . inside, I should wager."

A moment later, two pale-crusted figures emerged, blinking, from within the dark mountainside.

"Zetta!" Cyril hissed, making it sound like a rude word.

Juniper felt much the same, though she kept her voice neutral as she called, "Greetings, fellow candidate!"

Zetta looked up, narrowed her eyes, then relaxed—apparently seeing that Juniper had yet to start mining. For her part, Zetta hefted a large, cloth-wrapped bundle. Her muscular companion lugged one twice as big. Zetta gave a cursory nod and moved right past them on the path, heading back in the direction of the village with evident satisfaction at a job done well and early.

Juniper scowled. So Zetta had a jump on her. A *big* jump.

Still, sunset was hours off yet, and they had all the way till sunrise tomorrow to complete the task. There was plenty of time, and now they knew they were in the right spot. Juniper pulled her unlit torch out of her back and turned toward the cave.

Zetta paused in her walking. Leaning in to exchange a few words with her companion, she set down her bundle of sweetcrystal and scrambled across the rough ground to where they stood. "How fare you in your task?" she asked, with a grudging sort of concern.

Juniper tamped down her suspicions—why was Zetta acting friendly all of a sudden?—and answered honestly. It was no big secret, given the state of them. "We're well beat, if you must know. But we're here. The task to come won't be easy, but it's at hand and ready to be polished off. Not much more can be said than that!" She forced her lips into a smile. "Well done on your quick completion."

Zetta smiled wryly. "Gathering sweetcrystal is something I

have much experience with. When I was younger, some of us used to sneak out of a night and turn this very mine into a feasting hall. No provisions needed—all you could want for snacking to be found along the walls." She grinned, and even Cyril smiled in response. "You haven't really kicked up your dancing heels till you've done so in a mineshaft with the lights full out."

Stretching out her arms, she glanced back at her companion, who stood watching them, stone-faced. Zetta reached into her bag and pulled out a rounded, crystalline object. "Would you like to use this lamp?" Her mouth twisted as she spoke, as though two sides of her nature were fighting for control. "I don't know how much you know of the mines, but carrying an open flame in there is . . . not a good idea. There have been accidents, some deadly. Pockets of gas and so on."

Juniper and Cyril exchanged a glance.

"What do you mean?"

Zetta gestured toward Juniper's unlit torch. "I don't know all the specifics. Only that the chemical composition of the sweet-crystal—or the air within the mine, perhaps—does not mesh well with open flame. We only tried it the once . . ." She brought her hands together in a short, sharp clap. "Boom!"

Juniper jumped.

Zetta placed the lamp in her hands. "I have no great love for you, Juniper Torrence, but you are a worthy competitor, and a blood sister besides. I would not lose your life to ignorance. Nor your companion's." She pointed to a narrow opening in the lamp's underside. "There is a wick inside here—light it *before* entering the mines. The light is not bright, but it burns steady and true. And most important: It's covered."

"Th-thank you," stammered Juniper. How close had they come to a fatal accident?

Zetta nodded and turned to go. At the last minute, she swung back around. "Also, I wouldn't bother with this mine here—we've harvested everything in easy reach, and this is our tribe's main gathering spot, so it's well picked over. There's another mine entrance not a league back that way." She pointed in the direction of the bridge.

Cyril glared. "You're being strangely *nice*, all of a sudden. How do we know you're—"

"What you do is of no concern to me," Zetta snapped, apparently regretting this brief moment of helpfulness. "Explore this cave, take all the sweetcrystal you are able to find, and welcome to it." She lifted her nose and stalked away.

Juniper jabbed Cyril in the ribs, and he had the grace to look apologetic.

For her part, Juniper looked at the cave's opening, so deliciously near.

"We can't take her word for it," Cyril pointed out.

Juniper had been thinking the same thing. "Let's give it a look, then." But the rocklight Zetta had given them weighed heavy in her grasp, and with it, the vision of what could have happened had the other girl *not* interfered.

It didn't take long to see that Zetta's advice appeared right on target. The first space they reached, after a steep and painful climb, showed walls pocked with empty craters, barely glinting in the dull lamplight.

"We could push in further," Cyril suggested. "There must be more rooms like this one—they can't all be this empty."

But Juniper shook her head. How much more time would they lose investigating this cave? Zetta's help had been sound till now. What's more, the cave she'd mentioned was printed right in Erick's book, and wasn't far off at all. Juniper squinted back toward the narrow daylit opening.

"We'd best get moving," she said. "The sweet stuff's not going to come to us."

15

THEY REACHED THE NEW MINE AFTER ONE league's walk that felt like a dozen. Even with that accidental nap earlier, Juniper felt exhausted down to her core. To her annoyance, Cyril showed no signs of tiredness at all. What had happened to the sweaty, woebegone Cyril of this morning? Juniper wanted that boy back; this one made her look bad and feel worse.

All she could do was grind her teeth and struggle on.

But at last they arrived and stood blinking into the darkness of the new cave's entry. Just as with the last one, chalky sweetcrystal powder dotted the dirt leading in—though much less of it showed here—and the air held the same bewitching scent. So they were clearly in the right spot. This opening was narrower, though, and dropped in much more steeply.

Cyril relit Zetta's lamp and led the way, the flicker of light bobbing around him. Juniper watched the orange glow play across his features and off the rocky walls. She thought of the orange lights Jessamyn had seen around the horse thieves, which had so terrified her all those weeks ago; she looked again at the little orange lamp.

Well, that was another mystery solved.

She didn't have long to mull this over, for a minute later she heard Cyril call out, "Hello, *sweetcrystal*!" She followed him down a sharp incline and rounded a corner into a huge, wide-open space. In the dim light, the walls gleamed like the night sky, all pocked with shiny dabs of sweetcrystal. Juniper ran her hand over the nearest wall. There were dozens, hundreds, more little buttons of rocky sweetness than she could have numbered in a year of counting. But each one was pressed deep into the wall, like so many precious eyeballs tucked in so many dark sockets.

How were they going to get the crystals out? They might take a fortnight to extract the amount of sweet rock she'd seen Zetta and her companion carrying.

"Over here," Cyril called, and she turned from the wall toward the center of the room, where—Juniper gasped as Cyril's lamp shifted to illuminate a giant column squatting in the middle space.

It seemed to be made of solid sweetcrystal.

"Shall we dig in here, then, little cousin?" he said, with a smirk.

To her surprise, Juniper found she was enjoying the flare of kinship springing up between Cyril and herself. Nothing like a common challenge to nudge rivals toward a tolerant acceptance, she mused. Sometime over the last few hours, they really had become a "we."

"Let's," she said with relish.

They set to work.

And then . . . they stopped.

It took only a few minutes to realize that their methods were not proving successful. Juniper tried hacking at the wall with a variety of sharp stones, tried prodding it with a long sharp branch, even took a turn digging at the craggy surface with her fingers. Cyril alternated a slew of his own methods, with exactly the same level of success.

None.

Juniper's palm smarted under its bandage, still tender from the ceremonial slice. But the real problem was simply this: The sweet-crystal was the wrong consistency. It was gummy and slightly tacky, and while this should have made it easier to pry the crystals out, instead it made it harder. When Juniper managed to get any piece of it loose, the mass would crumble into a fine, sticky powder. Cyril finally spread out the cloth of their portable shelter to catch these drifts, but Juniper shook her head in frustration.

"It's no use," she said. "The Anju aren't going to spend the next year eating this mucky paste, all mixed up as it is with dirt and sweat. We need chunky crystal, masses of it. What's wrong with this stuff? Do you think Zetta steered us wrong?"

"It is uncommonly toasty in here," Cyril noted.

It *was* warm. Juniper had already shed her cloak, and now she loosened the collar of her overdress. She placed both hands on the pillar. "Is it coming from inside here, all the heat?"

"It could be from anywhere—some of these caves must lead down to the heart of the mountain. There are volcanic elements below the Hourglass, I know that for certain."

Juniper kicked at the wall. "Well, we *need* a way to get this stuff loose. Or the whole game is up." She stopped and glanced back at Cyril, who had a calculating look on his face. "What? What are you thinking? I can tell some sticky idea's oozing through your mind. Spit it out."

"Some *spectacular* sticky idea," Cyril corrected modestly. "Now, pay attention. We need a great heap of sweetcrystal, yes?"

Juniper nodded.

He waved a hand at the column. "Here we have just that. One enormous deposit of it. At our disposal—only waiting to be shaken loose. Only waiting for the right *incentive*."

"Incentive?"

Grinning wickedly, Cyril reached into his bag and pulled out his flint stones.

Juniper gasped. "You're jesting!"

"Not at all. I can't guarantee it would be a *safe* solution, but I do think it would work. Sensitive to gases, that Anju said? Awaiting a spark to shake them loose? Well. I say we *create* that spark. Break this block to bits, then we can take all that we need with ease."

"That's the worst idea I've ever heard!" Juniper sputtered.

"Only think on it." Cyril pointed toward the roof. "This is no support column. See that ruddy gap up there before the roof? And the walls around us are far as can be. We create just the smallest flame, nestle it up against the base of this pillar, and what happens? I'll tell you: a tidy little BOOM. A satisfying bite carved out of this great sugarloaf, and into our knapsacks it all goes. Challenge complete!"

"But—but—" This was *still* the worst idea she'd ever heard. But it was also their *only* idea. Was she actually considering it? She clawed again at the pillar. Nothing. She rubbed her hands on her skirts.

May the best prevail. Did she have what it took to be the best? Juniper closed her eyes. She pictured Odessa's face, her father's, her mother's. She opened her eyes and saw Cyril, studying her with a challenge in his gaze. *Now let's see what you're made of,* he seemed to be saying. *I bet you'll not go for this wild-hare idea. And then you'll fail.*

Love of country and pride of heritage were well and good, but sometimes it just came down to wiping the smirk off your nearest rival's face.

"We'll have to take every safety precaution," she said, her voice clipped. "All the sweetcrystal in the world won't be any use if we're scattered about missing our arms and legs."

The trick was getting the flame inside the cave without risking a too-soon triggering of the explosion in this enclosed space, wide though it was. (Though the very word *explosion* itself made Juniper shudder, bringing to mind as it did the images of distant flashes they'd seen on the far horizon during the first days of the Monsians' invasion of Torr.)

In the end, they just had to go for it.

They gathered up dry grass and twigs, layered them onto Cyril's neckerchief—almost too sweaty to use, but just functional—and set the whole thing atop a flat rock a safe distance from the cave. Then Juniper got busy kindling. Once the flame was thumb-high and burning stoutly, Cyril tied the kerchief's edges together tight enough so no heat would escape, but loose enough not to quash the little blaze.

From here, the fire would either catch, or it would suffocate and go out within seconds. It stubbornly did the latter; three times Juniper and Cyril jog-dashed it inside the cave only to find the flame had snuffed all the way out. The fourth time, though, after adding slightly larger twigs—and perhaps due to the drying out of Cyril's damp neckerchief—they got the bundle all the way inside and could see the faint orange glow still purring beneath the cloth.

"Now we run," said Cyril. He nudged the smoldering mass up against the column's base, turned, and sprinted for the entryway.

Juniper waited only a moment longer. The kerchief's knotted top grew dark as the flame inside chewed through its barrier. The smell of burnt cloth and charred body odor began to seep out.

She turned and ran.

She'd reached the cave's opening when the promised *boom* shook the floor. It wasn't as large as she'd feared—she fell only to her knees, despite being barely out of the mine. But Cyril looked satisfied. Though that may have had as much to do with her fall as the explosion.

"I'd call that a success," he said. "And well worth the sacrifice of my favorite scarf. Now, let us go inspect the goods."

They crept in together. Reaching the main room, Cyril held up the rocklight while Juniper scanned the thick, cloying air for the pillar. Her mouth dropped open. "It worked!"

It *had* worked—even better than they'd hoped, and far more than she'd expected from the low sound they'd heard from outside. They'd taken no mere chunk from the center pillar. Instead, the thing had crumbled in its entirety. The column was nothing but a rubble pile of sweetcrystal.

But something wasn't right.

"The ground!" Cyril yelped. "It's wet—and hot!"

Then Juniper saw liquid bubbling up out of the jagged stump where the pillar used to be. It was like they'd blown the cap off a bottle of ale, and now the contents were frothing up and slopping out everywhere.

"Oh, gads," said Cyril. "We'd best collect our prize and get out of here, quickit."

Juniper couldn't agree more. The floor was wet and edging toward swampy, so she draped the lean-to sheet across Cyril's outstretched arms and set to grabbing up every loose chunk she could find, until the tarp was piled high with tacky but still-solid sweetcrystal. While Cyril lugged his burden outside, she looped her cloak over her arm and kept on filling. The stuff was everywhere! When the bundle bulged nearly to the floor, she drew the edges tight shut. She tottered up the incline and out of the cave.

"Well, that's that," she said. She met Cyril's eye and saw his look mirror what she felt herself: the raw, uncut pride of accomplishment that comes from pushing yourself harder than you'd thought you could—and succeeding. In the next instant, though, the pride seeped right out of her, leaving behind a gas cloud of pure exhaustion.

A trickle of opaque liquid licked out of the cave behind them. Juniper looked up at the moon gleaming overhead. They had hours still until dawn, but the walk would be long and the bundles burdensome.

Juniper and Cyril set off, the weight of their success heavy on their backs.

16

"IT IS TIME FOR YOUR SECOND TASK!" ODESSA'S voice was sharp as the crack of dawn in Juniper's ears. She and Cyril had staggered into camp barely two hours before, depositing their loads next to Zetta's and Libba's, both of whom had come in hours earlier and were presumably enjoying a restful night's sleep in their rooms. Juniper noticed that Cyril's and her sweetcrystal pile held more than triple the other candidates'. If only the contest were being judged by volume, she'd have been the clear winner of this round.

Alas, the extra amount had earned only a pursed-lip scowl from Odessa and muttering from the Elders. They buzzed among themselves and motioned Juniper over, apparently wanting to question her on something or other. But Juniper was dead on her feet. Brushing the worst residue off her sticky cloak, she smiled and made her polite excuses, then slid away to the common area. There she collapsed across a lounge seat without even making it back to her room, blacking solidly out until dawn broke, what seemed like moments later.

Now they were gathered in the clearing, the three remaining candidates and their seconds. For the word was now official: Tania had not made it back in time, and a search party had just been dispatched to locate and rescue her from any trouble she might have met with on her way.

"More likely she is lurking in the bushes somewhere, all scruff-matted and nursing her lost pride," said Zetta smugly, casting a meaningful look at Juniper's disheveled figure.

Juniper looked at her rival, who had had enough leisure time to bathe and comb her long silvery hair into four practical braids, which were now bound up tight on top of her head. Her leather britches were fresh, and her pale fur wraps mud-free.

Zetta looked ready to take on the world.

By contrast, Juniper's layered underclothes were stiff inside her bodice, and her dress dark and dirt-scabbed. The hand-sewn peonies on her skirt were snagged and weeping embroidery thread like muddy tears. Her cloak was crusted with gummy, half-melted sweetcrystal, and her hair would have scared away a nesting rat. She'd tried to use her bone-handled comb on it that morning, but had finally given up. She'd ended up yanking it into a tail and using the last of her pins to jam it tight against her head, then had wound it all several times around with one of the velvet ribbons she'd ripped from her waistline. The dress was headed for the scrap pile anyway, more was the pity. What would her Comportment Master say if he could see her now? Juniper bit off a manic giggle, which almost made her dissolve into tears. Just thinking of her hated Comportment Master, her beloved palace, her precious endangered father was almost too much to bear.

Juniper's resolve hardened. She would bear all the mud in the world, suffer through every blister, and never sleep another night in her life if it would bring her through these Trials victorious, if it would give her a way to free her father and save her kingdom.

A way to make the Monsians pay.

Her mind skipped to Jessamyn's little spy cat. Was it still snoozing away in its hollow stump? Or could it have made its way to the Basin and back? Could it be waiting even now with a message tucked into its collar pouch?

Juniper realized that Odessa was standing in front of her, holding a crisp, newly rolled sheet of parchment. Juniper took it, fingers trembling as the last sleepy cobwebs brushed from her mind. The old woman's smile held a private look Juniper had come to recognize over the past few days: There were words hidden in the depths of her eyes, words Juniper could never fully make out but that burrowed deep in her mind, in her heart, in her spine.

I'll make you proud, Grandmother! she vowed.

She glanced at Cyril, who looked annoyingly well rested. And his hair freshly washed, to boot! When had he had time for that? *At least my dirt is warm and lived-in,* she thought miserably.

Juniper stifled one last yawn for the road. Then she unfurled the parchment sheet. Cyril leaned in, and they read together:

The Chieftain Trials: Test of Mind

Candidates shall proceed to the Memory Wall.

There, they shall contribute to the tribe's store of knowledge and history by creating a panel containing such events as bring value to the collective heritage.

The completed task shall be reviewed and must be approved by the Memory Keeper for accuracy and relevance.

Candidates shall return with this task accomplished in full before the morrow's sunrise.

May the best prevail!

From her tour of the Anju village, Juniper knew that the Memory Wall was a giant dropsy tree, impossibly tall, which held pride of place at the village's very center, not far from the Climbing Tree. The other two candidates were off like arrows; Juniper let them go. The task would likely be the easiest of all for the Anju contestants. They'd probably even been expecting it, living as they did with this monument in their midst. For Juniper, though, this test foretold only despair. What could she possibly hope to contribute to the history of a people she knew nothing about? In vain, she ran her mind over the tales her mother had told her as a child: They were nothing but stories. "The Girl Who Licked the Moon"? "Three Buffoons on a Barge"? "Two Went Up, Four Came Down"? Legends, all of them, fables, tall tales. Fanciful and dreamlike and perfect for listening to while curled up close to the person who loves you most in the world.

But right for inclusion on a historical monument? Hardly.

They reached the Memory Wall at last, and Cyril let out a low whistle. The giant tree had a smooth, pale, canvas-like bark, across which Anju history rippled out in the form of meticulous carvings, clearly done over the course of years and decades and centuries. Juniper walked slowly around the living historical record, letting herself take it all in. It seemed a lifetime ago that she and Zetta had breezed through their tour of the Anju village, with Tippy bobbing around them like a jaybird new from the nest. Back then, the tree had been a novelty, a wonder, something to admire and gawk at.

Now it looked suspiciously like the portent of her doom. The downfall of her entire country. For what could she hope to add to this cultural masterpiece?

Still, studying this treasure trove of lore, of information—this record of her past, her heritage—filled something inside her, pooled in hollows she hadn't known were there. This was part of the reason she'd come on this quest, after all.

And the other?

Juniper clenched her hands into fists. She wasn't giving up, not by a long shot. She had a whole day and a night ahead of her. Who knew what pertinent historical truths she might recall in that time? As for whether they passed muster—that would be in the hands of fate.

The trunk of the structure known as the Memory Wall was as wide around as the Great Tree back in the Basin. But where that tree was squat and stubby, the aptly named Memory Wall shot proudly into the sky. Thick, leafless branches cut straight out at regular intervals, and were hung with rope ladders and hammock seats, apparently for use by any who wished to view the historical artistry.

Today, however, the tree seemed to be reserved for the candidates, for they were the only ones upon it—though various onlookers milled around the ground and in the trees nearby, keeping an eye on the excitement.

Zetta was already hard at work. Perched up high, leather-clad legs dangling to either side of a branch, she was carving at the trunk with a sharp, pointed stone. Libba sat lower down, holding an equally suitable stone, but hadn't yet begun cutting into the bark. She seemed hesitant, and kept looking from side to side as though for escape.

Juniper didn't blame her. From her vantage point, she could see many of the exquisite carvings. Each was numbered to show its year, though they didn't seem displayed in consecutive order. Some names and other words were included—here Juniper saw *Torr* and there *Monsia*—but for the most part, the images told the stories. She saw a small group of people make their way from the far north, down through the mountain range. She saw them settle on the southwestern coast, establish themselves, grow populous. Juniper shifted, following the pictographic story as invaders swept in with forked swords and sharp-pointed helmets. She saw dead and maimed Anju scattered across the tree's scarred bark canvas. She saw survivors, few and bedraggled, make their determined way back north. She saw them carve out their own refuge in the mountains: safe, solitary, out of sight.

There was more—a lot more. She could see glimpses of sickness and disease, fires and floods, sweeping disasters and times of great joy. She saw tales of chieftain after chieftain and learned of their exploits. But there was one thing she didn't find. Juniper didn't realize what she'd been searching for until finally it crystallized.

She grabbed hold of a rope and started to climb. She ran her eyes across the bark, flitting from one historical record to the next, her excitement growing with every passing moment. On the ground, she could see Cyril frowning at her in puzzlement. He clearly had no idea what she was doing. But his hands were clenched in a gesture of unconscious solidarity; she knew he could sense her rising hope.

By the time she'd reached the top and circled all the way back around the tree's breadth, she felt her satisfaction bubble up and overflow.

She shinnied down the rope and landed with a bounce at Cyril's feet.

"What now?" he said. "You've got a face like a cat meeting a fishbowl. I suppose I'll have to hear you go on and on about some grand new idea you've gotten into your head." He waited expectantly.

Juniper beamed at him. "It's your lucky day," she said. "You get to help me tell the world about one of your favorite people."

17

WHAT WAS MISSING FROM THE MEMORY WALL'S chronicle was simple: Alaina, daughter of Odessa, almost-but-not-quite Chieftain of the Anju, Queen of Torr, and wife of King Regis. Mother of Juniper. There was neither mark nor mention of her from tap of root to tip of leaf.

Juniper couldn't have been more pleased.

Her mother's story was entirely at her disposal to tell. She couldn't have asked for a better opportunity. Cyril's mouth turned over when she shared her news with him. Oh, the moment was sweet! All that time Cyril had spent lurking in the shadows throughout Juniper's childhood, whispering taunts about her mother's heritage and bloodline. In his dark obsession, he'd become a sort of expert on the very person he so disdained. Now Juniper would use this ill-gotten knowledge to supplement her own and to help her craft a viable historical timeline.

"Cyril," she said briskly, thinking now of those cleverly sketched maps Tippy had found in his tent weeks ago. "You know your way around a stylus, I think?"

Distracted from his funk, Cyril looked up. "Top of my class," he drawled.

Juniper enjoyed a good list-making session. Her passion for schedules and timelines was embarrassingly well known. But one thing she could decidedly not do was *draw*. She thrust her stylus into Cyril's hand, then hunted along the ground until she found a stone that settled comfortably in her grip, and which came to a sharp pointed end.

"Let's climb up, then," she said. "I'll direct. You sketch. Then I'll carve the finished design into the bark. A team, yes?"

For a moment, Cyril seemed to teeter between his distaste at the subject and his enthusiasm for drawing. Finally he shrugged and gave a grudging smile. "A team," he agreed. "Yet again. But don't get used to it. I can't keep on bailing you out like this everyday of the livelong week! Why the goshawk you are the one running for chieftain and not myself, I've no idea. Surely I've done the draco's share of work on this infernal trek."

Juniper looped the rope around her foot and began to climb. "All part of the leadership process, my dear cousin! Utilizing the resources at our disposal. Making do with what we have and all that." She flashed him a grin through the branches. "After all, even a cracked bucket works when you need to pour."

The process wasn't *quite* as simple as Juniper had first thought. But once they settled into a routine, things moved smoothly. Juniper outlined to Cyril the story she wanted to tell, then they pared it down to its simplest essence. The bark was smooth by tree standards, but it was nothing like actual canvas or parchment, and Cyril's artistic skills were seriously put to the test. So Juniper kept to the basics: young Alaina's childhood and training amongst her people, her anticipation of the Trial (she mentally thanked Zetta for this new piece of information), her journey to the castle of Torr, her whirlwind romance and unexpected marriage to King Regis. Her heartbreak at being cut off from her people. Her longing and the wish she never lost, to her dying day, that she might hear word from them again. Despite this, her many good years in Torr. Her regal bearing, subjects who would travel from the far corners of the country to hear her speak, the clinics and care treatments she established to ensure that none lacked for any need that the royal family might be able to help secure.

By the end of her tale, Cyril paused in his sketching. He tucked the stylus behind his ear and gazed into the distance. "So, it's possible she may not have been *all* rotten fruit, that Anju mother of yours." His face reddened. "Don't think this constitutes an apology, by the way. And don't think that I'm not just waiting for the right moment to push you out of this tree, when it's to my best advantage."

"Never crossed my mind," Juniper said glibly. "But . . . thank you." She hefted her rock again and set to scratching.

To Juniper's wild delight, she and Cyril were the first to finish the test. They left Zetta gouging at her side of the bark—alone, for her brawny helper apparently lacked the artistic temperament. Libba still stared in clear despair at a blank section of the trunk, as though hoping to conjure a story from its silent sap.

The Memory Keeper was a wizened old man, who materialized out of a hollow in the tree's base as soon as Juniper's and Cyril's feet hit the ground. He introduced himself as Nolan, then looped a pair of crystal spectacles across the bridge of his nose.

"Please stay here and await my return," he rasped, then began a surprisingly nimble climb up the branches.

"Not bad for an oldster," said Cyril.

"You're leaking admiration everywhere these days," Juniper teased. "I hardly know you anymore! Wouldn't Palace Cyril be scandalized at this new turn of character?"

Cyril scuffed the ground with the toe of his boot. "Palace Cyril may not quite have been all he thought himself to be," he said, very softly. Juniper let the words hang in the air, too surprised to come up with a suitable answer, until she realized that none was really needed. In silence they watched Nolan, deftly tangled in the thick climbing ropes, as he scooted along their careful depiction from end to end. Partway through, he frowned, moved back to the beginning, and started again.

Juniper noticed that more villagers had gathered to watch. Nearest her was Tania, the contestant who had been eliminated the day before. The girl looked placid and composed, and Juniper felt a flush of awkwardness. Juniper hadn't had any part in the girl's loss, but the encounter still felt like a pothole waiting for a wagon.

Instead, Tania's voice was warm and hearty. "It's a good sign he

175

has been up there this long," she said in a low, confiding tone. "He can sometimes be up and back down before his rope's even stopped swinging."

"What does he look for?" Juniper asked. "How does he decide if the entry qualifies?"

"Many things. Content, foremost. If the story's already been told in any form, it cannot be admitted. If it's rendered inaccurately. If it's . . . visually unappealing." She rolled her eyes. "He's terribly fussy, but I suppose this work is his life. I can't imagine what will happen when he passes on and the task must go to another. He's a legend himself, as much as the Memory Wall."

"And if it's not suitable?" Cyril asked.

"Then it is stripped. The Memory Keeper files the top layer right off, to remove all trace of it." She pointed to a pale patch near the front middle of the tree. "This was one from the last Trials, I've heard. It was before my birth, of course, but I'm told it was spectacularly grotesque." Her mouth twisted in sympathy and she lowered her voice further. "'Twas Libba's mother's attempt. Artistically untalented to a most astonishing degree! The stuff of legend, that effort was. Libba herself is not near so bad an artist; only she believes herself to be worse yet, despite her mother's hiring constant instruction for her across all these years. I think Libba has spent a lifetime dreading that she might someday achieve a similar result and live on in infamy herself. Can you see her? She doesn't even dare to try."

The lank-haired girl was, in fact, sitting frozen in the identical position as when Juniper had first climbed down the tree. Only now, her face was wet with tears.

"She should carve in the story of her mother's Trial attempt," said Cyril lightly.

Juniper looked shocked at the idea, but Tania shrugged. "She could. It is a tribe legend already. But I don't think she will even lift her hand to start. She's that afraid of failure."

"There must be something we can do to help," said Juniper. "Can't we go over and . . . I don't know, encourage her or something? It doesn't seem sporting to just sit here on the sidelines, waiting for her to fail."

Tania looked at her frankly. "This is a test of leadership. We are looking for the woman who will be the leader of our tribe. A victory of this magnitude cannot be handed along gift-wrapped. It must be clawed out of the hands of destiny, or not at all."

Juniper had no answer to that.

"That's why, no matter how many of us were shocked at your entry into the Trials, we gave no true opposition. You are of the Blood. You even have training, of sorts. But most of all, you showed the type of brazen fire that our people need in order to survive. We do not live a comfortable life, Juniper Torrence. We are a people whose every hour is a life's tug with the elements. We need a leader who understands this, and who will bleed and fight and die alongside us. Whether you are that leader or no, I cannot say. But the ember is there, and that is a start. The rest, the Trials will tell."

The sound of a clearing throat pulled Juniper's attention from Tania's pointed stare on her one side and Cyril's sardonic raised eyebrow on the other. Nolan the Memory Keeper stood on a narrow planked platform, swinging gently below his observation branch. The clever device caught Juniper's admiration, and she wished Erick were here to see it, so he might sketch up some plans to try and replicate it in Queen's Basin.

Then Nolan opened his mouth, and all thoughts of the Basin fell away. "Juniper Torrence, candidate four. Your tale has been reviewed, and a decision has been made. In veracity: It qualifies. In originality: It qualifies. In representation: Here, too, it qualifies. I hereby judge this entry to be accepted."

With no further ceremony, he yanked the pull ropes to lower his pulley-swing to the ground. Then he turned and disappeared into the heart of his tree, slamming the door behind him.

"He didn't seem very happy to pass along that decision," muttered Cyril.

Tania gave him a baleful eye. "He values truth above all, so that would come before any personal preferences. In any case, you have passed this test—and before either of the others. Well done."

The excitement now over, the crowds began to melt away. Many faces looked as sour as Nolan's had been, but Juniper noticed a near equal number regarding her with open curiosity, some even with grudging admiration. A round, stern-faced man shepherded a gaggle of small children—Littles, she remembered Zetta calling them—who were all craning their necks toward the Memory Wall, hopping up and down in excited attempts to see the new story. But evidently they weren't allowed up for a closer look until the test was over.

Juniper turned to Cyril. "Well done, team," she said.

Cyril rolled his eyes. "You're welcome." But his smile was the most genuine one Juniper had seen from him yet.

Off to the side, Juniper caught sight of Odessa, staring transfixed at the newly added images. There was no way she could make out much detail from her place on the ground, but the look on her face—pain and regret and an exquisite sort of relief—told Juniper that she knew well what had been added.

And that she approved.

With the excitement over, Juniper felt her aching muscles turn to mush as the morning's exhaustion swept back. She was glad to be done early today, for her body screamed its need of a good night's sleep.

First, though, they had one more task to see through.

"Cyril," she said, "before we turn in for the day . . . how do you fancy a jaunt over to explore some stumps?"

18

THE JAGGED SNORING DREW JUNIPER TO THE
right stump immediately. She peered into the hollow, and her heart
sank: Fleeter was curled up in the identical position in which they'd
left him almost two days before.

"*Fleet*er, my bootstraps!" sniped Cyril. "Snoozer is more like it."

Juniper reached in and extracted the comatose cat, taking
a moment to stroke his stubbly back. Then—because why not
check?—she unhooked the clasp of the pouch that hung around
the creature's neck. Her fingers closed on a folded parchment
sheet. "Cyril! This isn't my note. Fleeter must have been and gone
already—he's delivered after all!"

Cyril raised an eyebrow.

"Aren't you a goodsy little spy cat?" Juniper crooned, tickling
the creature behind the ears and doing her best Tippy imitation.
The jollity did the trick, wiping the scornful look right off Cyril's
face as he let out a bark of unexpected laughter. Juniper grinned

in return. "Let's see what news our intrepid feline has to share, shall we?"

"How did he come back to settle again in this very stump? I confess I doubted that talk of super smells and such . . ." Cyril trailed off, shrugging like he didn't much care one way or another. But he was clearly impressed.

What with one thing and another, Cyril was becoming scarcely recognizable of late.

In the next moment, all thoughts of Cyril fled Juniper's mind, as she pushed the paper's edges apart and tumbled into the familiar, beloved world of the Basin.

Dear Juniper,

A lot has happened since the last time I wrote. First, everyone is well, and work continues at a staggering rate. In preparation for the out-journey, we've moved the horses up to the Cavern, and have all the saddles completely packed and ready to load on. This return trip shall come none too soon, I might add, for our food stores are dangerously low. Though Paul of the Garden informs us that pea shoots are peeping out (you see what I did there?), and we enjoyed our first official crop today: spiced radishes! Not everyone celebrates this peppery vegetable, but the freshness can't be beat. Root has also been having some success with his hunting—dwarf rabbits and quail thus far, but he has an eye out for bigger game, and we all (hungrily) hope for the best.

But what am I going on about? I have neglected the biggest news of all: We've had a wing from the palace! As Jess predicted, her sister, Egg, did indeed receive our message and has sent a brief note to state this fact. The missive had little news other than word of her safety and confirmation of the palace's takeover and the capture of her father, as well as yours. We are heavy of heart, yet take comfort in knowing for certain how things stand. We have sent back a reply and await more news.

I will keep you abreast as we learn more.

Something else is odd around here: The river's gone hot on us. That's strange, isn't it? I've been digging through my books to try and figure out the reason, and how I perish for want of all the study resources back at the palace! I know there's something I'm overlooking, for there's a familiarity to this that niggles but doesn't quite land. At any rate, we're unable to use the swimming hole at the waterfall—it's gone beyond warmth to a jolly unsettling hot. The stream is still tolerable—quite pleasant, actually, and most soothing on the feet with all those knobby stones to tread. Hopefully the temperature will rise no higher. I daresay this gathering heat has something to do with all the infernal sunstone hereabound, but I'm dashed if I know what.

You can bet I have my thinking hat on and will report as soon as I have further news.

> Till then, I remain,
> Your faithful friend (and chief adviser),
> Erick Dufrayne

Juniper released her fingers, and the parchment snapped shut. How she wished that she could just hitch up her skirts and fly-leap across the mountain chasm to land on that nearby peak! Queen's Basin was not far at all—just across this break in the mountain range. In fact, if Erick's book was to be believed, the Hourglass Mountains all shared a common spine that linked them right up from their cores. How quickly she could be home, with her friends. She could make it in hours, she knew, or even less.

"Juniper?"

She shook herself as Cyril's voice brought her back to reality.

The Trials. The Anju. The third test.

"It's not like they aren't *vastly* better off without you there, you know," he went on, only this time the dripping scorn was as fake as snow in summer. "Do yourself a favor and let them toddle on their own a bit more. Your little country will still be there when you're done knocking off this Anju task."

Juniper could have hugged him. She didn't, of course—that would just have been weird—but she refolded the parchment into a tight flat square and tucked it inside her waist pouch. She pried another sheet from the back of her journal, though it pained her to see the dwindling pages, and set down a few words about the latest in the Trials and what was still to come.

If all goes well, she wrote, *I shall complete the last task with the same success we have met thus far. But one way or another, all shall be resolved by the second sunrise from this one. Then we shall know what is in store for my future, and with it, the future of all Torr. One way or another, we must ready ourselves to head back in defense of the palace—and the king.*

Juniper looked up. Cyril had leaned in to read over her shoulder. She frowned and swatted at his face, but he just ducked and moved to a different angle and kept reading. She scowled.

I have determined that I cannot allow myself to fail in this task. We need this army, and I have seen nothing here thus far that I cannot overcome. For your part there, it is time now to gather everyone together, complete any final packing tasks, and make ready the provisions for our journey.

Torr Palace must be reclaimed. My father, and all the other captives, must be rescued.

Upon my return, we move out.

With luck, we shall have the Anju army at our back when we do so.

The walk back to the Anju camp was a quiet one. Juniper felt weighed down by all she'd spelled out in her letter. Why did it all feel so much realer, the burden somehow heavier, once she'd put her desires and intents into words? She recalled a memory of her mother pulling her aside after a particularly odious lecture from her Comportment Master, who had spoken at length about how young ladies must be seen and not heard.

Spoken words hold power, her mother had said, putting a hand on each of Juniper's little shoulders. *To say it is to believe it, and belief is the magic that makes anything possible. Don't ever let anyone tell you what you can or cannot do. Speak your dreams aloud, then go and make them happen.*

To this day, Juniper sometimes fought a nagging sense that assertiveness was not fully ladylike. And yet, was not confidence the spine of leadership? Self-belief didn't take any more energy than self-doubt, and it was a good deal more comfortable to live with.

She could not make herself win, but she could certainly walk a winner's walk.

As they left the clearing, the ground shivered slightly under their feet.

Cyril looked up. "Did you feel that? Where's it coming from?"

The shaking of the ground was no stronger than when they'd exploded the sweetcrystal mine, but Juniper couldn't tell where this rumbling originated.

"It's not coming from Torr," she whispered, squinting off into the horizon. The late afternoon sky was clear; there were no flashes or distant smoke like they had seen several weeks before, when Monsia had first invaded.

That didn't mean the enemy wasn't out there, though, scheming and plotting and moving ahead with their dastardly plans.

The ground shook again. Juniper looked sideways at Cyril, her thoughts still on Torr. "How could you do it?" she asked him. "Betray your country like that? You knew the attack on the palace was going to happen, and you never said a word. Helped them, even. Or your father did, anyway, which is much the same."

He bit his lip. "It's not that easy, is it? *You've* got your father and your country all on the same side, nice and tidy. It's easy to be loyal then, isn't it? Plain and simple. But split them up, put them on two opposite sides . . ." He shook his head. "Who gets your loyalty now? And what wouldn't you do for someone you love, when it comes right down to it?"

They walked back to the camp in silence.

19

The Chieftain Trials: Test of Mettle

The final test is upon you, candidates!

This test is the darkest and most risky of all, yet also holds the most potential for reward. This is where the true leader will rise above the rest. The task is simple:

You will identify the greatest danger to our people.

You will seek it out and engage it.

You will subdue and bring this element under your control so that it no longer poses any threat.

The one who brings demonstrable proof of the greatest threat so contained shall be the winner of this final Test, and shall be named chief.

May the best prevail!

Juniper's mouth dropped all the way open. "Danger?" she echoed, looking at Cyril. "What greatest danger?"

The last two candidates and their seconds—for Libba never

had begun her attempt on the Memory Wall and at daybreak had been disqualified—stood opposite each other in a loose semicircle, hemmed in by Odessa and the other Elders. A scatter of early-rising Anju stood nearby, ogling the action. Juniper herself had entered the clearing feeling ready to take on the world: Her gown and cloak were still hopelessly unkempt, but she'd slept long and soundly, scrubbed her teeth with a good chew of licorice root, and washed and combed her hair through twice with her own carved comb. She felt as bright as a newly minted coin.

This task, however, set her back on her heels. "I need more information before I can proceed," she said to Odessa. Zetta and her second were conferring avidly, waving their hands and nodding as though the task was already half done. Juniper crumpled the parchment in her hand. "Come on—it's only right."

Odessa opened her mouth, but Zetta stopped talking and stepped into the silence. "*Right?*" Zetta said icily, and in the next moment her controlled façade crumbled altogether. "I don't think *right* is a word that has any part in these Trials, does it? I'm not afraid of you, Juniper, daughter of Alaina the Deserter. Oh, hadn't you heard that name?" she said, into Juniper's flinch. "Yes, that's what we call her. Never mind that, though. I know you're not *one of us*, so how would you know of our dangers? I'll tell you what I've decided to tackle, shall I?" Zetta waved away an Elder's protest, her shoulders now shaking with barely controlled fury. "It's only *right*, isn't it? Now, listen up. The Claw. Perhaps you saw it as you dropped in the other day . . . ominous-looking mountain-tip? Smoky fissure in the rocks? Well. Something lives up there.

A creature, which happens to have been very active these many months, venturing down to attack our settlement and causing a great deal of damage."

Juniper squirmed, but Zetta's words came so hard and fast that she couldn't get a word in edgewise—nor, honestly, would she have known what to say if she could have.

"The creature of the Claw is something of an aberration, if you must know—a fire salamander. Never heard of that?" She laughed, a harsh grating sound. "How about *fiery draco*, does that ring any bells? Huge, lizardlike creature? Breathes fire if you get too near?"

Juniper blanched. A *draco*? Was this a practical joke?

"We've been a little too much on the receiving end of that *fiery* side, these last seasons. But no more. I am going to pay a visit to that mighty draco and see what can be seen. Now. What say you, blood sister?" Zetta clamped a hand on her guard's arm and turned to go. "Shall I see you there?"

"She can't be serious," Cyril whispered in Juniper's ear. But Juniper knew Zetta was telling the truth—she knew it from the desperate throb in her words, from the tremulous looks of the Elders, from Odessa's stern, skewering glare.

Zetta was going to face the mythical fiery draco in his den. And where was Juniper supposed to find a threat to top that one? This was clearly the Anju's number one concern. Juniper had no choice but to follow right alongside.

Oh, by the goshawk. What had she gotten herself into?

"One other thing." Zetta was almost out of earshot, and her words felt like an afterthought. But the calculating look was back in her eye, and Juniper's pulse quickened. What was her rival scheming up *now*?

Zetta barreled on. "Your little settlement? It's not nearly so safe as you think. If I were you, I'd finish up my test very quickly and get back over to deliver them a safety warning—*if* they're still even there by then."

"What?" Juniper shouted at Zetta's retreating back. "What are you talking about?"

Zetta shrugged without turning. "I just thought you should know."

"KNOW WHAT?" Juniper exploded. "Stop speaking in riddles, you fur-bundled monster of a girl! WHAT has put my settlement in danger?"

Zetta sighed dramatically and turned. "Why, the Peakseason Floods, don't you know?" She snorted. "Or didn't you wonder why that lovely, cunning little valley lies deserted when it should be a far more pleasant place for us to live than this scrub-covered mountaintop? It was an Anju settlement, long ago. Why is it no longer, do you suppose?"

Images clicked into place in Juniper's mind—a story she had seen on the Memory Wall but not connected. A rounded valley, well settled . . . a bubbling, raging spout of water clawing from belowground . . . a raging, steaming flood . . . people swept away . . . bodies, bodies everywhere—

"What's going to happen?" she shouted. "And when? *What is it we don't know?*"

"Zetta, daughter of Darla!" Odessa's voice cracked like a whip.

"Your actions are far out of line, and ill-befitting a candidate in these Trials." She turned to Juniper. "She is correct about the Peak-season Floods. Our people settled that valley a dozen decades past, and it is a lush living place most of the year round. But once a year, the lake overflows its banks; the wellsprings within the spine of the Hourglass churn up and release a torrent of boiling water—enough to flood the whole valley bowl, right up to the lip of the caves. The waters do not linger, but they rage fierce and swift, with temperatures hot enough to scald an ibex. Anything in its path is in grave danger."

"But—but—why wouldn't you have said something?" Juniper felt herself starting to run away, back toward the Basin. She had to warn them, had to—

"Child," said Odessa, putting a hand on her shoulder. "Settle, I beg you. It is a *peakseason* threat. There is no danger now, not for months ahead—we are in the heart of midseason. Zetta has no cause to rattle you so. You would do well to move your camp out of that valley before too long—or settle upon higher ground as the time nears. But while the flood itself is flash-violent, it is not entirely unexpected. First come days of heightened water levels, of steadily increasing river temperatures, unusual ground shaking. There is ample warning."

"Heightened water levels?" Juniper echoed. Her hand strayed to Erick's recent letter. "Increased temperatures? Shaking ground?" Her legs began to tremble uncontrollably.

Zetta saw, and smirked. "Oh, did I forget to mention?" She turned and bowed to Odessa. "My Elder: The sweetcrystal which my counterpart delivered two days past did not come from any of the recommended mines. She got it from the forbidden cave—from the *Core*."

Juniper stared. "But you—" Oh. Of course. *Zetta* had sent her to that cave . . . but *why*? What was this Core?

Odessa paled. "Child, what have you done?"

Zetta's voice took on an instructive tone. "The Core has a direct conduit to the underground wellsprings. Am I right in suspecting that you chipped away some of that large bundle you brought back from off the center pillar? Maybe even more than *some* of it?"

"We . . ." Juniper swallowed. "The pillar . . . Well, it sort of—"

"We had to explode it," Cyril cut in. "It was the only way to get the crystal out. The stuff was too gummy to extract otherwise."

Now Zetta went still. "Wait. You—the whole pillar? It's gone?" She looked aghast, as though the little schemer hadn't led them right into that trap.

"Will someone please explain exactly what's going on?" Juniper said, her sense of urgency mounting like the very floods under discussion.

"The Peakseason Floods happen naturally every year," said Zetta. She looked uncertain now. "But they can be precipitated, too. By peakseason, the accumulated heat and increased water pressure grows too concentrated within the Core, and pushes outward. The Core gradually dissolves, and that's what triggers the floods, eventually. It takes a long time—months more. But if you've blown apart the whole pillar . . ."

Juniper took a step back. Cyril put a hand on her arm, and she could feel his grip trembling violently.

"I fear for your kingdom, Juniper, daughter of Alaina." Whatever emotion had clouded Zetta's face, it was gone now. With the rock-hard air of someone making the best of a bad deal, she stepped closer and hissed in Juniper's ear. "Choose now—for you cannot have both. The floods will not delay; this I can promise you. Set your sights on this Trial if you will. Give your try at wresting the Anju away from me, and you will lose your precious Basin. Or else go now and save your people, and *leave me to mine*."

20

JUNIPER DIDN'T STOP TO THINK. SHE TURNED, pushed through the circle, and ran.

There was no analysis, no reckoning, no weighing of measures and balances. She just hitched up her split skirts, pumped her arms, and tore across the uneven ground like her life depended on it. And perhaps *her* life didn't, but others' certainly did.

She heard pounding steps behind her, but she ran on blindly. She didn't slow her pace until something snagged her arm and she stumbled and nearly fell.

"Juniper," Cyril panted. "Slow down! You'll never make it if you don't pace yourself."

"That scheming—evil—conniving—"

"She's all of those things," he agreed. "But we can beat this. We can save them."

The ground shook.

"Come on," said Cyril. "We'll make it in time."

They ran on together, stopping only when needed, and barely

even then. Finally at the rope bridge, Juniper doubled over, panting. Cyril collapsed near her, toppling flat out on the frosty ground. Below them and off to the side, Juniper could see the forbidden cave. Its opening was now the mouth of a wide, steaming river churning out and gushing over the side of the mountain. Presumably, more water was massing under the mountain, engorging the underground passageways toward the Basin right now.

Or maybe it was already there.

Juniper pushed onto the bridge, with Cyril right behind her. She didn't dare run, though. The structure was too precarious for that.

"You're giving up the Trials by leaving now," Cyril said, unnecessarily. "Are you sure you want to do this?"

"You're jesting, right?"

Cyril shrugged. "If it's a matter of warning Erick and the others, my legs are longer than yours. Look at you, barely keeping up! I say you go back and kill that beastly draco before Zetta does, win the Trial, and let me take care of sounding the alarm. You can have it both ways—don't you see?"

Juniper batted away the idea without a second's pause. "I won't risk it. There's too much at stake. We don't know where everyone is or how near the floods are. It'll take both of us to round everybody up quickly enough—and see what we can do to save the settlement." She started to jog again, although the bridge wobbled badly under her feet. She was forced to slow down, grinding her teeth in frustration.

"Your decision, I suppose. Only you've worked awfully hard to get this far."

"Don't *you* see?" Juniper exclaimed, turning to Cyril. She could feel tears stinging the corners of her eyes. "Don't you see that none of that matters without the Basin, without *them*? The Anju aren't my people, not really. There's Odessa, of course. But we're only just beginning to know each other. My heart's in the Basin, and I can't even think about another thing until I know they are safe."

"Fair enough," said Cyril quietly.

Their feet hit the stone embankment, and they set off running at full tilt again.

As Juniper burst out of the tunnel's opening onto the ledge overlooking the Basin, a wave of heat hit her like a slap to the face. Everything looked just as she'd left it, just as she'd known it every day of their stay thus far. The weather had been mild and pleasant always, with an almost charmed quality. Unusually warm, perhaps, given how high they were in the mountains. But never anything like this. This was like stepping onto the brick of an oven: a damp, sticky heat that wormed into her smallclothes and curled the fine hairs back from her neck. Without slowing her pace, she unfastened her cloak, which was stiff and heavy with layers of matted dirt, sweat, and sweetcrystal gum. Tugging the odious thing off, she threw it down on a boulder. She'd come back for it when this was all over.

Maybe.

Behind her, Cyril yanked at his own collar. "What is with this heat wave?" Sweat glistened between his brows.

"Zetta was right! This whole mountain is gushing out heat."

The stones that formed the mountain's crust had gone from their usual comforting warmth to the pale pink of oven coals. As Juniper dashed down the trail, she could feel a disturbing warmth seeping through the soles of her boots.

"They'll have already moved out by now. It's evident that something—"

"Oh, no," Juniper breathed. She and Cyril were partway down the slope and could see how the river bulged up, already slopping over its banks and rocking with little bubbling undercurrents. And at the center, just up from the Great Tree . . .

"They're *all* there!" yelped Cyril, sounding so shaken that Juniper would have done a double take if she hadn't already been flat-out running.

The entire group was gathered together. They scurried around with stones and branches and giant pots from which they were scooping big handfuls of clay onto a makeshift wall. They were trying to build a barrier between their settlement and the overflowing edge of the river.

"Hey!" Juniper yelled. But the sound caught in her throat, her voice a little parched butterfly that barely left the ground. It was, she quickly saw, impossible to yell and run at the same time. And she was just too far away to be heard.

Cyril grabbed her arm. "Run," he said. "Run fast and get them out of there. I have an idea."

Before Juniper could register what was going on, he'd turned and started back up the hill the way he'd come. "Where—" she puffed, then her feet nearly skidded out from under her on the stony trail. She had no idea what Cyril was up to, nor, frankly, any time right now to care.

She had to get to the river.

Far away—too far!—down the cliff and across the clearing, along the riverbank the wall was taking shape. Juniper could faintly hear the kids' cheers and calls of encouragement. They were working hard, pulling together, just like the incredible team they were.

Juniper's eyes stung. She ran faster, pushing through air so thick and soupy she was almost swimming.

She cleared the slope's last boulder and hit the valley running, not even bothering to go around the vegetable garden but cutting straight through the middle for the quickest route. Every few seconds, she tried calling out, but her voice held no volume at all.

Look around you! she thought at them desperately.

But they didn't, of course—why would they? Their full concentration was on their task, trying to save a settlement they had no idea was already doomed.

Then Juniper heard a dull bellowing sound. It came from above and behind her, so that she windmilled her arms and skidded a long stripe in the dug-up earth. The noise came again: the long, loud trumpeting bellow. She saw then—it was Cyril, perched on a rocky overhang, blowing on a hollow ram's horn and waving his arms madly at the faces down by the river that were now starting to turn in his direction.

Fearing she might collapse with relief, Juniper redoubled her speed. Sweat poured freely down her back and legs. But she'd been spotted, and the general enthusiasm ratcheted up a notch. The group let out a wild yell of joy—then set back to work with renewed zeal.

"Nooooo," Juniper moaned. She was so close now. "Listen up!" she yelled. "You need to——" But it was no use. They saw her; they might even hear that she was calling *something*. But how could she make them understand?

"STOP!" It was Cyril's voice, but loud and distorted. Juniper wanted to cheer—he was yelling *into* the horn. The resulting sound was disturbing, and only just barely intelligible. But he'd caught their attention.

"DANGER!" Cyril called. He paused, while Juniper noticed some of the kids stopping to look around. The bridge was just ahead of her now. She waved her arms.

"The river's flooding!" she yelled. "Go back! It's not safe!"

At the river's bank, the bubbling, roiling surface cast up long plumes of steam and mist. She flung herself across the bridge, coughing and gasping at the rising heat. The surging water heaved just below the soggy planks.

"FLOOD!" Cyril bellowed.

Juniper leaped off the bridge and nearly topped Alta. "Get everyone back!" she gasped. "There's a huge flood coming—boiling hot water—it's going to burst out and overflow everywhere. We need—to get everyone—to higher ground!"

Alta blinked twice, taking all this in. Then, while Juniper collapsed in a heap, gasping and trying to dislodge the sledgehammer from within her chest, Alta raised a loud call. "Everybody back! Our queen says the river's not safe. We've got to abandon camp and get to higher ground, NOW!"

"Let's move out, everybody!" called Erick, then rushed over to place a hand on Juniper's back. "Are you all right? And was that really Cyril up there? Being *helpful?*"

Juniper smiled, still panting. "Against all expectation, our Cyril seems to have done some self-improving over the last few days. Oh, Erick—I have *so much* to catch you up on! But now we've got to move out, and quick."

"The animals!" said Toby. "If there's a flood coming, they'll be in danger, too." He took off running toward the enclosure. Juniper considered the chickens and the goats—were they really worth risking the kids' lives for? Then again, Toby was already in for the slog; there wasn't much they could do but help.

She turned to look back across to the North Bank, her heart sinking. "Where are the horses?" she said. Those, they definitely couldn't do without.

"No fear," said Erick. "They're settled up in the Cavern already. Remember?"

Right. He'd said as much in his last letter. That was one less thing to worry about, at least.

"Oh, no!" came Sussi's voice. "LOOK!"

Juniper followed the direction of the girl's trembling finger, looked up past the roiling river, past the cliff to where the swimming hole had been. But it was a hole no longer. Above the rocky crest, around the bordering plants, the water swelled in a rounded, bulging mass—a heaving bubble of burgeoning liquid, just waiting for that one last drop that would shatter its surface tension and send it all raining down on the valley below.

On *them*.

"It's about to burst!" Erick called.

"Let's go—everybody, top speed!" barked Juniper. "Head for the trail. Toby's got the animal enclosure open already. Everyone grab the nearest creature and hightail it up the slope, double-quick."

They ran.

Filbert led the way, his long legs giving both stride and speed. Leena grabbed Sussi's hand. Jess held her skirts up and tried to avoid the muddy patches, while still making excellent time. Root slowed his pace to run alongside Oona, who seemed unwilling to be more than a few steps from his side. By ones and twos, with every animal accounted for, the group clattered up the ragged slope, heading for the opening to the Cavern. The animals moved just as swiftly, as if they could tell there was nothing good for them down below.

But something felt incomplete.

Juniper ran through the settlers in her mind, then her eyes popped opened wide. "Where is Tippy?"

"Tippy?" said Alta. "She—she was just here! I saw her rolling in the mud not ten minutes ago."

"TIPPY!" Juniper screamed.

Kids and animals streamed past, but Juniper pushed her way back to look out over the valley. "TIPPY!" she shrieked again.

"Here!" came a faint squeak, and to Juniper's inexpressible

relief, the little girl popped out of an apartment cave farther up the cliffside.

"What are you doing all the way over there?" Juniper yelled. "Come join us, and quick!"

Tippy bobbed a quick curtsey. "Right you are, O My Commander!" she chirped. Then she frowned. "That water don't look right, miss—I think—" She started running toward them along the narrow cliff's trail.

Juniper let the others rush past her as she waited for Tippy to catch up. Toby and a couple others were already in the Cavern, but many—*too* many—still struggled up the trail.

Then off to their west, up on the far bank, the surface tension took in its last drop. With a wet, smacking sound the giant water bubble burst, sending a volley of white-hot water catapulting across the clearing. Several others pushed inside the cave, but most of the kids—Juniper and Tippy included—were still too far away.

"EVERYBODY TURN AROUND!" Juniper yelled. "Face the cliff wall!"

"Keep a tight hold on the creatures," panted Paul.

There was a scream from Jessamyn. Erick tugged at her arm, and they jammed their faces into the cliffside.

The water struck, a searing wave that crashed hard against the lower Basin floor. Steam scalded the backs of Juniper's hands, and she felt a painful prickling through her stockings. Their position on the cliff's edge, however, shielded them from all but a smattering of the boiling liquid.

"Now move, everybody!" Erick yelled. The first assault was

over, but the overflowing river was now tearing up the ground below. The water level rose by the moment.

Grabbing Tippy's hand, Juniper dashed the rest of the way up the trail. A few seconds later, they reached the cave's opening and piled inside. The last of them hustled in, creatures and all, everyone dashing for the farthest side of the giant, echoing room.

The noise in the Cavern was deafening. But it was the knowledge of what was going on outside that tied Juniper up in knots.

"I've got to know how it is out there," she whispered to Erick after a few minutes. He nodded and followed her back down the short entryway to the cave's mouth. Moving carefully, and keeping her face well back from the blistering heat, Juniper parted the vines and looked down. She needed one last look at the kingdom they had so painstakingly built—this place she'd come to think of as home. Through the sea of steam and scorching vapor, she could just see the thatched roof of the dining area disappear under the unforgiving current.

Then it, too, was gone as Queen's Basin sank under a pouring cataclysm of waterfire.

21

INSIDE THE CAVERN, ALL WAS CHAOS. THE torches in the wall sconces had been lit, but everywhere was squawking, bleating, and whinnying. Kids shrieked and wailed. Some of the younger ones were crying. Juniper felt very near despair herself, thinking of all those hours, days, and weeks they'd spent building their kingdom. To see it all being swept away, very likely destroyed altogether—it was nearly too much to manage. But someone needed to stay calm, and right now, Juniper was it.

Yet what could she hope to do against all the fear and confusion tearing through the crowd?

That's when it came to her.

There was one thing that always brought them together, that calmed nerves and joined spirits—the very thing, in fact, that had launched them on this whole journey to begin with: music. Juniper smiled to remember that ragtag, all-kids group of musicians at her Nameday party back at the palace—many of the kids sitting here tonight, in fact—and how their melodies had called to her and whispered how much more she herself could be and do. And now here she was, seeing and doing and being so much more than she ever could have imagined.

What could be more powerful, more transporting than *music*?

Juniper began to hum, low in her throat. It took her a moment to find the right key, but when she did, she let herself sing out the melody more loudly. She herself was far from musical; she knew that for a fact. But it wasn't artistry she was after. Next to her, Erick noticed, caught on, and joined his voice to Juniper's. Alta came next. Then, one by one, each member of Queen's Basin quieted their fretful jostling and began to sing. The song was soft and gentle at first: a whisper of nights gone by, the ghost of arms linking with arms, the promise of a stronger tomorrow. The slow start built to a warmer middle, as flagging spirits rallied and dispirited thoughts clung to the bandied notes like a life raft on the waves.

So much was broken; so much had been lost. But here they were, still together, still well.

Still Queen's Basin.

The horses settled into their feedbags and the goats into a cordoned-off area Toby had set up for them. The chickens roamed freely through the group, pecking and squawking as though in time to the music.

Juniper let herself relax. They'd made it through this. Things were going to be all right.

Gradually, the roar outside hushed. Inside was quiet, too—everybody was sung out, though several smaller groups had pulled out decks of cards or started coin-toss games. Erick was halfway through a book with print so small that Juniper's eyes swam just looking his way.

Eventually, she pushed back through the vines to the outdoors. Staring out onto the valley, Juniper saw that the floodwaters—fierce and fast and hot as they still ran—had settled just below their cliffside trail. The worst of the flood seemed to be over.

It was time to assess the damage.

Glad that she was still wearing her tough traveling boots, Juniper stepped onto the drenched, steaming ledge outside the cave. Several others filed solemnly behind her, and together they took in the destruction of their beloved kingdom.

The waterfall still raged five or six times its usual size. The North Bank was so deeply submerged that the ground wasn't even visible. On the opposite cliff, Juniper could just make out a small figure in a muddy orange coat. Juniper felt a pang for Cyril, weathering out the flood by himself on the far side of the mountain.

The South Bank had fared a little better; it also had a lot more to lose. The kitchen supplies had gone first: Wooden crates and grain bags could be seen swirling in the current; a soup pot eddied and tossed like a miniature boat. The sturdy dining area posts held out for long minutes, then the first one bent and toppled before their eyes. The others folded seconds later. Here and there, a flat paving stone bubbled up from the loosened soil, turning over and over like a leaf in the wind as it was sucked downstream.

Tears dripped down Juniper's face. The Great Tree, at least, was unharmed. The giant stone wheel that leaned against its base, and which was so useful for climbing, had clearly weathered its share of floods. It hadn't even shifted in the onslaught.

"The damage won't reach the platform," said Erick, coming up behind her. "The water's all done rising. The Great Tree is safe."

"The Beauty Chamber!" exclaimed Jessamyn. "Look!"

As the repository for storing all their collected gowns, decorative trinkets, jewelry, and beauty supplies, the Beauty Chamber's main walls had been built strong and sturdy. And perhaps those walls alone might have held up.

But the Beauty Chamber also had an extension that dipped over the river, forming a delicious enclosed bathing room that Juniper had enjoyed often to great satisfaction. This feature was the building's undoing, for the floodwaters dashed mercilessly up into that opening. As they watched, the walls of the Beauty Chamber first bulged . . . then exploded outward, disgorging a volley of gowns and ribbons and creams and wood-slat walls.

"Ooohhh," moaned Oona. "All of them pretty things! All *gone*."

"Ahem," said Tippy. "Not *all* of them."

All heads swung in her direction. The little girl just crooked a finger and darted off down the trail.

"Wait up, you sprocket!" called Alta. "It's not safe to—"

"Sure 'tis!" said Tippy, stopping at the apartment cave she'd been lurking in just before the flood. "I'm only going just this far. See? Come in and peek, then, if you're brave enough. I promise you a good reward!"

In the minutes they'd spent watching, the floodwater's level had dropped slightly. It seemed safe to leave the Cavern, so Juniper stamped along the muddy trail—washed clean of its loose gravel, at any rate—with Alta and a handful of others behind her. Reaching the door of the small cave, Juniper peered inside. Her mouth dropped all the way open.

On the floor was a heap of dresses, slippers, undergarments, and a smattering of potted beauty supplies.

"What on the blooming earth?" said Alta.

"Everyone was rushing about building walls earlier," said Tippy. "I got myself rolled in the mud, and went off to have a clean in the Beauty Chamber afore I kept going. Then I got to looking around at all these good garments, and so much icky water a-lapping up through the dipping pool. I thought, 'Well, I could spirit some of it up a ways.' For safekeeping-like, don't you see? Get them away from all that wet. And so I did."

Juniper was lost for words.

"I didn't get a near fraction of all the goodness," said Tippy sorrowfully.

Juniper wanted to laugh. It was the most trivial of rescues, to be sure. No dress nor petticoat nor vial of rosewater could affect one single thing in any of their lives, one way or another. And yet, the simplicity of the gesture, the pure goodness (and love of finery) that had moved Tippy to act, warmed Juniper through like nothing else.

Her hug nearly squashed Tippy's breath full out of her.

"Well, well, well," came a dry voice at the cave's entrance. "Her whole kingdom is destroyed, but at least she has managed to keep her *party dresses* clean."

Juniper looked up. "Cyril?"

He stood in the door, thoroughly drenched and caked with mud, beaming from ear to ear.

Juniper dashed across the room and joyfully grabbed his arm. "You're safe!"

The rest of the group gaped at her.

"Queen's Basin," Juniper said, "I've got an all-new arrival to introduce to you today. Group, meet Cyril Lefarge. Cyril, meet the group. He's not a bad sort, as it turns out, this cousin of mine. And he can blow a mean warning horn."

The flood didn't linger. Within an hour, the levels were visibly down, and by late afternoon, the waters had withdrawn entirely, leaving behind a mud-strewn, debris-scattered wasteland. The kids shed their shoes and stockings, and Juniper and the other girls tied their skirts around their knees. (Let propriety be buttonholed for the day, Juniper decided. There was simply too much to do.) Then they all picked their way down the hillside to inspect the damage. The heat had been completely sucked out of the stones—for the first time since their arrival, the ground was entirely cool to the touch. Juniper imagined the heat would gradually begin to build inside the stones until next year's flood season.

No wonder the Anju had chosen not to live in this valley. It was an accursed spot, to be sure.

Or . . . was it?

She looked around. The Beauty Chamber was in shambles, and the animals' enclosure fully demolished. The walls of the kitchen and dining area were broken beyond repair. But the heavy sitting and table stones still sat in their customary spots. The Great Tree was untouched. And the water level hadn't come near the apartment caves. The bridge stood firm, and the new handrail had come through quite unscathed. Half the paving stones were gone, but they hadn't gone far.

Juniper lifted her chin.

This was still her kingdom. And she was not going to let anything—not even a boiling flash flood—wrestle it from her. She turned and let out a piercing whistle to get everyone's attention. Then she jumped up on the nearest boulder and flung her arms out wide.

"Citizens of Queen's Basin," she called, "we have faced down many challenges in our kingdom's short history, and this may be our biggest one yet. We are looking at the near destruction of our settlement, the loss of all our many weeks of work. Ruddy hard work, too, from early morning till late night. The elements themselves have conspired against us." With a little human help, but there was no need to go into that just now. "But shall we be overcome? Will fire and water take us down?"

She looked around the group. More than one face blinked uncertainly back at her.

"It does raise the question of safety," said Paul. "How do we know such a flood won't just sweep back on us again tomorrow? Or the day after?"

Erick cleared his throat. "I've been doing a lot of reading— first, I should say how sorry I am for not predicting this earlier.

The Peakseason Floods are all across my books, only I never connected them to our Basin. Also . . . well, it's not peak-season, right?"

Juniper grimaced. There was a lot she still needed to fill him in on.

"That's the one thing that bothers me," he went on. "If it weren't for that—well, I've never heard of any flood of this type taking place outside of that one time every year. It's a matter of accumulation. It takes all those months for the heat and pressure to build to where the water overflows its containment area."

"The timing won't be a problem in the future," Juniper said. "I will tell you all the story later of how this whole thing came about. But for now, you're right—if we know the flood only comes at peakseason, and if we know that it's coming when we build . . ."

"Then we can counter it," Roddy said. "I've got some ideas already—ballast and reinforced foundations. We're prepared now. We can handle this."

"Plus, there's masses of warning," said Leena. "Them banks were bulging for days, and putting out heat to sizzle the kettle besides! We just didn't know what to look for, so we didn't connect it to an actual threat. Now we know what's coming, there's plenty of means to get to safety once the signs begin to show."

Juniper nodded. "This is our country, settlers. This is our kingdom. Shall we give it up to the fiery elements? Shall we let ourselves be chased out of this home we've come to love, this place we've made our own?" She thrust her arms into the air. "I say NO. I say that we view today's events as a setback, nothing more. I say we join together and work to make Queen's Basin *better* than it has ever been before. And I say we begin *this very moment!*"

Her speech was met with a satisfying roar of approval, and without further delay, the group set to work. The final dregs of floodwater had drained out, and the lingering puddles were evaporating fast. Still, every bit of the Bank was mud-splattered, strewn with torn-up turf and uprooted plants. Tree limbs were everywhere.

There was no hope of getting this disaster area back to its pre-flood state anytime soon, of course. Nor was that really at the top of their minds, given their plans to journey soon out to Torr. But at least they could do the basics before they left. They could give the Basin a hearty freshening up. They could stake their claim and make it clear that this was *their* home and they weren't about to be scared away.

Juniper divided them into teams: Leena and Sussi attacked the kitchen area; Toby went to settle the animals while Filbert and Roddy rebuilt their fences; Paul traipsed off to the gardens to see if anything could be salvaged; Erick, Alta, Root, and—Juniper couldn't help a lingering thrill—*Cyril* worked on collecting debris and dragging the loosened paving stones back to be resettled in their spots. Tippy flitted from group to group handing out fresh rags, buckets of water, and other needful items.

Oona sidled up to Juniper and asked, in a low and bashful tone, whether she might not assist Root in his wanderings, for surely there was too much rubbish for him to collect alone. Suppressing an eye-roll, Juniper gave her permission. If Oona's crush had transferred from Cyril to Root, then so much the better. She just hoped the boy knew what he was in for.

As for Jess, no sooner had Juniper passed out the rest of the tasks and turned in her direction than Jess let out a yell, raising her arm to the sky. Sure enough, Juniper spotted the messenger, winging its way across the sky toward the Beacon.

The girl sure had the gift of timing!

Without further hesitation, Juniper passed the role of overseer to Erick and followed Jess up the slope. She didn't think she'd ever seen the stately girl move this quickly, even within her newly revealed persona.

After long minutes, they reached the tiny cave where the little ghost-bat messenger now roosted after its long flight from the palace. With a barely suppressed thrill, Juniper pulled a rolled-up message off the creature's leg.

"It's from Egg!" Jess exclaimed, scooting in to read along with Juniper.

To my faraway Sister and her Companions:

I send you greetings from the beset Palace of Torr. You requested a full news bulletin, and this I shall provide for you here. King Regis remains imprisoned. He is held captive in his very own dungeon—more the insult!—along with the entirety of his guard and armed forces, and any adult Torrean within the palace who did not swear allegiance to the Monsian invaders.

Those of us Torreans who remain free have been

213

reduced to servile tasks, a fact which quite pleases me for the free access I have to prowl the palace and gather intelligence. I am formulating a plan for takeover, but I shall require assistance in filling certain roles, for I do not imagine I might retake this place all on my own.

Or perhaps I could. But it would be more difficult.

In any case, King Regis is due to be transported to Monsia—there to be locked up much more securely, or worse!—sometime soon after the close of the grand Summerfest, which begins two weeks hence. We must therefore proceed with due haste, for if he is swallowed into the wastelands of that nether nation, he shall doubtless be as good as dead.

So, my sister, what can you do for me? You can convey all of this information to Princess Juniper at once, and beg her to gather me up such an army as she might possess, that we may retake the palace posthaste.

Bring me the people, and I will see to everything else.

> I remain your scheming, busily planning relation,
> Eglantine Ceward

There was so much information in this letter that Juniper had to read it three times to take it all in. The first thing she felt was an overwhelming sense of relief—her father was imprisoned, yes, but he was *safe*. As safe as he could be under Monsian guard, and certainly much threatened. But he was *alive!* All those fears she'd fought over the last torturous weeks were finally put to rest. So much peril remained at hand, so much hung over them all——but right now, just at this moment, he was well.

There was still hope.

"Two weeks," Juniper said, looking up to meet Jess's gaze.

The other girl nodded. "It's not long. And even a bit less, taking out a day for this message to reach us."

"Your sister seems like quite the dynamo."

"That she is," Jess agreed. "Egg talks a strong game. But one thing she has no use for is empty promises."

"So we can count on her to be truly building up a fighting plan?"

"You can count on her for anything."

Jess lapsed into silence after that, and Juniper herself appreciated the space. There was a lot to think about. More than anything, she wanted to leap to action, but first, she needed to come up with a plan for what to do. They clambered back down the mountain, where Jess joined one of the work crews (with just a token number of complaints; new-formed habits died hard, apparently), and Juniper set about her own tasks of scrubbing, dragging, and lifting. But all the while, her mind was leagues away, circling the palace of Torr, prodding and probing, angling for a way in. Assessing this newest and most puzzling of allies, Jess's sister, Egg. Picturing the third Anju trial, Zetta heading toward her fiery foe, Odessa's words: *The last of our proud line . . . You were meant to come here, to be here at this time.* Thinking of what might have been, had Juniper been able to continue the contest through to its end. And thinking, most of all, of their immediate need, more urgent now than ever.

An army to march in defense of Torr.

Where on earth were they going to get an army?

They worked all through the afternoon, through the dusk, and well into the night, thanks to hastily erected torch posts. By the time the full moon began tipping toward the far horizon, the Basin was in a tolerable state, and the group collapsed upon the dining area in one famished heap. Leena had dipped into their dwindling supplies that had been stored in the Cavern, and she and Sussi had produced a magnificent smoked-meat pie, with garlicky wild greens on the side. Their last bag of salt had been lost in the flood, but not a word of complaint was heard.

As they sat quietly munching, many kids half dozing off where they sat, Juniper considered next steps. The progress they'd made in their feverish work attack was astonishing. Of course, there was still much to do to bring Queen's Basin back to its pre-flood state. But the immediate tasks had been tended to. Their base was secure and their kingdom in good shape.

For right now, Juniper knew, their task here was done. Now they needed to turn their attention outward. Egg's letter had made one thing abundantly clear: The time had come to follow through on their plan. They needed to head out from Queen's Basin.

It was time to go and save Torr.

And there was only one way Juniper knew to do this. A

thread of an idea was forming in her mind. She had no idea if it would work, but truthfully? She'd ventured out on thinner ledges before.

She'd just have to take that step and see if it held her.

"Listen up, everybody," she said, and each tired face turned in her direction. "We've worked right down to the bone today, all of us. No one has ever better deserved a night's rest. So we're going to sleep hard tonight. Because tomorrow, we're going to rise early, eat a hearty breakfast, and then I'm going to take you on a little excursion."

A thin-ledge thread of an idea—that was all. She could only hope it would be enough.

It was time to take Queen's Basin to the Anju.

22

THE NEXT MORNING FOUND THE QUEEN'S
Basin group bright-eyed and wildly enthusiastic. In spite of all
they'd been through the day before and the short night of sleep,
everybody was active and alert as they set off on their expedition.
They put Juniper in mind of a tour group being paraded past a series of famous landmarks. The kids gaped at the winding tunnel
through Mount Ichor, shivered in delight as they crossed the sus-
pension bridge over to Mount Rahze (Tippy leading the way with
not a hint of her early terror), and marveled at the wide clearing
of stumps. Here Juniper led Jess and Tippy to the hollow where
Fleeter still lay, curled up and snoring outrageously. Jess squatted
down and gave a low whistle. The frowzy creature sprang to life
and catapulted itself into her arms. While Tippy clapped in glee,
Fleeter slung himself across Jess's shoulders with a purr of satisfaction so loud it was nearly a roar. They fit together, Juniper realized
with a rush—the clever cat and the cagey girl, each masquerading
their true natures under cover of their plain, everyday exteriors.

How remarkable a force was nature!

From there, the group pressed into the forest toward the Anju village. The air felt substantially warmer than it had in the days before. The sun was high and bright, but Juniper wondered whether the flood had caused any temperature shifts on this mountain, as well. To judge from the snowbroth they were now wading through, perhaps it had.

When at last they reached the hidden village of the Anju, the kids' necks arched back as they took in the ropes, swings, and structures that could be seen from the ground. The tree houses were all deserted, though, and Juniper knew why; she could clearly hear the buzz of conversation from the gathering spot at the village's far end. Despite all the chaos of the last hours, only a day and a night had passed since Juniper had stormed away from the Trials. Back on this mountain, the third and final stage of the competition had just come to a close. The Anju would be gathering to celebrate their new leader.

"Come on," Juniper said. "It's time we had some introductions all around."

"What do you have in mind, Juniper?" Erick asked nervously.

Juniper looked at him. More than anything, she wanted to pull him aside and tell him her plan—as rough and unformed as it still was—and get his opinion. Alta's, too. But, if she was honest, this scheme of hers was as holey as mouse-eaten cheese. Putting it into words might do it in altogether. If she stopped moving right now, she knew she could spend hours thinking, talking, strategizing, examining all sides of the issue, narrowing down the best thing to do. They'd come up with a great plan, she was sure—a plan infinitely better than the slipshod one she had now.

But time was passing.

All she really had right now was speed and the element of surprise.

"Just trust me," she said to Erick, "and follow my lead. If all goes as I'm hoping, we'll soon have a ripsnorter of a gathering on our hands."

They pushed out of the tree cover into the clearing at the far edge of the village. The first thing Juniper noticed was a vaguely sulfurous smell in the air. What on earth?

As Juniper had expected, the entire Anju tribe was gathered at the hillock. But while the mood at their last evening gathering had been one of relaxed revelry, this one held an air of frenzied excitement that bordered on mania.

Then she saw the reason: the huge, mud-gray mound of a body sprawled halfway up the slope and stretching down the other side.

"Is that . . . ?" said Cyril.

Tippy bumped up behind her. "Oh, Mistress Juniper, the feared draco! That girl has conquered it?"

Had Zetta not only defeated the draco, but managed to bring its body back to the camp, the better to display her victory? In spite of her fury at Zetta's betrayal, Juniper couldn't suppress a flicker of admiration. That girl had spine, all right!

Given the monster carcass in their midst, it took a few minutes for the gathered Anju to notice the new arrivals. But not long after, a shout went up, and heads began to swing in their direction.

Juniper's eyes were all for the draco. She could see only its rear flank from where she stood. It looked like a giant lizard, with a long neck and scaly skin that glinted bronze in the morning light. Its curved talons still gripped the earth, and its snout—Juniper's eyes widened. The creature's snout had been tied with a jaunty violet scarf. Upon its back sat Zetta, one leather-clad leg splayed out to either side of its wide neck. Her head was high and her eyes blazed. This moment was her stage, and she basked full in its light.

Zetta spotted Juniper.

There was a moment's hesitation, a blink of uncertainty. Then the girl narrowed her eyes and squared her shoulders.

Juniper pushed ahead of her group and strode across the open space. She shook off the glamorous image this moment created: Zetta, straddling the corpse of the defeated draco, the acknowledged ruler of her people. *No.* They were Juniper's people, too—her mother's people. This was her heritage. And these were the people she needed. Eglantine's letter had made that clearer than ever.

If she wanted to save Torr, to save her father, she needed one thing above all else: She needed an army. And there was nowhere she could get one but here.

Juniper stomped up to the center of the mound. Odessa and the three other Elders, who had been looking at Zetta, now turned toward Juniper. Their faces blanched.

As Juniper gathered herself to speak, Zetta slid down the draco's motionless flank, moving with practiced ease.

"Hello, blood sister," Zetta said. "Have you come to join in my celebration of victory?"

"Victory?" Juniper said calmly. "I'm not so sure about that."

Zetta cocked her head. "You must remember the third test. That parchment we all read out yestermorning?" She motioned behind her. "Greatest threat to our people, subdued and under control, as ordered." She winked. "Not quite so much of a threat anymore, hmmm?"

Juniper mashed her lips tight together, but didn't say anything. She let the silence spool out from her like a warm wind, renewing her strength and purpose.

"Well?" Zetta said. Her fingers tapped against the side of her thigh. "What are you waiting for? Why *did* you even bother coming back, after your cowardly retreat and abdication of the final test?"

Juniper waited another long minute, then she turned her back on Zetta. She faced Odessa and the Elders, who studied her intently. The Elders' expressions ranged from uncertain to openly hostile; Odessa looked like she'd had her chair kicked out from under her. "Elders of the Anju," Juniper said, "it is my honor to return before you this day."

"What is it you want, child?" barked a gruff man on the far edge of the row. "You are disrupting the proceedings, *again*. Will we ever be rid of you?"

A murmur went up at his words, something between agreement and discomfort.

Juniper's eyes narrowed. "No. No, you will not! My mother was Anju, and she never stopped being Anju. Adopting another culture

222

does not have to mean turning your back on your roots. Accepting a new present should not force you to reject your past. My mother *suffered* from lack of connection to her people. I saw evidence of this every moment of her life." She paused to compose herself.

"But that's not why I'm here today. If there is anything my mother taught me by example, it was the importance of honor. This same sentiment I heard echoed in your own words"—she inclined her head at Odessa—"upon the launch of the first test. 'Dignity and integrity,' weren't those the qualities we candidates were principally to emulate? 'Honor above all else'? Your chieftain should act 'always in support of her people, down to the smallest member'?"

There was a moment of silence.

Then Odessa quoted faintly, *"This is the primary rule, and the one that shall be paramount to all others."*

Juniper nodded. "That's what I heard, too." She turned and waved a hand toward the Queen's Basin group, which stood puddled at the far edges of the Anju's circle. "I have not come here alone to-day. I have brought the members of my own small colony, Queen's Basin, lately established in the valley over yonder. All of you likely know that I failed the third and final test—abandoned it midstream, as it were. But do you all know *why* I had to do this?"

"I don't see why that should matter!" Zetta said loudly. "I have completed the final test. I have—"

"You have lied, and cheated, and manipulated. You have not acted with integrity *or* dignity. Rather, you deliberately pointed me to a faulty mine—a *forbidden* mine, a fact of which you knew I was not aware—all in hopes of precipitating a deadly flood that would

223

force me to withdraw from the Trials. Evidently this worked even better than you'd expected, pulling me right out of a contest you must have known I would win."

Zetta opened her mouth to protest, but Juniper barreled on. "I rushed back to my settlement, yes—and I will have you know that Cyril and I barely made it in time. The flood came scant minutes after we did. Much of our colony was destroyed in the onrush, but I was able to bring every member to safety . . . with not a single moment to spare. Do you see?" She held up her hands, the backs still scoured red by the scalding steam. "Do you see how close we came? Do you see the cost of betrayal from this girl, this one who proclaims herself fit to be your ruler?"

Zetta looked stunned. "But I—it wasn't like that—I thought—"

"You thought only of *yourself*. You had no thought for anyone else. I would now ask the Elders whether that is the type of leader they would have over the Anju people."

The crowd buzzed. The Elders raised their eyebrows, leaned in, and began to mutter among themselves. Zetta turned her back on Juniper, shoulders shaking. Then she suddenly turned to face her again.

"No," Zetta said. "No, I do not accept this."

The Elders looked up from their discussion.

"Yes, Juniper, I led you astray on purpose. You should know that I did not intend to cause any danger or harm; clearly I miscalculated the force of your . . . *energy*. But I don't regret what I did, not for a moment. You say you didn't know any better than to proceed to that cave? If you were truly one of us, you *would* have." Zetta squared

224

her stance. "We are Anju. Say what you like, but we are not *your* people. I know of your war, this Monsian invasion that you want so badly to repel. You seek only to use my people, to seize them as a commodity and turn them to your purposes. And what will you do with us after that is accomplished? Move us into your precious palace to live your pretty packaged life?"

Juniper flushed. "Is that really how you want to gain your right to be chief, through such underhanded means?"

Zetta looked her straight in the eye. "I will do whatever it takes."

"Be that as it may. You've broken the bylaws of the Trial. I say that I am the only fair candidate remaining." Juniper turned to face the Elders. None of them would meet her gaze, except Odessa, who studied her thoughtfully.

"We recognize your challenge, Juniper, daughter of Alaina," Odessa said formally. "Now, give us some time while we reach a decision."

The verdict did not take long in coming. The Elders buzzed and chattered and stormed. But at last they all sat down, and the wizened old man who had spoken so curtly to Juniper raised his voice like a dirge. "So let it be recognized by the people. Zetta, daughter of Darla, has broken our most solemn custom of always acting first and foremost with truth and integrity and honor."

He turned toward Odessa, who spoke in turn. "Juniper, daughter of Alaina, you abdicated your role in the third test. However, now that the circumstances have been brought to light, it is evident that all is not as it first seemed. Your task was to identify the greatest danger to our people, to seek out and engage it, to subdue and bring this element under control and thus to eliminate its threat. It has been argued—" Odessa swallowed, and Juniper wondered if the arguing had come from her. "It has been argued that you followed this rule exactly. Those of your settlement are your people, and it is hard not to regard that out-of-season flood as the greatest of threats. Sacrificing your place in the Trials to save them showed true leadership, courage, and honor."

The elder resumed his speech. "So let it be acknowledged on this day: Zetta, daughter of Darla, is hereby disqualified from the Trials. The rulership of our people must pass to the next qualified candidate"—he barely choked on the words, to his credit—"Juniper, daughter of Alaina."

A stunned silence met his words, then a thin cheer arose. Juniper could see the gathered Anju sizing her up, measuring her worth. She checked inside herself, waiting for the rush of pure joy that should accompany such a moment.

She'd won. *She'd won!* She would soon be in command of the Anju people.

She had gained the army she needed to take back to Torr—and not just this small group, but the promise of a web of inter-connected warriors located throughout the Hourglass Mountains, every one of them at her disposal to descend upon the Monsian invaders and put them to rout.

She was going to save her father!

"The officiating ceremony will take place this night at moonrise. The oath will be sworn and the leather chieftain's band bestowed. For now, let us all adjourn and get the necessary preparations under way."

The Anju began to disperse, though more than one sidled up to clasp Juniper's hand and murmur words of congratulation and welcome. The Queen's Basin group clustered around, too, clapping and smiling at Juniper's success. Even Cyril bobbed his chin with a mock-scornful eye-roll that could not hide his pride at her win. It crossed Juniper's mind that pushing out Zetta was just the kind of underhanded maneuver he *would* be proud of. Immediately she felt ashamed of this thought.

Meanwhile, off to the side and all but forgotten, Zetta stood alone. One hand trailed on her fallen draco's flank. Her gaze was fixed upon the distant woods.

Juniper swallowed a lump in her throat. She reminded herself how Zetta had tricked her, how *she* had been the one who first stooped to underhanded means. Juniper had only acted in her own defense. She wouldn't feel sorry for that girl, she *wouldn't*.

Then a series of things happened in quick succession.

Zetta seemed to come out of her trance. With a glare in Juniper's direction, she circled around the prone monster. She scrambled up its flank and settled herself into the hollow of its shoulders.

The great draco . . . shook itself.

It stood up on all four paws.

Then it spread its mighty wings and lifted off into the glowering sky.

23

AFTER ZETTA'S DEPARTURE, JUNIPER HAD A hard time focusing on her surroundings. Once the shock of the draco's flight wore off, the other kids were quickly absorbed by the friendly Anju. They split into groups to explore the village, view the Memory Wall, or test their skills on the ropes course of the Climbing Tree. But Juniper, after several vain efforts at making pleasant conversation, finally gave up and excused herself. Try as she might, she couldn't shake off the image of Zetta astride the great draco, winging up like a projectile into the bright morning sky.

So, the monster had not been dead. That much was plain as crabgrass. It hadn't come as a surprise to the Anju, either.

But then how had it sat there so still through all the proceedings? Had Zetta drugged it? Or tamed it somehow? The more Juniper thought, the more antsy she got. While the rest of the settlers spent their time until the evening ceremony in various forms of exploring and relaxation, Juniper knew she wouldn't be able to settle until she learned what had gone on with Zetta.

Finally she whispered to Erick that she was going to go out for a bit on her own. She eased her way out of the camp. A light snow had begun to fall, and Juniper wrapped her cloak more tightly around herself.

She set her body in the direction of the Claw, and began to climb.

It took hours. The task was made the more challenging by the patches of ice and the sharp snowdrifts frosted all along the edges of her upward climb. She kept a hard pace, though, never stopping for more than a minute at a time, determined to reach her destination as quickly as possible. She wasn't sure she'd find Zetta there—but then, where else would she have gone?

At last she made it. The Claw loomed witchlike against the pale murky sky, with sunset rapidly approaching and the snow whispering down. Juniper scrambled up the narrow stone walkway that led to the topmost crag. The draco was nowhere to be seen, but a wisp of smoke curled from the shadowed opening. From within came a stuttering, snoring sound.

In front of the cave was a large rounded boulder. On the boulder sat Zetta, feet crossed beneath her, hands resting in the hollow of her lap. A pair of claw-tipped Anju boots sat neatly on the rock next to her. Zetta seemed to be awaiting Juniper's arrival, a fact that surprised Juniper until she realized that, of course, she would have been visible for the last hour or more of her climb.

She was doubly glad to have kept up such a stiff pace. Torreans were no flatland rats!

When Juniper reached the landing, Zetta moved over to make room on her boulder. Not knowing what else to do, Juniper clambered up beside her. They studied the powdering sky in silence for several minutes.

Finally, Zetta said, "So. I suppose I should congratulate you. That was a bold move, confronting the Council like that. Risky, but it paid off."

Juniper shrugged. She wasn't going to deny it. She'd fought for this victory. And she *needed* it, she reminded herself again. This was no trivial contest; it was a matter of life or death for a whole nation. She opened her mouth to say this, but what came out instead was, "What did you do to that draco? I thought you'd killed it."

Zetta laughed. "Killed him? Never."

"I thought that was the challenge. Get rid of the mortal enemy and such."

Zetta snorted. "One could argue that my greatest enemy is sitting right beside me."

She had a point.

Juniper glanced around the little promontory, just now noticing a rustic lean-to erected against the side of the cave. A scattering of dishes. An old blanket. A handful of half-wilted snapdragons in a small clay vase. Realization dawned on her. "You've been coming up here," she said. "Before the trial, even. You were preparing for this."

Zetta considered her coolly. She stretched her arms behind her and leaned back. "It's like they said. This draco has been the bane of our village for months. Flying by and torching the trees—our structures can take some battering, but not this much! Crashing into stuff. Generally wreaking havoc. Everyone was afraid of it. One of the Littles wandered off and was never found. The draco was seen on the wing shortly after, and everyone blamed the beast for poor Asha's disappearance."

Juniper was aghast. "It ate the child?"

Zetta shook her head and went on. "I wasn't so sure. There was talk of gathering a party to mount an attack, but it never came together. No one had any idea what we might do against a beast of this type. So. I began doing my own scouting. I crept up here day after day, spying on the creature, learning its ways. Before long, I understood everything there was to know about this fearsome, fire-breathing beast. I began implementing a plan for how I might bring him around to a more peaceful place. And then . . ." She swallowed.

"Then, Chief Darla grew ill. Of course, that consumed all my time and attention, caring for my mother and adjusting to her deteriorating health. I was in no mood to even think of coming up here for a good while. Then . . . she passed on. We came to the Trials. And you know the rest." Zetta tilted her head back and closed her eyes, letting the tiny snowflakes whisper down across her cheeks.

"That still seems pretty convenient," Juniper said.

"Convenient that my mother died so suddenly?" said Zetta, but her tone had no bite. "Or maybe convenient that I cared enough about my people to want to do something to stop their biggest threat, even before I knew it would be required of me?" She shrugged. "You can make what you will of that, I suppose."

Juniper bit her lip, chastened. "You're right, that was a terrible thing to say. Do tell me, though. How did you end up cracking that fiery shell?"

At this, Zetta's face glowed to life. "It's been an experience, let me tell you. For weeks I came up here—longer, maybe. Observing, like I said, then making a plan. Slowly I introduced myself to the draco, bringing what foodstuffs I could find, venturing a little nearer each time."

"That sounds dangerous."

Zetta tossed her head. "No more than I can handle, I assure you. Oh, I won't say I didn't feel the singe on more than one occasion. But over time . . . I suppose he became accustomed to me. And I to him. He's really quite a delicate beast, can you imagine?"

"Is that so," said Juniper dryly.

"Truly. And now, finally, after much time and more, he is become just as tame as you please. With me, anyway—I can't speak for anyone else trying to sneak up and game him. Didn't you see how I had that wisp of a thing around his great maw? A silk scarf, no more! He is a wonder, and I don't doubt at this moment he's my dearest friend."

Juniper digested this in silence. Despite herself, she was impressed. "So when that 'greatest danger' question came along—"

"Now you understand the way of it. What else could they have been thinking of when they wrote that? It's been some time since we've had any attacks, but that fiery threat looms large in our memory. I knew what was in mind when that charge was delivered. And perhaps I could have set them straight, explained that the danger they feared was no longer much of a danger at all. But it wouldn't have been necessarily true, would it? And how would they truly grasp his taming if I were not to show them in true and actual life?"

"So when the Trial came about, you simply . . . flew him on down?"

"Even so," said Zetta. "They're savagely intelligent, dracos. I had no idea, before I got to know my dearest. But taking the time to listen and observe, to find out what is important to him . . . What a magnificent creature! I've fallen for him rather hard, as you can see. We trust each other, he and I. I've even taught him some tricks." She shook her head ruefully. "Suns, but it feels good to tell someone all of this at last! But you can see why I had to make sure you didn't come up here with me, when it came time for the final test."

Juniper did see. And the evidence of this subterfuge—for there *was* something a little devious in the way Zetta had paraded her triumph over the draco as some sort of brutal conquest, even though the Anju had known he wasn't dead—should have made Juniper feel better about her own victory.

Strangely, though, it didn't.

"So," Zetta said, "you have your rulership. And I know you've got plans for that war down in your flatlands." She shook her head at Juniper's surprise. "Come on. That's no great secret. But what happens after that? Are you really going to settle up here in the mountains for good?"

That question had crossed Juniper's mind, too. "Actually, I've been thinking about that a lot. This place you have up here—it's so out of the way. And cold, too. I mean, this is your summer, right?" She frowned at the drifting snow and pulled her cloak more tightly about herself. "In Torr, we've got plenty of unsettled pockets of land. I might move everyone down there. Think how much more comfortable life would be—" She stopped at the thunderous look on Zetta's face. "What? What did I say?"

"*That's your big plan?*" Zetta said. "Take over my village and turn it into a silk-screen copy of your Torr? Subjugate my people to your superior customs and traditions, is that it?"

"No . . ." Juniper's excuses died on her lips. It wasn't like that. Was it?

"We have a life here," said Zetta. "A good life. And if it doesn't look ideal to you, then maybe you should think hard about whether you really are *one of us*."

Juniper had no response to that, so she focused her gaze down the mountain. Through the swirls of papery snow, she could make out the rooftops of the Anju village, peeking from the tree cover. She thought of the cleverly constructed dwellings, the care that had gone into their building and upkeep, all the little necessities of everyday Anju life of which she still had no idea. She thought of the weeks and months Zetta had spent learning about the draco, befriending and taming this wild creature without any thought that it might benefit her someday. Simply seeing her people's need. She remembered the looks on all the gathered faces as they had swiveled between her and Zetta.

The Anju. They were Juniper's *people*, yes . . . but—in a rush, she suddenly knew this for a certain fact— they were not her *subjects*.

And they never would be.

What would the future hold for the Anju with Juniper as their ruler? She'd thought about this a lot, of course, but Zetta's questions had crystallized things in a way that felt brand-new. Zetta had been willing to do anything to win, even going so far as to lure Juniper away from the last test. But her motivation had been the protection and safety of—and love for—her people. What was Juniper's excuse? Gaining command of their army to lead them out against Monsia—she would be *using them*, just as Zetta had accused. Wasn't that truly her main reason for wanting the rulership? A valid reason, a necessary and even noble one, from her view.

Nonetheless, it was *her* reason. Not theirs.

What would happen to them afterward? She tried to picture the whole tribe picking up stakes and moving into a wing of the palace or settling the deserted parcel of land down by Oleo's Bay, building up their own houses and barns and village stores. She tried to picture Mother Odessa shedding her furs for a frilled gown and satin slippers, Zetta and Tania and Libba walking sedately along the roads of Torrence town, or riding daintily on horseback.

She couldn't picture any of it.

Juniper had always prided herself in her ability to take one thing at a time, to assess the future in the broadest of terms and sort out the details later. But these particular details were somewhat bigger than those that usually lay on her horizon.

Now she tried to imagine herself actually ruling over this tribe, being responsible for hundreds of people—old and young alike—giving them guidance and instruction on their decisions and movements and everyday lives. Was she really going to continue as their ruler once Torr had been liberated and her father restored to his throne? Move up to the mountains and live here year-round—not in the Basin, even, but here in the treetops, the way a ruler of the Anju must?

And what about this war she was roping them into without their consent? What would this cost the Anju people, being conscripted to fight a battle that was not their own?

If that is the cost of victory, she thought dully, *is it truly worth its blood price?*

Suddenly she knew that if she let things go on as they were, if she let herself continue along this path, she would regret it for the rest of her life.

Juniper turned to look at the girl sitting next to her. "Zetta," she said, "will you take me for a ride? I find that I very much want to see how that draco flies."

The moment the draco ("Floris," Zetta screamed over the roaring wind. "I've named him Floris!") leaped off the crag and caught the wind current was one Juniper would vividly remember for the rest of her life. They flew up first, into the sinking sun, and Zetta proudly circled around the Claw several times, guiding him with just a gentle brush of the hand to one way or another. For Juniper's part, she clung to Zetta's waist in a death grip, her thighs squeezing Floris's flank so hard, her muscles ached.

But the flight itself—oh, it was *magic*! Faster than a horse's full tilt gallop, higher than the tallest treetop climb, the wind-rush far beyond any precipitous dive from a cliff-top pool.

This, Juniper thought, *this is a moment to shape all future moments!*

Too quickly the trip was over, and Zetta lowered her draco to settle again in the gathering area, half on and half off the main mound. There was a general shrieking and scuttling as the assembled crowd scurried off to both sides. The Queen's Basin group was all there, and Juniper waved jauntily at their gape-mouthed stares to see her astride so terrible a mount.

As Juniper began to climb down, Zetta leaned in and grabbed her hand. Having said her piece earlier, with the fight for rulership lost and her own future out of her control, Zetta now seemed reconciled to Juniper—friendly, even.

"May the best prevail," she said, "and you have done that. It was good of you to come up and talk to me. I won't say I don't still hate you for showing yourself stronger than me. But your gesture was well met."

Juniper opened her mouth, but Zetta barreled right over her. "My intentions were good insofar as they went, but I see now that the means of reaching a goal is every bit as important as the goal itself. It's no good to save the body if you must gut the soul to do so." She shook her head. "A hard way for me to learn this lesson, but what's done is done. As for the flood, I truly had no idea it *could* escalate that rapidly. I intended only to nudge up the pacing a kick or two. I heavily regret the loss of your settlement and any harm done to your people."

Juniper nodded. It felt good to have this acknowledged, to understand that Zetta had not intended the violence that had nearly befallen them. "We all came through it safely—that's what matters, I suppose. Anyway, how could you have known what the end result would be?"

"Still," said Zetta, "it was an inexcusable risk I took. The dangers of the Peakseason Floods are well known to us. You should have had weeks more to prepare—you could have brought everything to safety with time to spare. There's a reason that cave is forbidden; that's where the source is for the underground rivers. Oh, I had no idea you'd explode the whole place—I just thought you'd hasten things along a little bit, speed the heating process, and I could send you along with a warning to get you out of the way." Her mouth twisted. "You went above and beyond my wildest expectations. But I risked lives and livelihoods by my rash decision, and that is unforgivable—"

"Actually," said Juniper, "actually, it *is* forgivable. I didn't have to follow your advice. And blowing up a cave like that, knowing it was so volatile? Not my smartest decision. Let me be clear: What you did was awful. And it could have had the worst of repercussions. If it had . . . I might be speaking a lot differently right now. But providence was on our side, so how can I hold a grudge?" She smiled wryly. "I *was* trying to steal your throne. I had my reasons, but still. Anyway, I have an apology of my own."

Juniper let go of Zetta's arm, and they moved away from the draco, who had tucked his head under his wing, looking so much like an enormous monster chicken that Juniper was temporarily distracted. But she knew she had to move quickly, before she changed her mind.

This was the right decision, she knew it.

But, lands, it would not be easy!

She turned toward the assembled group—all the Anju, by now, and all Queen's Basin—who had hushed to silence and were giving the two rivals their full attention. Juniper raised her voice. "I have something to say to all of you today: I was wrong. I let my fear for my king and my country cloud my judgment. But here, today, I want to tell you the truth. I have come to realize one true thing—I am not cut out to rule the Anju. You *are* my people, yes, but I'm not the one who has lived with you, bled with you, fought for you." She took a deep breath. There was no turning back now.

She faced Odessa. "I know this goes against everything I said this morning. All of that *is* true, but there is one more thing that must be said. Zetta may have broken the rules, but her motivation was always for you, her people. I respect that you are so honor-bound that you would follow through, even to your own detriment, choosing me as your leader based on the precepts originally set down. But the fact is, I know nothing of your ways, not in their deep and true fullness." She kept her voice steady. "I would make a terrible Chieftain of the Anju."

Odessa's look was unreadable. "What are you saying, Juniper, daughter of Alaina?"

Juniper looked across the group, catching Erick's eye. He gave her a reassuring nod. "I'm saying that I wish to officially withdraw from this Trial. Please reconsider Zetta for admission in my place."

After this, things moved very quickly. The Elders leaped into the preparations for the officiating ceremony, as though afraid that circumstances would change yet again and their new leader would be spirited away from them for good. Zetta's face flashed through a rainbow of emotions—more than Juniper had ever seen her display—but even as she opened her mouth to speak, her minders swooped in and whisked her away. The look she sent Juniper, though—that look spoke whole volumes. Even Floris let out a bleat—truly, a *bleat!*—of evident joy.

How was it that a loss could be so much sweeter than a win?

It was, though. To her surprise, she felt a love for this people grow and swell inside, filling her full to bursting. For once, she felt truly a part of them.

In choosing to move away, she'd taken the first step toward truly becoming one of them.

When the ceremony was over, the Queen's Basin group decided to stay for the evening festivities before setting off back home. There were decisions to make and next steps to consider, but first they needed to close out this chapter. The fine delicacies that were served up topped even the ones they had enjoyed at the feast before the Trials. And the crowning piece, which four muscled young men bore out on a polished wood platter, was a web of fine-spun, sugary filament tangled over and all around a nest of succulent fruits of all types. The unprecedented amount of sweet-crystal brought in by the candidates, they heard whispered, had enabled this once-in-a-generation confection.

Juniper wondered if, even now, someone was storing up mental images of this memorable delight, for later depiction on the Memory Wall. After all, what better to capture for posterity than your finest desserts?

On the other side of the group, Leena made the rounds to several women in turn until she located the creator of the sugary masterpiece, where she began exclaiming, nodding, and writing furious notes on a scrap of parchment. Erick took a crystalline lamp and a sheaf of empty pages and set off for the Memory Wall with a history-lover's gleam in his eye; he'd probably have to be pried loose when it came time to leave. Tippy had found a cluster of Littles about her size and started up a game of honey-pots, the whole group of them rolling in frenzied turns across the quaggy ground. Even Cyril seemed to have a found a like-minded companion, making a stiff sort of conversation with Tania at the far edge of the fire pit.

Even across the never-changing throb of worry for her father and Torr, and the knowledge that all her plans would now need to be refigured, Juniper felt a deep satisfaction at this blending of her two peoples, her two worlds. If only all of life could see such resolution!

Finally, Juniper spread the word that they would soon head back to the Basin. It would be a challenging hike back in the darkness, but the snow had stopped. The moon overhead was bright and full as a rounded cheese. Now that this Anju chapter was closed, Juniper wanted—*needed*—to be gone. She had an invasion to plan—a very small invasion, now that they were back to settlers only. But it would have to do.

She would figure out a way to get her people back to Torr and save her father. She *would*. This was the most important thing in her entire world right now. Before they left, though, there was someone she needed to talk to.

She found her sitting at the base of a tree, looking out silently over the forest. "Mother Odessa?" said Juniper. She swallowed. "Grandmother?"

The woman looked up, smiling faintly. Juniper thought she looked twice as old as she had that morning.

"I'm sorry I didn't . . ." Juniper wasn't entirely sure what she was apologizing for, but she knew she needed to say *something*. "I know you wanted me to . . ."

"Say no more, child," said Odessa. "It's quite clear I was pushing my own plans hard—much too hard. Hindsight is the clearest sight, after all. I only . . ." She sighed. "It would have been good if you could have stayed here with us. With me. For a while, at least."

"You miss my mother, don't you?"

"I think—I *know* I didn't handle Alaina's departure well. I was so full of my own righteous anger back then. I could see nothing beyond my role as chief and her searing betrayal. When she left, I pronounced her dead to the Tribe. Forbade anyone to have any contact with her. She sent letters and parcels—so many, over the years! I ordered every one of them destroyed unread. Turned down all requests for a visit. After some time, I began to regret this decision, but how could I go back on the pronouncement I had made before all? Particularly as I was no longer chief, by that point." The old woman's shoulders drooped. "Then . . . there you were. And I thought, what a chance it would be! Not quite like having your mother back, but as near to it as I could get."

Juniper felt her eyes sting. Hindsight indeed!

Odessa squinted at the tree branches, then seemed to make up her mind. "Will you come to my dwelling? Do you have a few minutes to spare?"

"Of course," said Juniper. She looked back toward the clearing, where the others were still busy mingling. She did want to be on the road soon, but this was important. She might not get another chance.

The moonlight would keep a little longer.

She followed Odessa's example and strapped herself into a narrow leather seat that dangled down from the loblolly pine, then pulled herself up hand over hand until she reached the wide, high branch above. Two trees over, a burble of singsong voices chattered out a rhythmic melody. A whiff of incense crackled in the air. Stepping out of the harness, Juniper followed her grandmother along the well-worn tree limb walkway.

Odessa's house looked like a giant acorn: a fine wooden globe that swayed gently from strong suspending ropes. Juniper wobbled across a stiff connecting net and slid inside the cozy home.

"It's like being inside a hollowed-out egg," she marveled. She lowered herself to the cushioned floor and tucked her legs under her.

Odessa was digging in a chest and came out with a folded piece of bright white cloth. On top lay a small leather pouch, which Odessa put into her hand first. "This is for you," she said.

Juniper wiggled apart the drawstring opening, turned it over, and felt something heavy fall into her hand: a bright blue stone that winked and shone in the dim evening light.

"Oh," Juniper breathed. "It's beautiful!"

"That is to remember me by," she said. "It is a little thing I came upon many years ago. It has brought me luck—or I have found my own luck while I kept it near me—and I think the time has come to pass that on to you. And this is for you, too." Odessa slid the cloth into her hands.

Juniper's fingers moved to it automatically. The white was so bright that, in this dim space, it nearly hurt her eyes to look at it straight on. But the weave was dense and strong, and soft as finest silk.

"There's a story behind this cloak," said Odessa, "though I'm afraid I don't know it. It was your mother's dearest possession. It's made of a special weave—a rare milk-cotton plant. This fabric won't tear, or burn, or even stain. It's near indestructible, so far as I can tell." Her eyes softened in a sad smile. "Alaina loved it because it was the same color as her hair. She said it made her feel like a fairy of the legends. When she put it on, she said, she felt invincible."

"Invisible?" Juniper asked, puzzled.

Odessa's eyes twinkled. "Perhaps that, too. Who can say? If ever there was an object to make a body lean toward the mystical, that garment is it. Not that I believe in such things, mind you. You'll just have to try it out and see what it has to show."

Juniper shrugged out of her cloak and swung the new one over her shoulders. "I love it," she said. "I will wear it in memory of her."

Odessa nodded. "You should be going now. Your kingdom awaits." She turned away, and Juniper could tell the old woman wasn't much for good-byes. So she reached inside her waist pouch, pulled out her notebook, and ripped a sheet from the back. Writing quickly, she scratched a few lines, then signed her name with a small symbol at the end. She creased the sheet in half and left it on her cushion, atop her own neatly folded cloak. Maybe her grandmother would find in this small token some comfort, some warmth.

I'll be back soon, Juniper vowed fiercely, repeating the words of her farewell note. *I promise.*

Then she climbed out the door and strapped herself into the harness, tugged on the hand-ropes, and began to lower herself to the ground.

To her surprise, Zetta was waiting for her at the bottom of the tree. Around her neck she wore a thick leather band covered in runic designs. This must be the symbol of the chieftaincy she'd heard talk of.

Unfastening the harness, Juniper climbed to her feet. The two girls stared each other in the eye.

"I'm not going to thank you," Zetta said shortly.

"Nor should you," said Juniper. "I did what I had to, nothing more." She turned to go, but Zetta caught her arm.

"Just a second."

Juniper looked at her in silence. Finally she prodded gently, "You wanted to ask something?"

"About Monsia," Zetta said tentatively. "They are your enemy, are they not?"

"They are."

Zetta studied Juniper a moment longer, then she smiled. "They are our enemy, too, you know. And ruler or not, you *are* one of us." She paused. "Perhaps we should talk."

Epilogue

LATE THE NEXT MORNING, THE CITIZENS OF Queen's Basin gathered around the campfire back in their familiar, partly rebuilt dining area. Leena had made griddle cakes over the open flame, topped with a confit made with hazelnuts from Root's mysterious and apparently never-ending stash. The group buzzed with an excitement nearly live enough to warrant its own breakfast.

It was all settled: Zetta had promised to spread the word to the greater network of Anju tribes, who would put themselves at the group's disposal as needed within the next few weeks. Floris, too, might be called on to make his own fiery appearance if the occasion warranted. (If Juniper had anything to do with that, it certainly would.) The great draco might be tame when it came to Zetta and her friends, but those who saw his approaching wingspan and stood on the receiving end of his flaming breath would be none the wiser.

In the meantime, the Queen's Basin crew would proceed with

their expedition back to Torr—but Juniper had come up with the beginnings of a plan for that, too. She and Erick and Alta and Jess had been up very late the night before, after the rest of the group had collapsed on their pallets following the giddy walk home.

There were a lot of nails still to be hammered into this rough-built plan they were cobbling together. But the foundation was sure, the direction was set, and the company couldn't be beat. Now they just needed to forge ahead and hope it was strong enough to hold them.

As the settlers milled around now, snacking and chatting, swapping stories of the night before, and voicing hopes for what was to come, Cyril ambled over to Juniper.

"So," he said, "that Sussi does make a mean mud mask."

Juniper grinned. "She does, doesn't she? I must say, your complexion is looking remarkably even and bright today. Not a spot to be seen."

Cyril returned her grin, but the gesture was halfhearted.

"What's on your mind?" Juniper said. "You don't want to talk to me about mud masks. You look like a goat in a sweetbriar patch."

"I was just thinking about our deal. Do you remember?"

Juniper didn't want to confess that it had clean slipped her mind. The Cyril who had needed complicated deals and concessions to keep in line seemed so far removed from this boy who, for the first time she could remember, she wasn't ashamed to think of as her cousin.

"I do," she said cautiously.

"I was to help you win the Anju contest, and in return, you—"

"Would let you leave the Basin freely." Juniper swallowed. "But—I didn't win, did I?"

Cyril smiled wryly. "You did, actually. You won the contest. For a few hours, you were ruler of the Anju. It's not on my head that you chose to give that up to return to your little valley play-spot." The words were pure Palace Cyril, but the tone was light and without malice. What was more, Juniper knew he was right.

But . . . could she really just let him go? After all they'd been through on this journey, she'd grown closer to Cyril than she'd ever thought possible. But he still was—had been—a traitor. He and his father had worked with the Monsians, had betrayed their country straight out. Could she really let him leave, taking with him the knowledge of all their thoughts and coming plans, half-formed as they were?

Agreeing to this had seemed easy from a distance, but now the truth of it stopped her cold. Was this what leadership was, then? Making unmakeable decisions, choosing between the impossible and the unbearable?

There was no way she would go back on her word. She couldn't. And yet . . .

She felt a panic rising in her chest, felt her eyes filling with tears. How could she just let him go? Finally she managed, "Is that what you want? To leave us now?"

Cyril studied her, and she could see his face changing as he took in her expression. When he spoke, the lightness was gone from his voice. "No," he said. "No, I don't want to leave. But I wanted to know whether you would have let me. Whether you'd have honored your word."

Juniper opened her mouth to reply—of course she would have. How could she not, in the end? Whatever the price, a ruler's word was everything.

But Cyril didn't give her the chance. He spun on his heel and set off back toward the cliffside.

"Ahoy, all!" came a sudden yell. It was Paul, his voice coming from across the river on the North Bank. "Get over here, and fast. You won't believe this!"

Trying to put Cyril out of her mind—he would be all right; she'd talk to him soon and make sure everything was straight between them—Juniper jumped up and shielded her eyes against the midmorning's glare. She couldn't see clearly, but the grassy field looked . . . blue? Leaving her plate on her sitting stone, Juniper ran toward the bridge. Most of the others clustered along behind her. It took her until halfway across the bridge before she could see the ground clearly, but when she did, her breath caught in her throat. There stood Paul, in the midst of what had been the tattered remains of the vegetable garden.

But it was tattered and tired no longer.

For all across the sloped North Bank, where hours and days and weeks of painstaking work had been swept away in minutes by the churning floods—new life had begun.

Paul was standing calf-high in a field of brightest blue, bell-shaped flowers. "What do you think of this?" he trumpeted. "Night-bells! Can you reckon it?"

"Where did they come from?" cried Sussi. "How are they here?"

"It has to be the flood," said Paul. "It destroyed most everything it touched—and yet it also carried within itself the seeds of new life, and the mineral qualities to speed that process into the soil."

"Beauty from destruction," murmured Juniper. "And with an end, the hope for a new beginning."

If there was a better way to start the next chapter of her adventure, she didn't know it.

Acknowledgments

AS EVER, I OWE A HUGE DEBT OF GRATITUDE
to those who have worked so hard to help bring this book to
life. First and foremost, credit goes to my brilliant editor, Jill
Santopolo, along with the eagle-eyed Talia Benamy, Michael
Green, and the fleet of inspired designers, copy editors,
proofreaders, and others, without whom this book would be
nothing more than a puddle of ink on a page. To Erwin Madrid,
whose artistic cover masterpieces each manage to supersede the
last, to Siobhán Gallagher, for her exquisite design skills, and to

Dave Stevenson, whose mapmaking skills have brought Torr to life in such vivid detail. To Tara Shanahan, for all your efforts getting Juniper in the hands and hearts of readers far and wide.

To Erin Murphy, Tricia Lawrence, Dennis Stephens, Tara Gonzalez, and the rest of the EMLA team, my love and appreciation for all you do to maintain this nurturing creative space; and most especially to my clients, for your support and trust and patience with me as we walk this part of the road together. Kirsten Cappy, your creativity and enthusiasm know no bounds, and I'm so grateful to have you as a cheerleader! Helen Kampion, likewise, my thanks for your energy and efforts on Juniper's behalf.

My family and friends, as always, remain an invaluable part of the writing process: Zack, Kimberly, and Lauren—I love you more than I could say! The whole Paquette (and Askaryan and Clark) crew and the Neve family, thank you for your love and support and for believing in me. To my critique partners and writing buddies Nancy Werlin, Debbie Kovacs, Julie Berry, Julie Phillipps, Kip Wilson, Natalie Lorenzi, Sarah Beth Durst, and Diana Renn—you make it all not only possible, but enjoyable.

Writing a sequel turned out to be a more challenging experience than I'd expected. A finished first novel has been so finely curated, and so much care has been put into honing the arc and growth and resonance within that single unit; to open a fresh page and begin those threads anew, yet provide sufficient ties linking both backward and forward, tested me in ways I hadn't anticipated. Yet in the end, this book ended up being one of my most satisfying writing experiences to date. That's why my foremost gratitude will always be for YOU, my readers, who make it all possible. We're on this journey together, Juniper and her friends and you and I—this is just the next step in her adventures, but who knows what's lurking right around the corner?

Till we meet again, and soon, back in Torr!

PRINCESS JUNIPER WILL ENLIST
THE HELP OF FRIENDS, SECRET SPY CATS,
AND EVEN A DRAGON TO SAVE HER COUNTRY!

TURN THE PAGE FOR A SAMPLE OF THE ACTION-PACKED
CONCLUSION TO JUNIPER'S ADVENTURES:

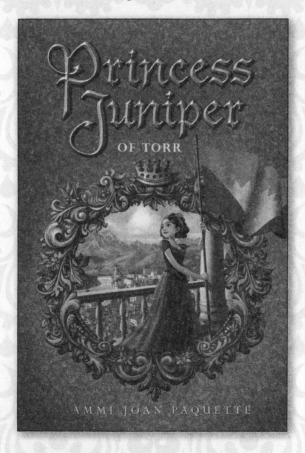

1

LEAVING QUEEN'S BASIN WAS PROVING HARDER than Juniper had expected.

She'd spent a little over a month as queen of her very own tiny mountain country, ruling over the best group of young subjects around. Even the superheated flash flood that had swept through just days ago had not beaten them. Their settlement wasn't yet re-built—that would take time, which they didn't have right now— but though a little scruffier and more pockmarked than before, it was still their bowl-shaped, sun-dappled valley home.

It was still Queen's Basin.

Now, though, it was time to turn their mind to bigger things: Time to face the enemy head-on. Time to save King Regis. Time to head back to Torr.

Their saddlebags were stuffed with the last of their food sup-plies, and the horses they'd got back from the Anju were rested and raring to go. Two days ago, an early scouting team of Alta and Jess had ventured down the mountain to see what they could learn about the state of Torr. The scouts were due back any time now; if all went as planned, the whole group would head out tomorrow morning.

Around Juniper, the valley was quiet in the dim evening light. But she could hear a buzz of activity coming from just up the mountain. With a grin, Juniper scrambled along the cliffside path. She pushed through the hanging bluevines into the Great Cave. There they all were: her fellow citizens of Queen's Basin. Her friends. Nearly a dozen kids were jumbled in the giant cave room, each one bright-eyed and yammering as they went about their tasks: packing and repacking, triple-checking, all desperately busy on this last night before the big departure.

"Princess Juniper!" called a deep voice to her left. It was Root, looking anxious. "Have you seen Cyril?"

"Cyril?" Juniper frowned. Since their return from the Anju adventure, her cousin had reformed his bullying ways and had stopped spying for his traitorous father and the invading Monsians. He'd joined the group for meals and done chores alongside the others. But when *was* the last time she'd seen him? "Not since breakfast," she said slowly.

"Nor I," said Root. "He said he wanted some time alone—I didn't think anything of it. But now . . ."

Juniper felt her stomach clench. Root was Cyril's best friend. If *he* didn't know where Cyril was, what did that mean?

"Come on," she said. "Let's figure this out."

Against the far wall, Erick stood under a flaming wall sconce, completely absorbed by a clothbound volume entitled *Treatise of the*

"We might have a problem," Juniper called out. Looking up and seeing them, Erick whipped the book behind his back, clearly ashamed to be caught reading at such a busy time. Actually, though, anything else from him would have been weird. Nearby, Leena stopped brushing her horse and moved in closer to see what was going on.

"Have either of you seen Cyril since breakfast?" Juniper asked them.

Erick and Leena exchanged a look. Both shook their heads.

"Could he have gone climbing and met some accident?" asked Erick.

"Not likely," said Root. He cleared his throat. "The thing is, his horse isn't where it ought to be. He keeps it tethered right next to mine. His saddlebags are gone, too."

"You think he's left us?" Erick said incredulously.

"Why, that leech-faced lout!" Leena exclaimed. "I *knew* his goodsy turnabout was too neat to be true! Once a traitor, always a traitor, that's what I say."

"Hold up, now," Juniper said. "Let's not jump to conclusions. Cyril's made some bad choices in the past, but that doesn't mean he's not changed. There might still be a reasonable explanation for this. He could have gone . . ."

There was an awkward silence. Juniper met Erick's eye. Where *could* Cyril have gone, with his horse and loaded saddlebags, and the group's departure just around the corner? And with no word to anyone of what he had in mind?

"There's nowhere he could be that he *ought* to be," said Erick quietly. "We move out as a group—that was always the plan. We all agreed."

Juniper thought of Cyril as he was weeks ago: hectoring, challenging, conniving. She thought of their recent exchanges, how he'd grown to be almost more of a brother than a cousin.

There must be some explanation. There *must*.

"We just hammered out our starting plan last night, didn't we?" said Leena. "Set up the details for how and when we'd get in to the castle: legging it with the crowds until Summerfest, then sneaking inside the walls during the open celebration. Well? No sooner did he hear the news but that boy saw his chance and skedaddled."

"No," said Juniper.

Seeing their next steps all set out in the open, had Cyril reconsidered what he owed his father, the traitorous Monsian ally Lefarge? Or, worse, had Cyril been lying to them, to *her*, all along?

Had Cyril ever truly been on their side?

"I don't like to doubt him," said Erick. "Maybe there's another explanation."

Leena snorted, and even Root looked pained. Juniper didn't like it either. Over the last few weeks, across the Anju Trials and all the difficulties there, Juniper had grown closer to Cyril than she'd ever thought possible. She'd seen a different side of her cousin than he had shown during their childhood. It seemed impossible to imagine him out there now, spilling their plans to the Monsians, bulking up the defenses around the captive king, and

4

preparing Torr Castle against their incursion. Yet what else could explain him sneaking away without a word to anyone?

The more they discussed and looked at all the angles, the clearer the plain facts stood out. Cyril was gone, along with his horse and his travel gear and up-to-date knowledge of how they planned to get inside Torr Castle.

Oh, the cut went deep! Juniper clenched her fists and stared at the wall, while the others muttered around her.

She'd been a fool to trust him. She saw that now. They just had to face the facts.

Cyril had betrayed them again.

2

WITH EFFORT, JUNIPER PULLED HERSELF together. She squeezed her churning emotions into a hard ball and flung them to the back of her mind. From now on, she wouldn't spare that blackguard one further thought.

Next to her, Erick was watching with a half grin.

"What?" Juniper said, startled out of her funk. "What's that gleam in your eye?"

Leena, too, cracked a smile. "Only you're that predictable, Princess Juniper," she said.

Erick nodded. "It's like a whole three-act play just unfolded across your face. We're now at the stage where our intrepid hero has settled upon a firm course of action and dives into it with verve and vigor."

Despite herself, Juniper laughed. "I wouldn't say my course is at all firm right now. But I'm hanged if I'm going to let Cyril botch up everything we've been working for. Let's get the rest of the team together, shall we? An emergency meeting is in order."

"Calling a meeting without your indispensable scouting party?" came a voice behind them. "I see we've made it back just in time."

"Why, 'tis our own Alta, alive and in the flesh!" Tippy's shrill voice trumpeted up from suspiciously nearby. Apparently she'd been lurking in their conversation. Now, though, her voice was loud enough to bring over the rest of the group as she bounded toward the new arrivals.

Alta was leading her magnificent stallion, Thunderstar, with Jess and the fine-boned Lady clattering close behind. The girls' eyes were bright and their cheeks flushed from the long tramp through the cave tunnels. With a squeal, Tippy launched herself at Alta, who reached down to enfold the younger girl in a full-body embrace.

"Well met," Juniper said to the scouts, once the hugfest was done. "Your timing could not be better."

"We're all packed up for tomorrow's out-leaving, only just awaiting your return, and also we've had Cyril gad off us, so he's a traitor all over again," Tippy summarized, all in a rush.

This was met with alarm from the larger group. Juniper waved her arms in the air. "All right, then, the news is out: It seems Cyril's gone and left us without a word. We don't know his reasons, but I think it's safe to assume the worst." Juniper sighed. "Still, we're set to head out tomorrow at dawn, and there's no way to push that any sooner. The scouts and their mounts need a night's rest, and we can catch up on their news meanwhile. Plus, we've some powerful planning to do. Which, as with anything, is better done with food near at hand. Shall we regroup at the dining area?"

The others agreed and quickly went about finishing the last of their packing before heading from the cave. Alta began tethering Thunderstar, but Jess went straight for a low pouch hanging between Lady's hind legs. She reached inside and pulled out a warm, purring bundle.

Tippy perked up immediately. "Fleeter! Ah, my own Fleeter is back, too! May I hold your little spy cat, Jess? I've missed him so."

Jess rolled her eyes, but still seemed to appreciate Tippy's enthusiasm. Certainly they were the only two who saw any appeal in the mangy creature (which legitimately looked part moth-eaten sweater and part undead corpse). Oblivious to Juniper's faint shudder, Tippy and Fleeter got busy nuzzling, so she left well enough alone and headed down into the Basin.

Within a few minutes, all the Queen's Basin crew had trundled down the winding cliffside path and settled themselves on the worn sitting stones. The torches had been brought from the cave and set up around their dining area, where the flames scratched long shadows on the ring of anxious faces. Leena passed around a basket of day-old biscuits along with Root's latest efforts at dried meat—quail and summer hare—which was extraordinarily tough, but filling. The effort of chewing also offered some distraction from the worries at hand.

"The meat needs more salt, I think," tried Root. He was looking around as though trying to gauge the success of his curing skills.

"Fleeter loves it," Tippy declared.

"Makes us work for every bite, is all," said Roddy, and a few others murmured agreement.

8

"I think it's quite perfect just as it is," said Oona. Her hand lifted as though she was going to put it on Root's knee (she was sitting so close to him that she barely had to move to do so), but at the last minute, she seemed to think better of it. She blushed and lowered her eyes.

"So," Juniper said, turning to Alta, "what news do you have to share of your scouting mission?"

"The journey went——" Alta began.

"Quite as well as expected," Jess cut in. Alta scowled at the interruption, but Jess barreled on. "We visited Sari first, as it's the nearest town to us and on our way. We passed quickly through, for as usual they have no concerns but for their own industry and care not a fig for the goings-on of the greater country."

Being the daughter of a renowned spy-for-hire seemed to have given Jess the right flair for this scouting mission, Juniper thought. "So you didn't stay over there?" she asked.

"Only an afternoon," Alta confirmed. "Then we made our way to Longton, arriving by nightfall."

Jess nodded. "Longton was its usual hotbed of useful information."

"How did you go about collecting it?" Leena asked.

"In my experience, the best information is gathered by spending time in public places—parks and festivals, marketplaces, alehouses."

"Surely not an alehouse!" exclaimed Sussi.

"Well, they didn't allow us in, being young and unaccompanied and all," Jess conceded. "But then we found a spot even better: an open-air theater putting on a play of *Belle and the Moon*."

"*Belle and the Moon?*" Juniper whispered. The others didn't know it, but this play—and its title song—had a very special meaning to her. It was not only her favorite musical performance, but also the last song she had danced to with her father, on that night that seemed so long ago, her thirteenth Nameday celebration back at the palace. Before any of this had happened—before Queen's Basin, before their departure.

Before the Monsians had invaded and taken her father captive.

It was all too easy to get caught up in the day-to-day stress and drama and tasks that needed doing, and to forget the harsh reality that was hanging over them. They were no longer out here to play and have a good time in their carefree summer kingdom. They truly had to be—or had to *become* at least—a compact fighting force, a miniature all-kids army that the enemy would not see coming.

Somehow, some way, they had to save the day.

Oblivious to Juniper's inner turmoil, Jess was still recounting the news they had gathered on their scouting expedition. "Word from across Torr is slim and grim. The Monsians did march down the White Highway some weeks back, but they made no stops other than to set some fields ablaze. And that seemed more to make a point than anything."

"Them's the fires we saw from here! Clouds of fearsome smoke everywhere!" Tippy shuddered and clutched Fleeter more tightly.

Jess nodded. "The Monsians brought their might against the palace, and were through the walls in a matter of days. It was an inside job, folks say, that's how they got in so quick. Betrayed from within."

None of this was news, of course. The betrayal of Rupert Lefarge, the king's chief adviser and Cyril's father, was the reason Torr Castle had fallen. But, oh, that did not make it any easier to hear. Those walls had stood for centuries! Down through countless generations of Torrence rulers, not once had the defenses been breached. Juniper clenched her hands into fists.

"Several armed battalions remain at the castle," said Alta, "perhaps one or two hundred soldiers."

Erick frowned, and Juniper could guess why. His father had been captain of the guard at the palace. If the Monsian soldiers were loose in the castle, what must be the state of the Torrean guards?

Alta went on, "Now, here's a curious thing. Apparently the palace is not being ruled by the Monsians, but by Rupert Lefarge and his wife, Malvinia. They've been putting out the word that everything across the country should carry on as normal. Including, and especially, Summerfest."

Jess nodded. "They've been sending out a great tide of pamphlets and proclamations, urging townsfolk and villagers to attend. Talking it up as an extraordinary spectacle like nothing that's come before it. And there is to be a particular announcement on the final day that no one will want to miss."

"It's good they're not changing the Summerfest plans," said Juniper. Their own palace entry relied on that festival, after all.

But she didn't like the sound of the rest of it. Not one single bit.

"And no one suspected your origins as you gathered your intelligence?" Leena asked.

Jess raised both eyebrows, as if the question was beneath her. She walked over to Tippy and picked up the sleeping Fleeter, settling the cat in the folds of her skirt. Then she pulled a small jar from her pocket and began dabbing her face with cream.

Alta said, "We stayed the night in Longton—this antiquated costume shop owner we sat next to at the show was selling off his stock and taking in boarders, saving up to pursue his lifelong dream of becoming a squid trawler." Juniper blinked at this information, and Alta shrugged. "It gave us a base for launching our investigations, with no one the wiser."

"So there's the news," said Juniper. The meal had wound down, and Root was passing around a bowlful of hazelnuts. Doggone things—where *did* he keep getting them? Now with bellies satisfied and this new information heavy on their minds, the settlers were getting restless.

"We *had* ourselves a sound plan," Leena said, her voice sharp, "before Cyril ran amok on us. What do we do now?"

"Yes," said Oona. "How does all this change things for us?"

Jess screwed the lid back on her jar and waited with the rest.

Juniper climbed to her feet. The truth was, she had no idea. But what she did know was their starting point. And as any good list maker knows, once you scratch that #1 on the page, you're as good as halfway to your goal. "All right. Listen up, Queen's Basin," she said. "Let's recap what we know. Starting with Summerfest."

"Summerfest!" trumpeted Tippy, popping up to bob around Juniper like a gourd-doll set to rocking. "Only the most glorious time of the year! Seven days of food and frolic in the summer sun."

"Kicks off in just over a week," said Leena. "Back in my palace days, we were sweating in the kitchen for ages leading up to it, getting everything ready for the crowds."

Juniper nodded. "It has always been my father's favorite festival," she said quietly. "It's a tradition that goes back to his father's father, who wanted a time when the citizens of Torr—so many as cared to join in—could mingle and refresh themselves all together in one place." Juniper had so many memories of Summerfest in years past: watching the slippery butterfight wrestlers duke it out for the crowds, the taste of sticky spun-sugar confections on her tongue, the tangled riot of noise and crowds that gave off a gauzy freedom she felt at no other time. Summerfest had always been one of the highlights of her year. But this year, things could not have been more different.

Thousands of townspeople and villagers from all across Torr traveled every summer to the castle for the chance to attend— or even to be on the outskirts, for not all of the gathered thousands could make it into the castle proper. In the weeks building up to the end of summer, tent cities were erected in the fields outside the castle grounds. Closer to the gates, the shopkeepers, tradesmen, and performers set up their stalls. These next few weeks would be packed with people and buzzing with activity. And this year, it looked like there might be even more attending than usual.

In short? There was no better place for a small rebel group to hide in plain sight.

"So the grand palace opening on Summerfest Eve has been the linchpin of our plan thus far," said Juniper. The Queen's Basin group had planned to lurk among the festivalgoers during the week leading up to the festival, using the cover of the crowd to gain information on the Monsian presence in the palace: enemy plans, placement, fortifications. They would then make their move during the grand feast that was traditionally held the evening before Summerfest. In all the hullabaloo of partying crowds, no one would notice a stealthy stream of kids joining the greater throngs to gain access to the palace. Once inside, the kids would go right to work freeing the king and reclaiming the castle.

The details of said rescue, admittedly, had yet to be worked out. That first step was solid, though.

Or at least, it *had* been.

Juniper sighed. "But now we need to rethink everything. Cyril knows our plan. He'll be expecting us. So let's think about it: What will *his* first step be upon leaving here?"

"Make a beeline back to the palace," said Erick. "Spill our info. Then have all the guards lined up and ready. On Summerfest Eve, they're alert and on the lookout. They spot us; they pounce."

"Even more than that," said Alta, "I bet he'll send guards into the festival grounds well before the fest begins. He'll be looking for you and us all so he can foil our plans before they start."

"He won't even let us set foot in the castle," said Sussi, her voice quivering.

14

"We should count on more security around King Regis, too," said Jess, "now they know someone's set to try a rescue. And we should probably prepare for the worst: The king wasn't to be moved until after the festival? If I were the bad guys, I would try to get him out sooner. Pack him right off on his way *before* it even starts. Stop any chance of subterfuge cold."

Juniper felt the familiar tightening inside her chest. *Don't lose focus,* she told herself. But how on earth could they best an occupying army? They were just thirteen kids, after all. Zetta of the Anju had promised help if it came down to a fight, but she wouldn't march her people in blindly without knowing what was going on. No, their only weapons had been secrecy and the element of surprise.

And now what were they left with?

Juniper looked around her at the ring of dispirited faces. This had been hard enough when they *did* have a solid plan. Now the group felt perilously close to falling apart.

Still unsure what to do, Juniper cleared her throat. The chatter died away.

"Oh, boy," said Tippy in a dramatic whisper. "It's time for a speech, innit?"

Juniper smiled weakly. "You know me well, Tipster!" She cleared her throat again, sharpening her focus. *All right,* actually she was stalling for time. Finally she said, "I'm not going to lie to you: This is a low blow we've been dealt. Cyril's duplicity has us right back at the starting gate. But we've been well pummeled before. And have we let that stop us?" A mutter went around the circle.

"We've faced storm and flood, we've built a country all our own, we've lived alone in the wild, and we've *thrived*. We are overcomers. We are the children of Torr! And now? Without a doubt, we are Torr's only hope. So." She paused. Something was niggling at her from earlier in the conversation.

And with it, the spark of an idea.

Juniper turned to Alta and Jess. "I've been thinking about that place you stayed in Longton," she said.

Jess made a hawking sound in her throat. "That renegade silk-stitcher."

Juniper beamed. "Ah, yes. About the silk. And cotton and velvet and leather and lace! That's *exactly* what caught my attention. Now listen up, for I have a new plan that might help us not only outsmart Cyril but get the jump on our whole enemy besides. First, we'll need to break into two groups."

"Huh?" Tippy's eyes were round as an owl's.

"Yep," said Juniper. "One group will head straight for the castle. And the other? Will do a little dressing up."